DULCIE CROWDER GETS HER MAN

DULCIE CROWDER
GETS HER MAN

•

Sarah Richmond

AVALON BOOKS
NEW YORK

I dedicate this story to the hero of my life: Mike Gross.

Published by Avalon Books,
an imprint of Thomas Bouregy & Co., Inc.
New York, NY

Library of Congress Cataloging-in-Publication Data

Richmond, Sarah, 1948–
    Dulcie Crowder gets her man / Sarah Richmond.
        p. cm.
    ISBN 978-0-8034-7617-2 (hardcover : acid-free paper)
    I. Title.
    PS3618.I356D85 2011
    813'.6—dc23
                                            2011025771

PRINTED IN THE UNITED STATES OF AMERICA
ON ACID-FREE PAPER
BY RR DONNELLEY, HARRISONBURG, VIRGINIA

Acknowledgments

I wish to thank my critique partner extraordinaire, Jessica Ferguson, for all her wonderful suggestions, and my brother, Tom Winchester, for his help with firearms. Also, a big thanks to Bill and Kay Steffen at the Blair Sugar Pine Bed & Breakfast in Placerville for pointing me in the right direction and the docents at the Placerville Historical Museum, 524 Main Street, Placerville, for keeping history alive for our generation.

Earth's crammed with Heaven,
And every common bush afire with God,
But only he who sees takes off his shoes;
The rest sit round it and pluck blackberries.

—Elizabeth Barrett Browning

Chapter One

Deputy sheriff Tom Walker spotted the corner of the black ace peeking out from under Willie Crowder's frayed sleeve, but he didn't let on he knew the old boy was fixing to end the evening with a winning hand.

Willie laid four aces on the table as easy as you please and looked up at Tom with a twinkle in his eye.

Tom shook his head and threw down his cards. "You've cleaned me out," he said. "I never did see a man with such a string of good luck at cards."

Willie chuckled as if he and Lady Luck were on intimate terms. He scooped up his winnings into a hefty pile.

"Another cup of coffee?" Tom stood and stretched.

"Don't mind if I do," Willie said with a voice full of gravel. He drained his mug and handed it over.

Tom exited through the open cell door and poured two mugs full. The coffee had brewed for hours on the cast-iron stove and was as thick as creek mud.

The sky had gone from black to gray, and a few birds were twittering, but Tom refrained from looking at his watch. Willie was going to hang at eight o'clock. Jasper would be along when it was time.

Hangtown had begun to settle down into respectability, the hangman's noose being the preferred way to deal with criminals of all

1

stripes. Dang it all if he hadn't taken a liking to old Willie, a fatal flaw in a lawman sworn to bring law and order to the El Dorado.

He handed Willie his mug.

"I'll send over to the Blue Stocking for some bacon and eggs," Tom said, leaning against the iron bars of the cell.

Willie scratched his stomach. "Not for me. I'm off my feed."

"Suit yourself," Tom replied with understanding. Willie never wasted a drop of water or a crumb of his food. He didn't intend to make an exception this morning.

Willie took out a dirty square of kerchief from his frayed shirt pocket and gathered up his winnings.

"Sheriff, I do have one last request."

"Shoot," Tom said. He was the *deputy* sheriff. The *sheriff* lived in and ran things from the county seat of Coloma. Tom had corrected Willie a time or two, but the old man insisted on the promotion.

"A small claim, my mule, and a Kentucky smoothbore flintlock are the full extent of my worldly belongings, along with this cash money." He nodded at the handkerchief tied up in a bundle. "I've left my daughter up at the claim. Could you take the mule and weapon and my winnings to her?"

"This is the first you've mentioned you took a wife and had a child," Tom said.

"My missus died birthing our girl. Dulcie is all the kin I've got." Willie warmed his hands on the mug and became thoughtful. "I reckon I could've done better by both of them."

It was the only regret Willie had given voice to.

Tom was more than willing to help him. "Don't you worry about your girl. I'll go fetch her and bring her into town."

Willie should've looked relieved, but doubt creased his forehead.

"Fair warning, Sheriff. Dulcie has a mind of her own. She'll not take kindly to any suggestions she's not capable."

"A girl shouldn't be alone with desperadoes wandering these hills," Tom reminded him.

"I don't think she'll take to city ways too easy," Willie said.

"She'll need supplies one of these days. She'll have to make the acquaintance of Hangtown sooner or later."

Willie rubbed his scrawny beard, which was salted with stiff white hairs. "I reckon you're right."

Tom knew the old boy prided himself on being self-reliant and was as tough-minded as any man he'd come across. No doubt Willie's daughter was more of the same. As a deputy and as a man, Tom had a natural inclination to protect womenfolk, and he was confident his use of Walker charm would coax Willie's daughter to safer surroundings.

Willie slurped his coffee. "She'll be as angry as a hornet at what I've done," he said. "After she grieves, of course."

"Losing a loved one is never easy," Tom answered. He emptied his mug and stepped back from the cell to let Willie mull over what must be a heavy heart.

Two newly deputized men pushed through the door, freshly washed and shaved.

Jasper Jenkins, no more than a pup, was eager to do his best. Riley Gibbs, a Sidney boy who had some book learning, was more thoughtful about his duties. Riley had a way of overthinking the situation when it came to confronting the criminal mind. Tom feared that one day Riley's bookish ways would get him killed.

Both boys carried shotguns loaded with buckshot and could stop a man at close range, but Tom doubted they'd be able to quell a riot.

The citizens of this town expected justice, and there were those who were more than willing to take the law into their own hands and put that noose around Willie's neck themselves. Tom was duty bound not to let them.

Tom opened the middle drawer of the oak desk and took out his pa's Colt .36 single-action repeater. He buckled the leather gun belt and let it settle on his hip. He shucked the six-shooter into the holster.

Tom was ready. He'd learned to be careful and was fully prepared for surprises. There'd be no vigilante lynching in Hangtown while he wore the badge.

Willie wiped his face with a chapped hand and rose to his feet.

"I thank you kindly, Sheriff, for all you've done. You've been a friend to this weary traveler, and you're a man your pa would be proud of."

Tom was touched by the man's praise. During the long evenings waiting on the judge to arrive, he and Willie had swapped stories. He'd told Willie about the old days when Tom's pa had worn the badge. Those had been dangerous times. The town had been called Old Dry Diggings by the miners scratching the earth for gold. His pa had been one of the first to bring law and order to the territory.

Sheriff Walker had caught a bullet in an ambush over by Spanish Hill for his effort. The territory had become part of the State of California. New laws had been made. Tom had taken over for his pa, proud to defend the town and its God-fearing residents. Sheriff Walker had left a better place for having lived, and Tom meant to carry on his legacy.

"Wish things had turned out differently," Tom said. It was small consolation.

"Don't you fret none," Willie said with a wink. "I'm ready to meet my Maker."

Willie held out both hands, showing the scars from a lifetime of hard work, lately placer mining in the El Dorado. Tom slapped on a pair of handcuffs. He'd like to remove the leg irons. Where was a man Willie's age going to run off to?

Tom stepped back to give Willie room to leave the cell. He watched as the old man shuffled toward the door, his shoulders straight and his chin up high. He usually saw fear in a man about to die, or defiance, but Willie seemed as cheerful as a man headed out to a Sunday school picnic.

Tom picked up his hat and squashed it onto his head.

Jasper opened the door to angry voices.

Ezra Dixon and a few other Hangtown citizens congregated on the boardwalk.

When they saw Willie, they glared at him with feral eyes. Willie didn't flinch but stared back, giving as good as he got, Tom reckoned.

"Ezra," Tom said, acknowledging the leader of the Hangtown Vigilance Committee.

"Morning, Deputy." He made no move to let them pass.

"Is there something you need?" Tom asked.

"Just thought me and the boys would take this no-account off your hands this morning," Ezra said.

There were murmurs of agreement.

"Let me do my job, Ezra," Tom replied with irritation.

"Don't get your dander up," Ezra said. "Before your pa took up the badge, the Vigilance Committee took care of these ne'er-do-wells in swift order and without any coddling."

"I reckon those days are over," Tom said.

Ezra stepped closer. "All I'm saying is, there's no need to spend hard-earned money sending for a judge and the expense of a trial like you did for Crowder here for what us law-abiding citizens can manage."

Tom faced him. He'd heard the argument a hundred times. Ezra was a respected member of the community, but Tom wasn't about to be bullied. "A fair trial is the only way to deal with accused criminals."

Ezra's eyes narrowed. "The Vigilance Committee sees things differently."

"Step aside, Ezra. I won't ask you again."

Ezra remained rooted to the spot. "Just so you know, Deputy, I intend to run for sheriff come election time."

"That'd be your right. Now, you and your men clear out," Tom said, his patience about used up.

Ezra stepped back. The other men moved off the boardwalk, muttering.

Tom motioned for Jasper to lead the way. The boy jumped to the front, holding his shotgun across his body. "Riley, you cover our back."

Tom grabbed Willie by the shoulder. "You keep your eyes straight and your mouth shut."

Willie nodded. "I won't provoke Ezra or them others. I'll leave the honor of hanging me to you, Sheriff."

Tom caught the irony of Willie's words. It didn't make his job any easier.

He marched Willie up the boardwalk. Clumps of citizens turned shaded eyes on the prisoner. They wore their Sunday best, men in top hats and ladies twirling parasols. Their faces were twisted in hate and reproach toward the old man who'd found himself on the wrong side of the law.

When they rounded the corner, Tom spotted a brass band assembling directly across from the hanging tree. Jasper looked back at Tom. Tom could only shake his head.

The band started playing "Oh! Susanna," a favorite of the locals.

Willie seemed to be enjoying the performance. A lazy smile cut across his whiskered chops, and he began to sway in time with the music. Tom realized that acceptance of things that couldn't be changed was part of Willie's character, and he meant to make the best of his last hour of living.

They stepped off the boardwalk into the street. The hangman's noose was knotted and ready. The undertaker's buckboard had been called into service.

The crowd pressed closer, and Jasper cleared a path like Moses parting the Red Sea.

Two youngsters roosted on the roof of the livery, their legs dangling over the edge. Tom turned to Riley. "Get those boys off of there and send them on home."

Riley looked relieved by his reassignment and headed in the direction of the livery.

Tom and Jasper hauled Willie up onto the back of the buckboard, and Tom climbed aboard. He helped Willie to his feet.

Preacher Evans said a few words meant to comfort the condemned. Whether Willie listened or not, Tom couldn't say. The preacher ended with a short prayer.

Next Mayor Coates climbed up onto the buckboard. This being an election year, the mayor said a few words about the importance of law and order. After his speech, the crowd broke out into enthusiastic applause. He jumped down and started shaking hands.

Tom fitted the noose around Willie's neck. The old codger refused a blindfold. He wanted to exit this life, he told Tom, with a view.

"Any last words?" Tom asked.

Willie shook his head, his gaze fixed on the horizon. Was he thinking about his girl left alone in this savage land?

"Don't you worry about Dulcie. She'll be well taken care of," Tom assured him.

A peace seemed to settle over the old man. He looked at Tom with satisfaction.

Tom stepped down. The undertaker looked at him, and Tom nodded. The undertaker gave the reins a shake. The gelding moved forward.

Tom shook off his tiredness as he packed his saddlebag with jerky, dried apples, and a sack of ground coffee. He could use some shut-eye, but he'd made Willie a promise he wasn't about to break.

Willie'd showed mighty poor judgment leaving a girl up in the lawless hills by her lonesome, in Tom's considered opinion. The country was rife with thieves and scoundrels, and bringing her to town couldn't wait.

Young Jasper Jenkins burst through the door, panting heavily. Tom had sent him to the livery to fetch Willie's mule. That boy never did anything slowly.

"Done like you asked," Jasper said. "Willie's mule is saddled and ready."

"Good. I'll be gone the better part of the day," Tom explained as he pulled on his gloves and threw the saddlebag over his shoulder.

"Do you really think you'll find Willie's daughter?" Jasper asked.

"That's my intention."

Jasper broke into a toothy grin. "What if she's skedaddled?"

"Willie was sure she'd stay put."

"What if Miss Crowder won't give up the claim?"

"She won't have to, but I want her here in town where she'll be safe." Tom headed for the door.

"Go get her, Tom."

He looked back at Jasper. "I'm depending on you to keep the peace around here while I'm gone."

"Don't you worry. I'll knock heads together if need be."

"Don't go borrowing trouble," Tom warned him.

Jasper's grin widened.

Tom didn't doubt the boy's ability. Young Jasper was too green to have given the danger of this job his full consideration. No amount of counsel would budge the boy from his need to prove himself.

"See you before dark," Tom told him, and he picked up his hat from the peg and settled it on his head.

Tom opened the door and stepped outside. The weather had turned warm. He was more than ready for spring, and that was the truth. He paused to unbutton his coat. The town seemed to have settled down from the morning's festivities, the men's bloodlust cooled.

Mr. Paisley swept the boardwalk in front of his dry goods store. Other citizens went about their business. They were decent folks, working hard and expecting Hangtown to be a good place to raise their families.

The public hangings did a fair job of providing security to the town. The ne'er-do-wells and no-accounts had, for the most part, moved on.

What Ezra Dixon had told him stuck in his craw, though. Tom had no doubt a man must stay vigilant, and a town must be dedicated to taking the necessary steps to keep the streets free from lawlessness, but justice would only prevail by means of a fair trial. No man had the right to interfere with the rule of law.

He threw his saddlebags up onto his horse. The mustang tried to pull his head up, but the reins, tied to the hitching post, held fast.

"Whoa," he said firmly. The mustang was only just broke and flighty, but Tom needed a sure-footed mount where he was going.

He didn't know what he'd find at the Crowder camp. Claim jumpers might've run the girl off. There were plenty of men in the hills fueled by greed who'd slit a throat to settle ownership of a piece of land.

Jasper came outside and stood in the doorway, holding his shotgun in his left hand. Tom gathered the reins of Willie's mule and mounted his mustang. Jasper saluted.

Tom nodded and turned his horse, headed for his ma's house. He had something to talk over with her before he went searching for the Crowder girl.

Ma had raised a ruckus when he'd pinned on the deputy's badge. He'd been unable to convince her the job was his calling.

Being the middle of three rambunctious boys, Tom had managed to evade most parental expectations. Jack had taken off to prospect for gold in the south diggings. They hadn't seen or heard from him since the summer of '48. Richard had headed for Denver to study the law. He'd died from a fever only two months shy of receiving his degree.

Ma still grieved for Pa and Tom's brothers. So did Tom. He also understood her fears. They were all afraid of the violence and killings in a lawless land.

Tom's ma had no objections to law and order; she understood the necessity of having a town sheriff and a slew of deputies. She just didn't want Tom to be the one risking his neck to bring troublemakers to justice.

His pa had stood up to gangs of bandits and killers. Tom would do the same.

He arrived at the Walker homestead inside of ten minutes. Ma came out onto the porch, her hound at her feet. Her gaze drifted to the mule and then back to Tom.

"You look a sight," she said.

"Spent the night playing cards with Willie Crowder."

"Is he gone?" she asked.

"Yes, ma'am. Right on schedule."

She frowned. "God rest his soul."

"Amen."

"Come on in, and I'll fix you some breakfast. I just took a batch of sourdough out of the oven."

Tom was tempted. He'd skipped breakfast, and he loved nothing better than his ma's sourdough biscuits straight from the oven.

"Can't," he said. "I've got a long ride ahead of me. Turns out Willie had a daughter. He asked me to look in on her."

"A daughter? There's a surprise."

"I suspect he didn't want anyone to know about his girl."

"Will you bring her to town?"

"Yes, ma'am," he answered. "A girl shouldn't be working a claim alone."

"What makes you so sure she'll be willing to leave it?" she asked.

"I'll just have to persuade her," Tom answered.

His ma fought a smile, but there was no mistaking it. "No doubt you will."

"Could she stay with you for a spell?" Tom asked.

This time her smile came easily. "I suppose I could use some female company."

Tom had been thinking along the same lines. He hadn't expected his ma to turn him down. Ma could be counted on to help those in need.

"I'll be back before sunset," he said. He tipped his hat in farewell.

Her smile collapsed. "Make sure you are."

Tom didn't have any words to reassure her. They'd spoken often enough of the danger, of the ruthless killings born in the rush for gold.

He aimed to clean up the El Dorado. It was his duty as a Walker and as a man.

He paused to remove his coat and tie it down to his pack. With a nudge of both knees, he urged his horse forward. They'd plenty of ground to cover before they reached their destination.

He headed east on a heavily rutted road that climbed into hills crowded with sycamore saplings bending in the wind. Last fall's leaves crackled underfoot. Blackbirds, disturbed by his presence, flew off squawking.

He'd never been one to express himself without some clumsiness, and he couldn't ever put words together to describe what he was feeling, but in this hostile land he'd seen God's majesty, and that could humble a man.

The wilderness was changing. Since the discovery of gold over at Sutter's Mill, new arrivals from all parts of the world had staked their claim to this land, trying their luck panning for gold ore, believing there was plenty to go around.

Some folks were lucky, but most came up empty.

In the process, they'd stripped the hills for lumber to build sluices and littered the countryside with their castoffs. He hated to see the earth ravished this way, leaving nothing but bare patches of rock and dirt.

He turned off the road onto a path just wide enough for his horse and the mule. A constant wind swirled trail dust into his face. He pulled up his bandanna to cover his nose and mouth and pulled down his hat.

He climbed steadily. His horse was game, and the mule didn't give up any objections.

The road narrowed and then disappeared. Tom pulled up and checked the wide expanse of thick pine forest around him. Wherever Willie'd built his lodgings, he'd taken pains to keep hidden. The old boy's need for secrecy worked against Tom.

He was about to turn back and follow a more northerly trail when a bullet ricocheted off a boulder not ten feet ahead. The mustang screamed and reared back on its hind legs.

"Whoa," Tom said as he pulled back on the reins. His horse backed up into Willie's mule, who sent out a loud protest and started bucking off Willie's gear. Tom let the critter go and drew out his six-shooter.

He settled the mustang down with a word or two and looked around him. All he could see were sugar pines reaching for the sky. His horse's hide rippled beneath him.

Tom scoured the rocks for the culprit who'd tried to bushwhack him. Then he caught sight of a gun barrel poking between two boulders, and cold certainty coursed though him.

He'd missed all the signs that someone had been watching him, a lethal mistake in the El Dorado.

"Drop your weapon," a voice shouted from behind the wall of granite. Tom couldn't tell if it was a young male or a female.

He dropped his six-shooter into the dirt, where he could reach it if and when he dismounted.

"And your rifle."

Tom pulled his rifle out of the scabbard and tossed it to the ground next to the shooter.

"Now put up your hands where I can see them."

First Tom yanked his bandanna from his mouth, ready to announce who he was and what he was after, and then did as he was told.

Chapter Two

Laughter had bubbled out of Dulcie Crowder as she'd watched the intruder fight to stay in the saddle as his mount tried to buck him off. She didn't lower her weapon. Pa had warned her to be cautious when strangers came calling. Dulcie never needed to be told twice.

The stranger had gained back control with a fair amount of competence and now sat tall in the saddle with his hands in the air.

"Will you take a look at him?" she said softly. She'd been talking to herself a lot lately, living alone the way she did.

He wore a dark brown woolly shirt settled on broad shoulders and a red bandanna around his neck. Dark hair sprouted out from under a short-brimmed hat. He needed a shave.

Coal black eyes showed the weariness of a man who'd traveled a distance. Most likely he'd not slept.

He carried a pistol, which he'd smartly tossed to the ground. A rifle, stowed in a scabbard behind his saddle, had joined it.

She'd caught him by surprise, so he hadn't been expecting to find her here. Most likely he was just passing through, but she wasn't taking any chances.

"Who might you be?" she asked in a gruff voice. She made a poor imitation of a man, but she was banking on the stranger being too scared to notice.

"Tom Walker, deputy sheriff out of Hangtown."

Her gut tightened. Pa had taught her to be suspicious of lawmen. The law had a way of taking what hardworking folks rightfully owned.

"What are you after?" she asked.

"I've come to pay my respects to Miss Dulcie Crowder," he said.

"You found her." Dulcie stepped from her hiding place.

His gaze connected with hers. There was no fright in him but no meanness either.

"Don't you know any better than to come sneaking up on a homestead?" she asked.

"I sure do, ma'am, and I'm sorry if I caused you any concern."

The deputy talked polite, but she didn't loosen her grip on the shotgun or remove her finger from the trigger.

Her gaze strayed to the mule, and she recognized him. Chester had a scar across his muzzle turned white where his previous owner had beaten him with a bullwhip.

"What are you doing with my pa's mule?" she asked, looking back at him.

He kept his gaze steady on her, and she was struck by his manliness.

"That's why I've come," he said. "I've brought bad news."

Dulcie faltered. Bad news could only mean one thing.

"You get off that horse slow and easy."

He lowered his hands and dismounted.

She stepped out of the shadows.

"Ma'am," he said, and he pulled off his hat and held it to his chest. His dark hair was mashed flat. In other circumstances, she would've burst out laughing, but his deep scowl convinced her this was no time for frivolity.

"Say your piece. I'm listening."

"I'd be obliged to, but first, won't you put down the weapon?"

Tom shifted his stance. Women could be skittish when it came to handling firearms.

For sure, he didn't want to tell her the distressing news about her pa with double-barrels pointed at his heart.

She did as he asked and lowered the shotgun but kept it tucked under one arm. She stood no more than five feet and looked to be eighteen or nineteen. The weapon was too big for her. A small, thin hand grasped the barrel. A blast from it would most likely knock her off her feet.

Her brown hair was braided down her back, and large brown eyes watched him with suspicion. She wore a man's canvas britches and a faded wool shirt with the sleeves rolled up to her elbows.

Still, there was no hiding the woman underneath.

Willie had a looker for a daughter. No wonder he kept her hidden up here on this hill, away from the pack of lonely men in town.

"Well?" she asked impatiently. He saw her lower lip quiver. She'd already guessed what he'd come to say and looked frail in a world that had suddenly gone empty.

"Your pa is dead, Dulcie," Tom said with regret.

Her eyes filled with grieving, and big tears ran down both cheeks.

"I'm sorry," he said simply, knowing there weren't any words that would comfort at a time like this.

"I appreciate you saying so," she replied. She wiped her face with the palm of her hand.

Tom removed his bandanna and handed it over.

She took it with a shudder and a sigh.

"He was a good pa," she said, blowing her nose. "And a good enough man."

"That he was."

"You knew him?" Her brown eyes glistened, her pain reflected in their depths.

"Your pa and I got acquainted over the last couple of days," he said. "I consider him a friend."

She nodded. "I'm glad to hear you say so."

"He told me about you being up here by yourself. He asked me to look in on you. Your pa thought about you right up to the end."

Dulcie's mouth twitched. "Pa sent you?"

"Yes, ma'am."

She set the shotgun against a stump. "Sorry about the shooter. Pa taught me to be careful around strangers."

"Your pa taught you right," he said.

Tom decided she had a trusting nature, something Willie had needed to warn her about.

"Pa didn't have any say in when he was going to die," she said with reflection, "but I know he put up a fight."

Tom looked away. He should tell her the details, but they could wait. She'd just heard her pa had died, and that was enough to chew on in one bite.

"I suppose he's buried in Hangtown?" she asked.

"He is." Tom didn't tell her where. The folks of Hangtown were particular about who could be buried in the church cemetery. Willie's final resting place was out of town with the outlaws, saloon dollies, and gambling men.

"Where's my manners?" Dulcie said with a sniff. "You've come a fair distance to return my pa's belongings and his mule. I expect you're ready for some grub."

"A hot cup of coffee would be appreciated."

She picked up a bowie knife measuring a good twelve inches from tip to bone handle. Tom gulped. For a little gal, she sure kept an arsenal of oversized weapons.

"I was skinning a hare when I heard you coming." She wiped the blade on the nearest chickweed bush. She stowed the knife in a leather sheath tied around her waist.

Tom grabbed his Colt and shoved it into his holster. He shucked his rifle back into its scabbard.

She'd disappeared inside a lean-to. The sorry-looking shelter was made of pine logs and rocks with nothing but pine-bough roofing to keep the elements out. She shoved aside a horse blanket that served for a door.

Tom had seen this kind of hard living before. The thousands of miners who roamed the El Dorado cobbled together what they could for shelter.

He led his horse and the mule over to a stone cistern. He scooped up a hatful of cold water and gave both animals a drink. He pulled off the saddle and hobbled his horse with a leather strap. The mule had already helped himself to some dried-up snakeweed left over from the winter's kill and looked content.

Tom splashed cold water on his face and ran a handful through his hair. How had Willie come to lay claim to this piece of land? Tom hadn't heard of any gold found this far east.

He'd no doubt Dulcie was brave and resilient. Folks living up in these hills had to be. All alone, though, Tom knew she would be taken advantage of. He hoped she recognized how vulnerable she was up here and how isolated. It would make his task of convincing her to come with him to town easier.

"Take a load off," she said, indicating the nearest tree stump.

Tom smiled. It was something Willie would've said.

He sat down next to a ring of stones. A fire smoldered there. She set the shotgun against another stump and put on a feed sack for an apron.

Using the hem of her feed-sack apron, she removed a blackened coffeepot from a flat stone and emptied the grounds into a tin pail. She ladled fresh water from a tin bucket into the pot and added new grounds. She set the pot back on its perch, close to the smoldering fire.

She did all these things as if this were a cozy kitchen instead of an outdoor campfire on a blustery spring day.

Soon the air smelled pungent with coffee brewing.

Tom was confirmed in his opinion that Miss Crowder should go back to town with him.

This was no life for a woman.

Dulcie stole a sideways look at the Hangtown deputy sheriff. He sure was a sight to see. He'd washed up, and the hairs on top of his head stood up straight. She could offer him her wooden comb, but she didn't think combing would improve matters. She wished she'd used that comb on her own tangled locks that morning.

There was confidence in the set of those broad shoulders and the way he sat astride that stump. She never faulted anybody who believed in himself.

The question front and center in her mind was, what kind of man rode all the way up there to do a favor for a man he'd known only a couple of days? What was Tom Walker after?

Pa'd been so sure the claim would make them rich. Being a homebody, she hadn't been as enthusiastic about trying their luck in the El Dorado. She'd endured the long winter and unbearable loneliness. There were many days she thought she couldn't take any more.

Now Pa laid buried in a patch of earth in gold country. Ma's grave was in the churchyard back home.

Dulcie might as well face facts. She was an orphan and dependent on the kindness of strangers.

She'd no interest in working the claim. She expected, at some point, to find a husband and raise a herd of young'uns. Meeting an eligible man was a difficult task, given she lived a good day's ride from civilization. When Pa left for town, she'd wanted so fiercely to go with him. Pa'd told her to stay with the claim so nobody would take it from them. She'd done as he'd asked.

Now here was this handsome deputy come to bring her the news her pa was gone, and she couldn't help but wonder if the deputy was a good man or bad.

"I'm frying up some rabbit. You're welcome to what there is," she said.

"Thank you, ma'am, but I can't stay."

She nodded. The visit would be a short one.

Tom folded his hands and hunched forward. "I've got to get back to town. I'd like you to come with me."

"On what account?"

His expression was kindly enough, but he battled fatigue and looked in no mood to argue. "On account of you can't live up here alone."

She picked up two dented tin cups off the ground and poured them full of steaming coffee. She set both cups on a rock. The deputy helped himself and blew on the dark brew.

Dulcie sat opposite him. "Because I'm female?"

The deputy's stern gaze pierced right through her resistance. "Living up here alone isn't safe for anybody, man or woman."

"I've managed well enough so far," she replied. She didn't want him to think she'd no backbone.

"You'd be doing me a favor," he replied.

"What kind of favor?" she asked suspiciously.

Tom examined the coffee grounds in the bottom of his cup. "My pa died a few years back. Ma lives by her lonesome. She's agreed to let you stay with her." He looked up and smiled. There was something about his smile that set well with Dulcie.

"Ma needs somebody besides me to worry about," Tom said. "I'd be obliged."

His thoughtfulness toward his ma touched her down deep. Truth be told, Dulcie wasn't a solitary creature either.

"Thank her kindly." Dulcie didn't want to seem ungrateful. "But I've got no means to live in town."

"What about selling your claim?" he asked.

"Is that what you're after? You want to buy this claim?"

"No, ma'am. I'm no miner."

"Claim's not worth much anyway," she admitted. "I suppose a mule would bring a hefty sum."

"Enough for a new start."

Dulcie nodded. He'd seen the core of her druthers. She wouldn't be a burden. She turned away, blinking madly to keep away fresh tears.

"Of course the decision is yours," he said.

Dulcie wiped her eyes with the kerchief and blew her nose. He'd let her have the final say in the matter. She couldn't help but think Tom Walker was an uncommon man.

"Are you married?" she asked.

"Nope."

"You must be sweet on someone."

He scratched the stubble of his day's worth of beard. "I reckon I was a time ago."

"If you don't mind my asking, what happened?"

He looked at his hands. "She married somebody else. I'm not the marrying kind," he said.

"What the heck does that mean?" She'd never heard such a fool notion in her life.

He didn't answer. No doubt he'd accepted the notion without any thought.

Dulcie's string of questions caused some awkwardness between them, which she surely hadn't meant to do.

"You'll have to forgive me. Pa always said I did enough talking for two. Although my pa could talk the leg off a rooster," she said. "He told many a knee-slapping good story without any encouragement."

The deputy pushed his hat back on his head. He looked amused by what she'd said, and she didn't even mind. She liked a man with an easy temperament.

"More coffee?"

Tom handed over his cup. "Thank you."

She'd make herself useful in town. She could trap rabbits and shoot deer and put up the meat for winter. She could keep a clean house and have supper on the table. She could do all that was expected of her and then some.

Those were good skills for a woman whose aim was matrimony.

"I'd like to come to town with you," she said. "I'd like it fine."

The deputy's smile spread to his eyes. He sure was a handsome man.

"I'd hoped you would."

"To tell the truth, I'm not overly fond of living up here," she said as she poured him a second cup.

"Your pa told me you wouldn't care for town living."

"Pa could be overprotective at times."

"I reckon most pa's are."

Dulcie swallowed hard. Tom Walker was a wonder, understanding like he did.

"Your pa was one of a kind."

"I believe he was. I was proud to take care of him. Now's different. Time I found a husband."

Tom frowned. Had he misunderstood what she was trying to say? Maybe not.

"What I mean is, you seem like a real nice fella. I'd like to get to know you better."

"I am," he said without any false modesty. "I'd like to get to know you too."

That was all the encouragement she needed. She wanted to get hitched. Here sat the likeliest candidate of any man she'd come across. "I was hoping you would."

Tom threw the coffee grounds in his cup into the fire and stood. "We'd better get started."

Dulcie faced him toe to toe, although he stood head and

shoulders taller, and she had to look up a distance. "I'd like nothing better."

The deputy backed away until he almost tripped over a stump.

This was her pa's doing, sending the deputy up to their camp, and she thanked the old man for thinking of her future.

"It won't take me long to pack what little I've got," she said as he gathered up the reins to his horse. He surely was in a hurry.

She picked up the half-skinned hare by the back legs. It'd feed three hungry mouths for sure. "I'll bring supper."

Chapter Three

As Tom led the way, his thoughts wrestled with two vital questions. What kind of situation had he gotten himself into? And what was he going to do about Dulcie Crowder?

She was lonely, maybe even desperate. She'd just learned the worst kind of news. Of course she'd attach herself to the first man who came along.

He needed to put a stop to any such female notions, but he didn't want to hurt her feelings.

Dulcie would soon find out he couldn't be a husband. He'd decided when he took on the job that he wouldn't put a wife and family in harm's way.

He looked back. She sat astride Willie's mule as well as any placer miner, a woman who knew how to get by with little. She'd turned up the brim on her faded hat. Her shotgun rested against the pommel.

She caught him staring at her and winked.

Tom swung his gaze to the rock-strewn path in front of him. He didn't know how to handle this girl, and he hated being unsure of himself.

They made good time, and when they reached Bailey Creek, Tom stopped. Dulcie rode up beside him.

"Our mounts could use a rest," he said.

"So could my backside," she replied. A sheen of perspiration wet her face, and her cheeks glowed pink and fresh. He didn't think he'd ever seen a prettier sight.

He turned away before she made more of his interest than was safe for a man.

They dismounted and walked a short way. He heard the gurgling water of the winter's snowmelt off the hilltops and pushed through underbrush until they came to a fast-flowing creek. Shafts of sunlight danced across the water.

Dulcie put her shotgun against the trunk of a cedar and sat down on a rock. She pulled off boots worn down at the heels and stripped off woolen socks. She rolled up her britches to her knees, exposing delicate feet and shapely ankles. Either she didn't know what effect such a sight would have on a man or she knew darned well.

Tom needed to keep his wits about him.

"Aren't you going to come in?" she asked. She splashed water in his direction with her bare feet.

Tom shook his head. "Too cold for me."

"Come on. The water'll wake you up."

Tom stayed put. He was uncomfortable with the situation. She was entirely too friendly with him, a man she'd just met.

She waded down the middle of the stream, hands outstretched to keep her balance on the slippery rocks. A gust of wind blew off her hat. Tom jumped to his feet and scooped it up as it floated past him.

She spun around and almost lost her balance. She righted herself, laughing. He liked hearing her laugh. A hank of wispy hair escaped her braid and whipped around her face. He stood there like a tongue-tied schoolboy, holding on to her dripping hat.

She blinked at him with those brown eyes.

He flung the hat onto the bank and started off in the opposite direction. He wondered if Dulcie had any remaining kin. With the money the mule would fetch, she could go back East and make a good life for herself among family who'd take care of her. She'd be better off in a place where violence wasn't a way of life and she could find a good man who could give her what she needed.

He'd suggest it when they arrived in Hangtown and she found out for herself the town had nothing for her.

Tom walked upstream to where the mule had wandered. The animal had found a patch of newly sprouted grass. He checked to make sure the cinch was tight and secure. He led the critter back to where Dulcie sat on a rock. She'd pulled on her footwear and turned up the brim of her hat.

"You ready?" he asked.

She gave him a quick, assessing gaze and grinned. "As ready as I'll ever be."

Dulcie itched for conversation, but ever since they'd left the creek, Tom Walker had worn a long face. Maybe he was pondering all the responsibilities of being a deputy, or maybe he'd something on his mind that was no business of hers. There was more than one way to shift a man's sulky mood.

"What's your horse's name?" Dulcie asked, riding up alongside him.

"He doesn't have one."

"Every critter ought to have a name. Even old Chester, as ornery as he is, has a respectable name."

Tom didn't reply.

"I think if I were to give your horse a name, I'd call him Shooting Star on account of the dab of white between his eyes."

The beginnings of a smile parted his lips. It was the kind of smile that made a girl's heart palpitate. She was happy she'd given him something to smile about.

"Of course, you can call him Star for short."

"Star it is," Tom replied.

Dulcie liked that he'd thawed some and finally was agreeable. They were going to get along just fine.

She spotted the town below them, nestled in a ravine, an assembly of tents, shacks, and wood buildings, tall and short, crowded together. She'd seen bigger towns coming out west through Missouri and Kansas, but Hangtown was big enough. This was Tom's town, and now it was her town. It would be a good place to be from.

"Looks like we made it," she said.

Tom nodded, keeping his opinion to himself.

They descended a rocky road as the sun set in front of them, blinding them for a minute or two before it slid behind a layer of clouds. The dusk quickly enveloped them, and she shivered, hating the dark as she did.

They turned onto the main road. Lamplight poured out of windows, and campfires burned rosy and welcoming. Wagons headed out of town, weighed down with supplies for the camps. Riders on horseback and mules passed them in both directions.

This was where her pa had come and where he'd taken his last breath. A deep sadness threatened to bring on a bout of crying, but she held her tears back. She needed to make a favorable impression on the folks of Hangtown.

Before long, Dulcie lagged behind. She couldn't help but wonder at everything there was to see. The town burst at the seams with commerce, as both sides of the street were crowded with businesses. She'd no doubt she'd arrived in an exciting place.

Ladies strolled along the wooden walkways, carrying parcels, and stopped to greet their friends. Men stood in clumps smoking pipes, talking loudly and laughing.

Some folks congregated on the boardwalk and gave her sideways glances. Of course, they'd be curious about a newcomer in town. She wouldn't be a newcomer for long. She couldn't wait to meet each and every one of them.

A man wearing a black suit and top hat pointed at her. She cast him a friendly smile, but he and the lady who clung to his arm turned away.

Another group of ladies, carrying baskets and chatting like magpies, stiffened as she rode by. Those women muffled their opinions behind gloved hands.

Tom kept his eyes on the road, and she understood why. He was used to being around women with fancy dresses and feathers flapping in the breeze. She was dressed like a trapper and not smelling like a rose. No use pretending otherwise.

Her education in town ways was lacking, but she was a quick learner. She'd ask Tom's ma to teach her. She'd show these citizens of Hangtown that Dulcie Crowder could be a lady.

Tom would notice her then, and he'd be proud to be seen with her. He'd come a-courting, and she'd be the happiest woman in all of California.

He pulled up in front of one of the wooden buildings. A young man came out carrying a shotgun. His long black hair was combed back off his forehead. His dark eyes sparkled good-naturedly. He was good to look at but not half as pretty as Tom.

He wore a tin badge just like Tom's with DEPUTY SHERIFF engraved on it.

"Howdy," he said to her, and he swept his hand through his hair. He turned to Tom. "You found her."

"Jasper, this is Miss Dulcie Crowder."

The deputy cast her a welcoming grin. Dulcie returned his kind attention with a smile of her own.

"Aren't you a surprise?" Jasper said.

"I guess I am."

"If there's anything you need, you ask for Jasper Jenkins."

"Thank you, but my needs are spoken for."

Jasper looked to Tom for an explanation. He didn't offer any.

Instead, Tom leaned on his pommel. "Anything happen while I was gone?"

Jasper set his weapon against the hitching post, his gaze stuck on Dulcie. "A telegram came from the sheriff in Coloma. You want me to fetch it?"

"Anything important?" Tom asked.

"Nah. He just wanted to know about this morning."

"It'll keep," Tom answered sharply.

"One thing you oughta know. Ezra Dixon found out about Miss Crowder. He's been saying some harsh words about you bringing her to town."

Tom scowled something frightful.

"Who's Ezra Dixon?" Dulcie asked.

"A man not to be crossed," Jasper answered.

"Did he have a run-in with my pa?"

Jasper and Tom exchanged glances. She'd guessed correctly.

"Ezra means to have your badge for leaving Hangtown without informing the town trustees," Jasper said.

Tom huffed.

"I should have a friendly talk with this Ezra," Dulcie said. She hated to be the source of trouble for her soon-to-be betrothed.

"You'll stay away from him," Tom cautioned.

"What harm would a little neighborly conversation do?" she asked.

"He doesn't like strangers," Tom replied.

Dulcie opened her mouth to remind Tom she wouldn't be a stranger for long. Tom knew Ezra Dixon well, and she'd heed his warning, even though she was mighty curious what her pa and Ezra had had words about.

"I'm taking Dulcie to my ma's place," Tom told Jasper. "I'll be back shortly."

Tom gave Star a word of encouragement and headed up the street.

"I'm pleased to meet you," Dulcie said.

Jasper lit up like a firefly and twirled his hat on one finger. "Ma'am."

She would've liked to talk more with Jasper Jenkins, but Tom was in all kinds of a hurry. She shook her reins, and Chester, bless his heart, broke into a trot. When she caught up with Tom Walker, she slowed Chester to a walk.

"Jasper seems real nice," she said.

"He is."

"I'm going to like this town."

"There are good people here."

He'd get no argument from her.

Tom kept looking ahead, his jaw clenched. Most likely he hadn't liked Ezra Dixon questioning his authority. Ezra Dixon's threat was uncalled for, to her way of thinking. What Tom had done, riding the better part of the day to tell her about her pa's sudden passing, was a kindness.

It seemed to Dulcie that kindness could use more cultivating in this world.

Chapter Four

The Walker place was at the end of a cluster of the most beautiful homes Dulcie had ever laid eyes on. They were arranged in a neat row like peas in a pod. Mrs. Walker's house rose two stories to meet the tops of the tallest trees. There was a big porch wrapped around on three sides, curtained windows, and plenty of trimming painted white. There was a real door made of oak. About fifty feet away a pole corral and a freshly painted stable had been built. Shading both stood a giant oak tree.

There was a look of permanence here, something Dulcie had longed for ever since she'd arrived in this part of the country.

A big black dog leaped off the front stoop, barking his fool head off. Chester balked and wouldn't go any farther, and no amount of sweet-talking would change his mind.

"The hound won't hurt you," Tom said. He pulled up his horse and dismounted.

"Your hound doesn't scare me," she said, in case he'd gotten the wrong impression. "Chester's of another opinion."

The dog reached her and circled the mule. Chester kicked out a hind leg to show his estimation of the ruckus. The dog was smart enough to stay out of reach.

"This dog have a name?" she asked, trying to make herself heard above the racket.

"In fact, he does. Ma named him Baron."

"That's a lofty name," she replied. She held on to the reins tighter as Chester acted ready to jump out of his skin.

With a sharp word from Tom, Baron quit his yapping and went

back to the house. He settled down on the porch, but his gaze never left Chester.

"Those two are going to have to settle their differences, one way or the other," she said.

A woman came out the house. Light from inside pooled around her. She was plainly dressed in dark muslin and wore a white apron and cap. She looked at Tom as if he were ten feet tall and made of gold ore.

Tom regarded her with weary eyes as he wrapped his reins around a hitching post.

"Ma, this is Dulcie Crowder, Willie's girl."

Chester cooperated after a persuasive nudge in his ribs, and they closed the gap.

Mrs. Walker's eyes were the same as Tom's, dark and brooding. Her face was framed in white hair drawn up on the back of her neck and secured with the neat cap on top. She looked kindly at Dulcie.

"Pleased to meet you, Dulcie."

"Same here, Mrs. Walker."

His ma looked inquiringly at Tom. "Any trouble?"

"None to speak of."

Mrs. Walker's gaze swept over Dulcie.

Dulcie knew she looked a sight, and she flushed with embarrassment.

"You can stay here," Mrs. Walker said without further hesitation. "I've got the room, since Thomas moved out."

Tom laid bare a halfhearted grin. "That'll be just fine," he said. "Come on, Dulcie."

Dulcie got down from Chester. She was grateful to be out of that saddle.

Tom reached for her reins. "I'll take the mule to the stable."

"I'll tend to him," Dulcie replied. "As long as I'm living here, I'll do my own chores."

Tom's dark eyes bore down on her like a summer storm. Her poor heart fluttered. She didn't know what she'd done to make him testy. She always spoke her mind. She didn't see any reason not to.

Chester was a responsibility she wouldn't shirk, and she couldn't let Tom think otherwise. She held on tightly to the reins.

Surprisingly, the deputy didn't try to argue. The storm clouds lifted.

"Are you staying for supper?" Mrs. Walker asked him.

Tom turned to his ma. "I can't. I've been gone all day, and Jasper's been on duty since daybreak."

Mrs. Walker stiffened. "Do as you like."

"Will you come by later?" Dulcie asked.

"No," Tom said, and he jumped into the saddle.

His ma turned on her heel and went into the house.

Dulcie felt awkward standing there. Obviously, Tom and his ma were feuding. She hoped it wasn't because of her.

Tom tipped his hat. It was all the good-bye she'd get. He pulled Star's head around and pointed him in the direction they'd just come from.

Dulcie watched him until he disappeared from view. Whatever the argument between Tom and his ma, it had put him into a sour mood, but he'd depended on his ma when he needed a helping hand with an extra mouth to feed. The family ties were strong. She'd do all she could to be agreeable and not be a source of trouble.

Under a canopy of a million stars, she started off for the stable with Chester in tow and thought about her pa. She wished Pa could've seen this place. He would've liked a house this grand just fine.

As hard as her pa had worked all his born days, he'd never had much to show for his trouble.

She came upon a carriage with a seat upholstered in black leather parked in front of the stable.

"Will you take a look at this?" she told Chester.

She ran a hand along the smooth, cold leather. The cloth top was fringed with bits and bobs, as fancy a carriage as she'd ever seen.

"One day I'm going to have a carriage just like this one," she said. The dream of riches was the gold-rush fantasy her pa had spoken of time and again.

Dulcie's stomach tightened. Pa would never realize his dream. He'd left her to do her best to fulfill the promise of the El Dorado.

Chester snorted.

"Don't you fret. I won't use no scrawny mule with my new carriage. I'll buy a sleek black gelding to pull me along in style."

Of course, a carriage and horse took a lot of money, and she didn't have much to speak of. How she would make her fortune remained to be discovered.

A short man wearing his hair in a long ponytail hurried out of the dark recesses of the stable. He bowed his head.

He wore a cap made of crimson silk and a shirt without any buttonholes. Instead, the shirt fastened with loops of braid hooked around the buttons. The man's getup looked strange to Dulcie, but she kept her comments to herself.

She remembered Pa talking of odd-looking men who came from the other side of the world to work in the gold fields.

"Are you a Chinaman?" she asked.

The man bowed again.

"My name is Dulcie Crowder."

"Eng," the man replied.

"Mr. Eng, if you'd show me where I can put up my mule, I'd be grateful."

Mr. Eng bowed a third time. Dulcie figured this was his way of replying in the affirmative.

She followed Mr. Eng down the short, rock-strewn path to the stable. He struck a match against the rough wood and lit a lantern hanging on a hook.

He lifted the lantern off the hook and motioned for her to follow him.

The stable had two boxes, one of them occupied by a dun-colored mare. Mr. Eng opened the door to the other box, and she led Chester inside. Mr. Eng hung the lantern on a nail and left her.

She pulled off the heavy pack and flung it to the ground. She removed the saddle, blanket, and bridle and set them in a corner next to her weapons.

Chester was crowding her as she rubbed him down with a handful of fresh straw.

"Move over, you ornery mule," she said, and she bumped him with her hip. She looked up and was startled by a man standing in the doorway, his face hidden by shadows.

She shot a look at her shotgun propped up in the corner. How could she have been so careless?

"You the Crowder woman?" he asked, his voice thick with menace.

"I am." She squinted to see him better. He wore a black coat and a short-brimmed hat.

"We don't want your kind in Hangtown," he said. "You Crowders only foul the air."

Dulcie gulped. "Who are you?" she asked, stepping back. She struggled to keep her voice from going all wobbly. The man would take on false courage if he knew she was afraid.

"That's not important. There's a lot of us here in Hangtown feel you'd better get on that mule and head out of here."

The coldness in his words gave her gooseflesh.

In a flash, she reached for her shotgun and raised it. But the man was gone.

Mr. Eng, with a bucket of oats, came into her sights.

She tucked her weapon under her arm just in case the stranger returned.

"Did you see a man when you came in just now?" she asked.

"Eng no see."

"Right in the doorway," she replied. "You must've bumped into him."

Mr. Eng shook his head.

Maybe it was for the best that Mr. Eng hadn't come across the stranger. No telling what the angry man would have done to him.

Dulcie decided she must tell Mrs. Walker about the visitor. She didn't want Mrs. Walker booting her out because of the threat Dulcie had brought to her doorstep, but Mrs. Walker deserved to know who came calling at her stable.

Mrs. Walker was standing by a back door. The house was flooded with light now, a warm and welcoming beacon in the darkness.

"I had a visitor just now in the stable," Dulcie said without preamble. "He told me to leave town."

"Did he give you a name?" Mrs. Walker asked.

"No, ma'am."

Mrs. Walker frowned.

"I surely didn't mean to bring you trouble," Dulcie said.

"You haven't," she replied, but without conviction.

Dulcie feared she'd already worn out her welcome.

"Don't you listen to men like him," Mrs. Walker said kindly. "Some folks are jittery about what happened this morning. They're liable to say anything."

"What happened this morning?" Dulcie asked.

Mrs. Walker sighed. "You don't know?"

"No, ma'am, I don't." Dulcie waited for an explanation.

"Let's not concern ourselves about all that now," she said with a wave of her hand as if she was shooing away a pesky fly. "I'll let Tom explain."

Dulcie wondered what the big mystery was, but she guessed she'd find out soon enough.

The stranger's message had been clear. Some folks didn't like newcomers in their town. She'd have to work hard to convince the Hangtown residents that she could be a good citizen.

"Take off your boots before you come into the house," Mrs. Walker said, her nose wrinkling. She turned and went inside, clearly troubled.

Dulcie sat down on a wooden bench and pulled off her boots, glad to be rid of them. She wiggled her toes. Her big toe stuck through her sock where she'd worn a new hole. She stripped both socks off, shaking her head. They'd been mended so many times, there wasn't enough yarn left in them to sew together.

She tucked her socks and boots under the bench and went inside to the kitchen. The stove radiated heat, and the room smelled of good things cooking.

Mrs. Walker's gaze settled on the sheath of her bowie knife. "You won't be in need of hunting gear while you're staying here."

Dulcie unbuckled the sheath belt and set the knife on the table.

Obviously, city ways were different from country ways, but Mrs. Walker would get no quarrel from Dulcie.

"I expect you're hungry," Mrs. Walker said in her friendly way.

Dulcie remembered the rabbit in her pack. She headed for the back door. "I've brought a rabbit ready for stewing. I'll go fetch it."

"Eng will bring your things in," Mrs. Walker replied.

"He's a Chinaman," Dulcie said as she turned around.

"Yes, Dulcie. Eng and his wife work for me."

"I've never met a Chinaman before," she said.

"There's all kinds come to Hangtown." Mrs. Walker ladled hot water out of the reservoir on the stove into a china pot. "Sit down, Dulcie. You must be tired after your ordeal."

Dulcie was bone weary and sore from the ride, but she didn't like being idle, especially with supper to be readied for the table. She pulled a chair away from the table and sat anyway. She didn't want to be a poor guest either.

Mrs. Walker set the pot and two cups and saucers on the table next to a pot of brown sugar cubes. The cups and saucers were white with pink roses. She went outside and came back with a white pitcher covered with a clean cloth. She put down the pitcher opposite Dulcie and removed the cloth. The pitcher contained sweet cream. That and the bowlful of sugar cubes was surely a sight.

Dulcie could've wept from the kindness. The lady had a fine set of dishes and luxuries to eat, and she didn't hold them back from the likes of Dulcie Crowder.

Pa had never taught her how to act at a tea party, so she'd watch Mrs. Walker and do exactly what she did.

"I'm so sorry about your pa's passing," Mrs. Walker said. Wiping her hands on her apron, she took her own seat.

Dulcie looked away and blinked rapidly. She wouldn't cry in front of Mrs. Walker.

The good lady reached over and patted Dulcie's wrist. Her touch was warm and a comfort.

"You've had a hard time, I know," Mrs. Walker assured her, "but that's behind you. You'll be safe here with me."

Dulcie looked at her and managed a smile. "My pa tried his best, and I don't hold his dying against him. Did you know him?"

Mrs. Walker frowned. "I'm sorry to say I didn't."

"I'll do my best to make him proud."

"I'm sure you will." Mrs. Walker withdrew her hand. There was no mistaking that something worried her.

"We'll take some getting used to each other, my ways being different from your town ways." Dulcie settled her hands in her lap. "Don't you fret, though. I intend to be a lady and a model citizen."

Mrs. Walker picked up the pot and poured brown tea into both cups. "I expect you will."

Dulcie marveled at Mrs. Walker's confidence. She wouldn't disappoint this woman.

She eyed the sugar.

"One or two?" Mrs. Walker asked.

"One's plenty." She didn't want to seem greedy.

Mrs. Walker picked up one with a pair of silver tongs and dropped it into Dulcie's cup. She picked up the white pitcher. She hesitated above Dulcie's cup. Dulcie nodded as her mouth watered in anticipation.

Mrs. Walker added a dollop to Dulcie's cup, which near to overflowed.

As any guest would, Dulcie waited for her hostess to pick up the delicate cup before she dug into the rich tea steaming in front of her. She knew her manners.

"Hangtown's a small community," Mrs. Walker said, "but we're growing."

"I reckon to add to their number," Dulcie replied.

Mrs. Walker stirred her cup.

Dulcie picked up a silver teaspoon and carefully swirled the brew.

Mrs. Walker picked up her cup. "Have you thought about your future?"

Dulcie copied her. "Yes, ma'am. I intend to settle down with a husband and raise a herd of children."

Mrs. Walker arched her eyebrows and took a sip of her tea, and Dulcie did the same. The sweet black tea tasted like heaven.

"As you'll find out, we have all different sorts of folks living in the El Dorado," Mrs. Walker said pleasantly. "Some come from as far away as Australia, a country most couldn't find on a map. A few people call these men Sidney ducks, but that's not a complimentary way of addressing them."

"I won't call them anything but their proper names," Dulcie assured her.

"You'll find Mexicans and Californians, folks who've lived here all their lives. Some of us came from back East. Some came from Chile. That's in South America. Most are law-abiding."

"I look forward to meeting all of them." Dulcie couldn't have been more sincere.

"You'll have an opportunity come Saturday night. There's a town social."

Dulcie could've jumped for joy, but she was a lady now and remained in her chair.

Mrs. Walker studied her. "We'll go to town come morning and find material for a new dress."

"That'll be expensive."

"Never you mind about the expense."

Dulcie wouldn't take charity. Crowders never liked to be beholden to anyone. She'd find a way to repay the woman. What did a girl with a worthless claim, a cantankerous mule, and nothing much else have to offer a fine lady such as Mrs. Walker?

"You must be careful in town," Mrs. Walker said. "Women are in short supply. Lonely men can be dangerous men."

Seemed to Dulcie there was an abundance of loneliness in this world.

"You don't have to worry about me. I know how to take care of myself. I've got my shotgun and now my pa's .36 gauge, and I know how to use them."

Mrs. Walker smiled, but weakly. She was a worrier, sure enough.

"How old are you, Dulcie?"

"I'm all of eighteen," she said between sips.

"You've got time to find a good man to marry."

"My ma was sixteen when she and Pa got married. I reckon eighteen is old enough."

Mrs. Walker nodded. "You'll have your pick of many good men in this town."

Dulcie set her cup back in the saucer with a steady hand. "I reckon I've already met some."

Mrs. Walker blinked. "Dear me."

"I need your help," Dulcie said, surprising even herself.

Mrs. Walker patted her bosom. "I'll do what I can."

"I have to become a lady," Dulcie explained.

Mrs. Walker's worries seemed to take flight. She smiled broadly. "We'd better get started."

She rose from her chair and started clearing the dishes before Dulcie even had a chance to empty her cup.

Chapter Five

Tom headed for town, regretting he'd exchanged harsh words again with his ma.

He figured it was a stroke of luck that Dulcie Crowder had been willing to leave her claim and come to stay in town. His ma needed a female to talk to, and Dulcie could carry on a conversation with a cigar store Indian.

Most important of all, Ma would have somebody else to worry about for a change, and that would give Tom some peace.

Tom dismounted in front of the sheriff's office. Jasper bolted out the front door, threading his left hand into the sleeve of his buckskin coat.

"Thank the Lord you're back," he said. "There's trouble over at Mary's."

"What kind of trouble?" Tom asked as he wrapped his reins around the hitching post.

"Two trappers, by the look of them, are raising Cain. You'd better come quick."

Tom drew his rifle out of the scabbard and followed the agitated deputy up the middle of Main Street. When he turned the corner, he could hear tinny music and shouting coming from the two-story building. MARY'S HOTEL AND FINE DINING stood out in bold black letters across the front windowpane.

Tom knew two things townsfolk could count on about Mary's. The owner served the best vittles in town, and she didn't allow piano music except on Saturday nights.

Tom pushed open the front door. Mary was standing by the

37

kitchen door, wringing the life out of a kitchen towel. Cyrus Littman's girl, who helped serve dinner, grimly pounded out a tune on the piano. Two burly men sat at a table grinning at her, a bottle of whiskey and two full glasses in front of them.

The other tables were empty.

Both men looked at Tom as he headed in their direction, spurs jingling with each stride. They wore clothes that'd been slept in. Their smell would raise nit flies come daylight.

They hadn't bothered to remove their fur hats.

"Join us?" one of the men asked. His face was red and sweating. He wrapped his hand around the glass in front of him and raised it to his gaping maw. He swallowed a mouthful and set the empty glass down on the table a little too quickly.

"Time you two took your business to the Blue Stocking," Tom said.

The Littman girl stopped playing and scuttled behind the piano.

"We ain't et yet," the man replied. He wiped his mouth with a corner of the tablecloth.

"You can take your feed over at the saloon," Tom replied, his anger rising.

"You've got no call to kick us out of here," the other man said loudly.

"I'm the deputy sheriff in this town," Tom said evenly. "I'm not asking you again."

"Tell me what laws we broke," the man demanded belligerently.

"We treat ladies with civility in Hangtown," Tom answered. He yanked off the stranger's coon hat and slapped it against his chest. "And we take off our hats at the supper table."

The man clung to his hat, his bloodshot eyes bulging.

The other man chuckled. "I don't see any *ladies* around here."

Tom had heard enough. "On second thought, this town doesn't need your business at all." He grabbed the man by the collar and yanked him to his feet. The bottle of whiskey tipped over, rolled off the table, and hit the floor. The shattered glass studded the floorboards, and the edges of a braided runner turned brown.

His partner reached for his knife, secured in a leather scabbard on his hip.

"I wouldn't do that," Jasper said. He raised his shotgun, and the unmistakable click as he thumbed back the hammer brought the man's head up.

The man wisely reconsidered unsheathing that knife and put both hands in the air.

"That's better," Tom said. "Now, on your feet."

The man rose slowly, and Tom shoved him and his partner toward the exit. Both stumbled and then righted themselves.

Jasper stepped aside. One of the men elbowed the door open, and they passed through.

Tom followed them outside, Jasper at his heels.

The trappers climbed into the saddles of two surly-looking mules and glared at Tom. There was still fight in these men, Tom could plainly see, and there was no telling what a man with too much whiskey in him might do. He and Jasper stood shoulder to shoulder, weapons ready.

The men were smart enough to live another day.

They headed out of town, cursing at their mounts.

"They're pretty riled," Jasper said, expelling a lungful of air.

"They'll get over it." Tom watched as the two men reached the end of the street and turned south. They'd go past his ma's place riding that way. Ma and Dulcie were alone.

"You want me to take your horse over to the livery?" Jasper asked.

"Nah," Tom replied. "I think I'll follow those boys until I'm satisfied they won't do anybody any harm. Can't be too careful."

"I'll go back inside and help Mary clean up," Jasper said.

"Get some supper while you're at it," Tom said.

"What about the sheriff's office?"

"I'll lock up on my way," Tom replied. "I shouldn't be gone long."

"The first thing we need to do is get you out of those clothes," Mrs. Walker said.

With those words, Dulcie's transformation into a proper lady started.

Mrs. Walker talked as she washed up the cups and saucers and set them on a strip of flour sacking. "I have some dresses put away that might fit you. If not, we'll make an alteration or two. Do you sew?"

"My mending skills are considerable," Dulcie stated proudly.

"I'm glad to hear it." Mrs. Walker wiped her hands on her apron.

"Let me dry those dishes and put them away," Dulcie offered.

"Don't bother. Time you had a bath. I'll see to the hot water."

A woman pushed open the back door with her hip and came into the kitchen carrying an armload of split wood. She was a thinner and shorter version of Mr. Eng but wore a plain gray skirt and high-collared blouse like Mrs. Walker.

"Howdy. I'm Dulcie Crowder."

The woman stopped in her tracks. From the look on her face, she hadn't expected a friendly greeting.

The woman bowed her head and then dumped her load into a willow basket by the cooking range. When she finished, she stood at attention.

"Dulcie, this is Mrs. Eng."

"Pleased to meet you," Dulcie said.

Mrs. Eng shot a look at Mrs. Walker.

"Likewise," Mrs. Walker said.

"Yes," Mrs. Eng said, bowing again. "Likewise."

"I hope we can be friends," Dulcie said.

Mrs. Eng looked doubtful.

"Go and haul in the tin tub hanging on the back porch," Mrs. Walker told Mrs. Eng.

Mrs. Eng hurried out of the room.

"I already figured out that bowing means yes," Dulcie said.

Dulcie had never had trouble communicating and couldn't imagine how the Engs managed.

"Her English is improving," Mrs. Walker replied.

She opened the door on the range and stuffed in several sticks of firewood. Then she opened the flue. Heat poured into the room.

"Do you think she gets the gist of what I'm saying?"

"She will in due time," Mrs. Walker said as she ladled hot water from the reservoir into a tin jug.

"I've never seen the likes of her, except for Mr. Eng, of course."

"I suspect Mrs. Eng has never met anyone quite like you either."

Dulcie understood her meaning. "I meant what I said about being friends."

"I'm sure you did." She'd filled the jug, steam wetting her face. "It's your behavior toward her that'll count."

Dulcie agreed wholeheartedly and vowed to do her best.

"This surely is a lot of fuss for me," Dulcie exclaimed, embarrassed to be causing her hostess extra work.

"You want to smell like a lady, don't you?"

"Yes, ma'am."

"Good." Mrs. Walker's eyes were bright. She seemed to have found renewed energy. "I'll go find you some clean towels and a bath sheet."

Mrs. Eng appeared at the doorway hefting a tin tub. Dulcie helped her carry it into the kitchen. They set it by the stove, the warmest place in the house.

She wanted to say a few words to Mrs. Eng, but the woman kept looking at the floor and hurried back outside. Some folks shied away from being friendly, but Dulcie suspected Mrs. Eng kept her distance because of her poor language skills.

Dulcie would help Mrs. Eng as much as she could with her English. It was a neighborly thing to do.

Mrs. Walker returned with a stack of folded clothes. She dropped them on the kitchen table and began looking through the pile. It didn't take long before she pulled out a dark brown broadcloth skirt.

"This looks to be the right size," she said. She held the skirt up to Dulcie's waist for good measure.

"You wouldn't know it to look at me now," Mrs. Walker said with a girlish laugh, "but I used to fit into this skirt."

She set the skirt across a chair, smoothing down a wrinkle or two with a brush of her hand. She did the same with a high-necked shirtwaist with ruffles around the sleeves and neck.

There was a brand-new chemise, a petticoat stiffened with cord, and cotton drawers.

Mrs. Walker's forehead creased as she examined the yellowed hem of the petticoat.

"This won't do," she said. "Maybe a good soak in vinegar and hot water will brighten it up."

Dulcie acknowledged the woman's efforts with a nod. The petticoat would've suited her just the way it was. The clothes were as fine as anyone could hope for.

Mrs. Walker turned her attention to the tub in front of the stove. "You get into that bath and have a good scrub." She took a square of soap out of her pocket. "This is lavender-scented. I was saving it for a special occasion."

Dulcie took the soap and sniffed spring flowers, a welcome change from the soap they'd used, and used sparingly, up at the claim.

"Thank you kindly," Dulcie said, filled with gratitude that Mrs. Walker had given her the soap she should've rightly used for herself.

Mrs. Walker left the kitchen humming.

Dulcie picked up the bucket of cold water and poured all of the contents into the tub. The water splashed onto the rag rug. She looked up to see if Mrs. Walker would come running back with words of caution. It wouldn't do to get off to a bad start with this lady.

Mrs. Walker was busy doing other things. Hopefully her rug would be dry by the time she returned.

Using a dish towel wrapped around the handle, Dulcie lifted the heavy jug of hot water and added enough to take the chill off. She tossed in the square of sweet-smelling soap.

Mrs. Walker had seen to what Dulcie needed right away. A bath was the first requirement of her becoming a lady, and she wanted to smell as good as Mrs. Walker smelled.

She quickly stripped off her shirt and britches and left them in a heap on the floor. She pulled off her wool undershirt. The cool air made her shudder. Quickly, she unbuttoned her drawers and kicked them next to the pile. She stepped, big toe first, into the clean, warm water and sat down.

The bath was a comfort after riding Chester the better part of the afternoon, and she laid her head back against the rim of the tub. She examined her fingernails, broken and with dirt wedged underneath. She stretched out her legs. Her toenails could use a good trimming. But she had no doubt a lady existed beneath all the trail dust and grime.

Tom would come courting in earnest after he took a whiff of her after this bath.

"Just you wait and see," she mused aloud.

She lathered up the bar of soap. A bubble burst, and she sneezed. Unbidden tears ran down her cheeks. The cold certainty of her loss was never far away.

She wiped her nose with the back of one hand. She sure would miss her pa.

Chapter Six

Tom followed the two trappers.

The pair were drunk and, no doubt, as hungry as bears getting ready for winter. This time of night lamplight burning in a house would be a welcoming sight and a sure sign supper was on the table.

If they veered off the road for any reason, if they gave him any cause at all for concern, he'd round them up and haul their sorry hides to the jail for the night to sleep off their contrariness.

The two men reached a fork in the road, and they turned in the direction of Diamond Spring, heads down, probably half asleep. Tom stopped, satisfied he'd seen the last of them.

He wasn't far from his ma's house. He should head back to town, but it wouldn't hurt to check in on the women.

He didn't have to go far before he reached the house his pa had built. He felt the stirrings of contentment, seeing the place lit up by the soft glow of lamplight. The fire in the stove would take the chill out of his bones. He could almost smell good food cooking.

Ma most likely had baked a pie. A hot meal would take the edge off a long day, even though there'd be a lecture about the dangers of his work accompanying it.

Nobody came out onto the porch to greet him. They were busy in the kitchen, most likely, and hadn't heard him ride up. Even the dog hadn't bothered to greet him. No doubt that mutt had gone soft with two women coddling him and was sleeping off his feed out in the barn.

Tom dismounted. Shooting Star—what a name for a horse. Women surely had romantic notions, Tom reflected.

"Well, Star, it's been a long ride. You deserve a dry blanket and feed."

The mustang agreed with a shake of his head.

Mr. Eng came running out of the darkness carrying a kerosene lantern and obliged Tom by taking the reins.

Tom headed for the house. He kicked off his boots at the back door. It sure was inconvenient, but his ma'd skin him alive if he wore spurs across her plank floors.

He left his boots where he'd shucked them. Someone talking caught his attention. His gaze lit on Dulcie Crowder at the stove, dressed in a dark skirt and pretty, high-necked shirtwaist. Ma hadn't wasted any time taking charge of Dulcie.

He stood in the doorway, knowing he should announce himself. But he couldn't stop staring.

Dulcie had taken her hair out of the braid. It fell in waves to her shoulders. The brown color was burnished with gold in the flicker of firelight. Her skin took on the hues of wildflower honey.

Tom's throat tightened.

She stirred a big pot, and the steam reddened her cheeks and the tip of her nose. A man could get used to coming home to a kitchen filled with warmth and welcome.

He stopped himself right there. He'd no right to think of Dulcie that way.

A man in his line of work couldn't take a wife.

Tom backed out of the door and shut it quietly behind him. He gathered up his boots and hurried to the front of the house. He stumbled on the first step of the porch, stubbing his big toe. It served him right. He tossed his boots aside.

The front door was unlocked. He stood in the threshold, undecided if he'd stay.

His ma came down the stairs with a thimble on her index finger and a pincushion tied around her wrist. She held a lady's stiff petticoat under one arm. She opened her mouth to say something as her stern gaze moved to his stocking feet. Seeing no need to scold, she looked at him instead with a questioning gaze.

He cleared the logjam in his throat. "I thought you ladies would like some company."

His ma lifted her shoulders slightly. "I expect you want some dinner as well."

His ma was as testy as ever.

Tom scratched the back of his neck, but he'd no doubt the women were cooking up more than dinner.

"Dulcie settling in?" he asked as casually as he could get away with so as not to encourage the woman.

"As well as can be expected," Ma replied, folding the petticoat in two.

"I've no doubt she'll take to living here with you until she decides where she's best off."

Her gaze hardened. "Don't you go suggesting she'd be better off elsewhere."

"That wasn't my meaning," Tom answered.

His ma eyed him wearily. "You didn't tell her about Willie being hanged for murder this morning, did you?"

"No, ma'am. Telling Dulcie her pa had died seemed to be enough news all of a sudden."

"You can't put off telling her much longer," Ma said. "She's bound to hear what happened, and the telling had better come from you."

"I know that," Tom replied, irritated at himself for the omission. He hadn't wanted to see any more tears. He'd wanted to spare Dulcie the additional heartache.

"She's already had someone stop by and demand she leave town."

"Who'd do such a thing?" he asked.

"I don't know, and neither does Dulcie. He came out to the stable when she was putting up her mule."

Tom frowned. He'd known that some folks wouldn't want Dulcie here. He'd hoped that once they met her, they'd change their minds. He hadn't expected threats.

"She knows there's something we're keeping from her."

"I'll tell her after supper," he said.

Ma huffed. "See that you do."

"Luckily, she has you to lean on," he replied, trying to smooth her ruffled feathers. "Hearing how her pa died won't be easy."

"She's stronger than you think," Ma said, her gaze softening, "but the longer you delay in telling her, the more difficult it will be for her."

Tom nodded. Ma never hid from the truth, of course. She'd weathered her share of bad news in the El Dorado and borne her losses with unquestionable strength. He wasn't so sure of Dulcie's reaction. He needed to prepare himself for an emotional outburst he'd no confidence in his ability to comfort.

"Supper's almost ready. You wait out here," Ma said, leaving no room to argue. "Dulcie will help."

Ma always had a bit of a general in her. She left him hat in hand and stocking-footed. He dropped his hat on the hall tree and made his way into the front parlor, a cozy room with a blazing fire putting out good heat. Baron was stretched out in front of the fender with a full belly. The hound picked up his head to see who'd intruded on his peace and then flopped down and went back to sleep.

"Some guard dog you are," he said.

Tom paced the room, wondering if he should get going while the going was good. He was outnumbered, that was for sure.

But running would be a cowardly thing to do. Dulcie was only a scrap of a girl, he reminded himself, and he'd promised his ma he'd tell Dulcie what had happened to Willie.

He sank into a high-backed chair instead. He was convinced now that Hangtown was no place for Dulcie and she'd be better off with kin. He was about to doze when Dulcie came out of the kitchen, his ma not far behind. He sprang to his feet.

When their gazes connected, he recognized his own need. She looked up at him the way a woman did when she had more than a passing interest in a man. Her lips parted in the playful half smile, half come-hither expression she'd shown him that afternoon. Again he found it difficult to resist.

He couldn't help but smile.

"I'm glad you came back," she said.

"Thomas, don't you think she's the prettiest girl in Hangtown?"

"Yes, ma'am." He'd seen her potential right off when he'd met her up at the Crowder claim. "I'd have to say you've done wonders."

Dulcie's brown eyes sparkled as she soaked up his compliment. Tom swallowed, his Adam's apple bobbing like an adolescent's.

"The food is ready," Ma said crisply. "Tom, you go on into the dining room and sit yourself down. Dulcie, you come along with me."

With a swish of her skirt, Dulcie followed his ma back into the kitchen.

Tom headed for the dining room. The table was already set for three with his ma's best china on his grandma's homespun table-cloth. There was honey and gooseberry jelly on the table, his favorites, along with a slab of butter. A plate, covered with a cloth, had been placed at the head of the table. He lifted the edge of the cloth. Sure enough, there were plump baking-powder biscuits, enough to feed an army.

Without a doubt, these two ladies had put out a spread that would weaken any man's resolve.

Tom took his seat. He hadn't thought about marrying since courting Maryanne. She'd waited for Tom to make an offer of marriage, but he'd kept putting off asking for her hand.

He'd thought then that he had poor makings for a husband. He thought so now. A woman would be a fool to take up with a law-man, especially in hard times like these.

Still, he couldn't deny the yearning Dulcie had awakened in him.

The ladies came into the room carrying steaming bowls of vittles and set them down in front of him. He stood and rubbed his hands together.

Then he pulled out his pa's chair and sat back down. He had to admit, it was satisfying sitting at the head of the table with two females fussing over his needs.

Dulcie filled the glasses with goat milk, already moving around the table with the grace of a woman practiced in city ways. Ma opened a covered dish. He smelled rabbit stew and gravy. His ma took her place opposite him.

"Dulcie, you sit next to Thomas." There was a lilt in Ma's voice, a happiness that hadn't been there since his pa had died.

Tom was surely pleased to hear his mother so content, and he silently congratulated himself on bringing these two together.

Dulcie did as she was told and sat down, prim and proper.

Tom couldn't help but think she'd adjusted quickly and well to city living. Maybe he'd been hasty in his thinking. Maybe Dulcie Crowder would take to Hangtown just fine.

Chapter Seven

Dulcie would have liked to scratch where the ruffles of the high-necked shirtwaist chafed against her neck, but she restrained herself in present company.

If only Pa could see her in this getup. Wouldn't he be surprised? She was on her way to becoming a real lady.

She did wonder what had brought Tom back to his ma's place after he'd turned down the offer of a meal when they'd arrived that afternoon. He seemed like the kind of man who, once he made up his mind, didn't change it.

Her stomach rumbled. Except for the sugar-and-cream-laced cup of tea, she'd only eaten a strip of venison jerky first thing that morning.

She scooted her chair closer to the table and sank her stocking feet into the thick rag rug. Thank goodness Mrs. Walker hadn't insisted she wear the buttoned-up boots that town ladies wore. Dulcie never could stand to wear shoes, even when the weather turned cold and the ground snapped with a layer of frost.

Everything in the Walker dining room was a wonder. The chair seats were as soft as clouds, and the polished wood gleamed in the lamplight. The cloth on the table was snowy white, and there wasn't a chip or crack in any of the plates or glasses.

The spread laid out on the table was enough for a dozen men. This must be the kind of supper Tom was used to. Dulcie would do well to learn all she could.

She waited to see what happened next, even though waiting had never been her strong suit. The dishes were passed and plates filled. She picked up her knife and fork, one poised in each fist, ready to dig in.

"We say Grace first," Mrs. Walker said, and Tom and his ma bowed their heads.

The Walkers gave thanks before they ate, and Dulcie would do the same. She knew exactly what she'd say.

Tom said a few thankful words. Mrs. Walker added that they'd plenty to be grateful for. Dulcie took a deep breath and thanked the Lord for providing the plump rabbit and asked that He look kindly after her pa, even though he'd often been a backslider.

Tom's ma ended the blessing with a soulful "Amen."

Dulcie opened her eyes and looked at their faces. Both Tom and Mrs. Walker beamed proudly at her.

Mrs. Walker shook out a proper cloth napkin and draped it across her lap. Dulcie did the same, even though she reckoned the napkin would do more good tucked into the neck of her fancy clothes.

She was eager to make a good impression on the Walkers, especially Tom, and she knew she must follow Mrs. Walker's lead.

Tom split open a biscuit and slathered on a healthy helping of butter and thick honey, which spilled over the side. He licked his fingers before he popped a bite into his mouth.

Dulcie's stomach growled, but she wasn't going to start before Mrs. Walker.

Finally the good lady picked up her fork and tucked it under a piece of rabbit. Dulcie copied her. Instead of a fork and knife in each fist, she held the fork like a pencil and pierced the nearest piece of tender meat on her plate. She had it halfway to her mouth when a drop of rich gravy slopped onto the clean tablecloth. She shot a look at Mrs. Walker, who hadn't noticed. Dulcie pulled her plate closer to cover the grease spot.

She didn't despair even though it would take a lot of doing to learn everything she needed to know about table manners and such.

For starters, it was all very peculiar eating one bite at a time, chewing with her mouth closed, and swallowing without making a peep. But she'd do whatever was expected of her. She was determined to be a lady.

She thought the meal delicious and made all the better by the company. She smacked her lips in appreciation until she saw Mrs. Walker's tiny frown. So she swiped her tongue around the corners of her mouth and patted her lips dry with the clean napkin.

This action seemed to meet with Mrs. Walker's approval, as she nodded her head when Dulcie had finished.

It was going to take some doing, but nobody ever said a Crowder couldn't learn the basics of eating proper.

Despite her missteps, she liked being here. Tom gave one-word replies as his ma spoke of the people in town—folks Dulcie would become friends with soon, she was sure.

When Tom cleaned his plate, dragging his second biscuit along the edges, his ma encouraged him to take another helping.

"No, thank you. I've had plenty." He pushed back from the table. "That was a bountiful spread."

His gaze hit Dulcie full force. She could tell he meant every word. "The praise belongs to your ma," Dulcie said.

Mrs. Walker tut-tutted. "Now, don't you go giving me the credit. You did all the hard work, Dulcie."

Mrs. Walker had stretched the truth of the matter, but Dulcie understood her intentions.

"Rabbit stew has always been one of my favorites," Tom said.

Dulcie about busted her buttons to hear him say so.

"I expect if you took up farming, you could sit down to such a supper each and every evening," Mrs. Walker said to Tom.

Dark clouds gathered on Tom's face. "I reckon that's a fact. But I'll never know regular hours. I'm a lawman and hope to be all of my life."

Mrs. Walker jabbed at the corners of her mouth with her linen napkin and laid it next to her plate. "I don't know why you're so opposed to taking up farming. It's honest work and respectable."

Tom didn't look surprised at the comment. He settled his arms on the armrests and leaned back in the chair.

"There's work to be done bringing law and order to the El Dorado," he said.

Mrs. Walker's face tightened. "There's plenty of other men to do it. I've heard talk Ezra Dixon's planning on running for the office of El Dorado County Sheriff."

"He told me so himself," Tom replied. "I've a notion to put my name on the ballot too."

"Have you?" Mrs. Walker's voice held a challenge in it.

"Yes, ma'am."

Dulcie couldn't hold back any longer. "Could I ask something?"

Mrs. Walker shot her a look of pure river ice and then turned back to lock horns with her son.

"Winning the sheriff's office would mean moving to Coloma," she said.

"Not if the voters decide to make Hangtown the county seat," Tom replied.

"Do you really think that will happen?" Mrs. Walker asked.

"It's a possibility."

"What's wrong with Ezra Dixon doing the job?" she asked.

"His brand of justice has nothing to do with the law," Tom said.

Mrs. Walker showed no signs of giving in. "Let someone else run against Ezra, then. There are many men in this town who could do the job."

"Nobody else will oppose Ezra and the Vigilance Committee," Tom replied. "It's up to me."

"I suppose you want my blessing, Tom Walker. You won't get it."

Tom rose to his feet and threw his napkin onto the table. His cheerful disposition had evaporated, replaced by a terrible scowl.

He tromped out of the room, stocking feet and all.

Mrs. Walker had gone red in the face. "Well!" she said, and she exhaled loudly.

They'd shut Dulcie out of the conversation, but now Mrs. Walker turned to her. "He'll come around. Just you wait and see."

Dulcie rose from her seat. All she'd wanted to ask was that they consider each other's feelings. She hadn't wanted the evening to end in anger.

"Let me go and talk to him," Dulcie said gently.

Mrs. Walker sat straight as a hat pin, her gaze averted.

Dulcie followed Tom outside. He was pulling on his boots.

"I hate to see you at odds with your ma," she said sincerely.

"She doesn't understand I have a job to do."

"She understands, but she's afraid. That'd be natural."

He stomped both feet and straightened. "I know."

She felt small standing next to him and suddenly shy.

"You look pretty tonight," he said. His face was half in darkness, but she could see that his anger was gone.

"I reckon that's your ma's doing."

"She's a good teacher."

"I've got a lot to learn." Dulcie lifted her chin, half hoping the deputy might give her a good-night kiss.

Tom turned away and looked out in the direction of the stable. She couldn't understand why he kept his distance. Hadn't he just said she was pretty?

"I've got something to say," he said.

She heard the reluctance in his voice.

"It's about how your pa came to die," Tom went on.

A sudden chill came over her. Dulcie crossed her arms. "I guess you'd better tell me."

He turned to look at her. She saw the same kindness in his sleep-deprived face that he'd shown her that afternoon up at the claim. Whatever he needed to say would hurt her.

"You might as well blurt it out," she said.

"Willie killed a man over at the Blue Stocking Saloon. They'd been playing cards, and according to witnesses, Willie'd been caught cheating. There was a fight, and the other fella got the worst of it."

For the first time in her life, Dulcie was at a loss for words. She couldn't believe what Tom was telling her.

"I sent for the circuit judge, so there'd be a fair trial," he continued. "It didn't take long for a jury to make a decision. Your pa was found guilty of murder and sentenced to hang. I had to carry out the sentence this morning."

This strange series of events fueled an uprising of emotions in her. "Seems to me you all were pretty quick to dispense with my pa."

Tom shifted his feet. "That's the way justice is carried out in the El Dorado. Sure and swift. That's the way it has to be. Otherwise there'd be vigilantes doing the hanging, and without even bothering with a trial. Law and order wouldn't be worth two bits."

Her knees went as wobbly as those of a newly born fawn.

"I'm sorry," he said sincerely. "I liked your pa, but I'd no choice after the judge passed sentence."

Dulcie was sorry too. She was sorry her pa had seen fit to fight a man over a game of cards.

"Who was this man my pa killed?" she asked, choking on the words.

"His name was Billingsly. By all accounts he was a short-card artist out of east Texas."

"My pa fought a gambling man and bested him?" Her pa's fighting abilities must have considerably improved of late. "A Crowder's way of handling a dispute is usually to cut his losses and run."

"He landed a lucky blow."

"An unlucky blow, as it turned out."

Tom stood over her. She could feel the heat of his body, hear his breathing, but her sight was blinded by hot tears.

"I told him gambling would be the death of him," she said. She hated that her pa would be remembered as a killer and not the man she knew.

"You listen to me. Your pa's thoughts were on you his last hours. He asked for you to be well taken care of."

Hearing her pa's last wishes expressed opened the floodgates. Dulcie began to blubber and couldn't stop.

Tom drew her to him. He held her against his thumping heart and stroked her hair. There was warmth in his embrace and tenderness she hadn't thought any man capable of.

He meant to comfort her, but she couldn't take comfort in the arms of the lawman. She was too full of humiliation for what her pa had done. She shrugged out of his embrace and gulped for air.

Tom stared at her with concern, which only added to her embarrassment.

"Why didn't you tell me earlier?" She swiped at her eyes with the frilly hanky Mrs. Walker had given her.

"I couldn't bring myself to."

She blew her nose loudly.

"I'm not fragile," she said, wiping at her nose. "I wouldn't have broken in two."

"I've come to find that out."

She'd no reason to doubt his sincerity, and that quelled her anger. "I know you meant well," she admitted.

Fresh tears escaped.

Tom reached out to brush the tears away with a calloused thumb.

She was too full of humiliation to let him continue.

"I think you'd better go now," she said. "There won't be any more tears for you to wipe."

Tom jerked his hand away and threaded his hat though his hands instead.

"I'll say good night, then," he replied, looking away.

"Good night," she said. Her voice croaked like a toad's.

He clamped his hat on his head and stepped off the porch.

She watched him walk to the stable, a little bow-legged, Mexican spurs singing. She didn't blame him for being the one who'd put the noose around her pa's neck. He'd done his duty as a Hangtown deputy must.

She stood there until he came riding out of the stable. He raised two fingers to his hat and turned Star toward the road.

She sat down on the first step. She wasn't ready for Mrs. Walker's words of condolence either, for surely she'd known what her pa had done. Everybody in town had known when she'd come riding in on Chester.

They'd seen her and asked themselves why she was there. One man had even gone so far as to express his doubts about Tom's judgment in bringing her to town. No doubt he held what her pa had done against her.

She heard whimpering, and Baron used his bulk to push the door open. He came out onto the porch, tail wagging. The dog nudged her hand, and Dulcie patted his head.

Pa often thought the worst of folks, but he never raised a hand in anger. Coming to the El Dorado had made him more fearful than ever. He'd become suspicious of anyone who ventured near their camp and watched over Dulcie like a she-bear protecting her cub.

She loved her pa, and what he'd done would never change that love.

"There's no disputing my pa killed a man, but I hope folks around here understand we Crowders aren't a murderous clan," she said to the dog.

Baron rested his head in her lap, and she stroked his silky ears.

"I know it's a tall order, but it's up to me to convince them."

Chapter Eight

M y, don't you look pretty," Mrs. Walker said, sunny as the new morning. Her anger at last night's supper table seemed to have been put aside.

"Morning," Dulcie replied cautiously.

"You surely were a picture last night," she went on without hesitation. "Don't think Thomas didn't notice."

Dulcie thanked her. It wasn't the kind of greeting Dulcie was used to first thing in the morning, but she appreciated that there'd be no dwelling on the past.

She'd thought long and hard about how she could repay the Walkers for all their kindness, and she'd come up with a solution. Mother and son were the two most bullheaded people she'd ever come across, and neither was likely to back off from their opinion about Tom's work as a lawman.

Dulcie feared that, come election time, if Tom did run for sheriff, the divide between them would only widen. There must be something Dulcie could do to keep that from happening.

"Don't you dawdle over your breakfast," Mrs. Walker said from the stove. "As soon as you've eaten, we're going into town."

Dulcie smoothed down her skirt. She'd had a job putting all this gear on. She wore striped stockings held up by leather contraptions buckled above her knees and drawers that buttoned at the back. The chemise was short-sleeved and glided on, and next came a corset, which seemed to Dulcie an unnecessary layer of clothing, but Mrs. Walker had insisted. She liked the results. The corset enhanced her natural assets.

Finally, she'd tied on a petticoat. Mrs. Walker had found a lacy one that made crackling sounds when she moved, and Mrs. Walker had made alterations so the hem wouldn't show.

When Dulcie had finished dressing, she'd felt trussed up like a Christmas goose, but she wasn't complaining. She'd hoped to make a favorable impression on a certain lawman, and all this getup should make him look twice.

In addition to the fancy clothes, she'd stowed a few coins her pa had left her in a leather pouch, tied it around her waist, and tucked it under her waistband, out of sight and safe from thieves and other no-accounts.

She sat down and, using a button hook, buttoned the ankle-high black boots Mrs. Walker had dug out of a big trunk in her attic. The boots pinched her toes, but Mrs. Walker expected that they be worn.

Mrs. Walker brought the frying pan to the table and slid two eggs and a piece of fried bread onto a china plate.

"Did you sleep well?" Mrs. Walker asked.

In truth, Dulcie had had trouble falling asleep, after what Tom had told her about Pa.

"Yes, ma'am," she said. "Your bed reminds me of home. I had a mattress stuffed with chicken feathers and the softest pillow you ever could lay your head on. That's not to say our house was as grand as yours."

Mrs. Walker's smile was motherly. "Where are your people from?"

"The sweet hills of southern Ohio," Dulcie replied. "My folks came over from the Old Country, but I'm an American, born and bred."

Talking about home brought on a spasm of longing to go back. She stifled a sigh.

"You're homesick," Mrs. Walker said.

"I guess I am," Dulcie admitted.

"I suppose we all miss those we've left," Mrs. Walker said.

And those who have left us.

"I still mean to call Hangtown home," Dulcie hurried to say. She didn't want there to be any misunderstanding.

"You'll feel better after you've made some friends your own age."

Mrs. Walker's face radiated a conviction that eased some of Dulcie's inner turmoil about whether the good citizens of Hangtown would want anything to do with her after what her pa had done.

"Yes, ma'am."

"You eat your eggs. Nothing like a hot breakfast to put a person right for the day."

Dulcie picked up the fork and dug in even though her appetite had left her. She didn't want to seem ungrateful.

Mrs. Walker returned the pan to the back of the stove.

"I found a bonnet for you," she said as she poured milk into a glass. "All Hangtown women wear bonnets or straw hats when they go to town."

"I appreciate the loan of a proper bonnet. My hat has seen better days and wouldn't look fitting with this getup anyway."

Mrs. Walker set the tall glass on the table in front of Dulcie.

She was a child again, being taken care of by this kind lady. Not that Pa hadn't tried, but his mothering skills just hadn't been the same.

Still and all, Mrs. Walker's efforts made Dulcie uneasy. She could've made her own breakfast and seen to milking the she-goat. She'd have made sure the milk was strained properly and brought into the house in time for breakfast. She could've gathered the eggs and candled them. There were a host of chores she could do if Mrs. Walker would let her.

Instead, she'd slept in, like one of those ladies she'd heard about back home. Dulcie hoped Mrs. Walker's pampering would only be temporary.

"I'll go fetch that bonnet," Mrs. Walker said as she left the room.

Dulcie finished the eggs, sopping up the last bit of yolk with the bread until her plate was clean. She stuffed the bread into her mouth.

Mrs. Eng came into the kitchen carrying an empty slop bucket.

Her mouth full, Dulcie bobbed her head.

Mrs. Eng bobbed her head back.

Sure enough, there was work to be done, and here she sat idle. She swallowed her breakfast and jumped from her chair. She gathered up her plate and glass and set them carefully in a dishpan.

Mrs. Eng watched her.

Dulcie smiled. She and Mrs. Eng were the same height—a welcome change from so many others always towering over her. Mrs. Eng smiled back, a little shyly, but the smile came through.

They were communicating as well as any two people, Dulcie reckoned. Mrs. Eng seemed to warm up to Dulcie, which was a relief after the chilly reception yesterday.

"How about we wash up these dishes together?" she asked.

Mrs. Eng shook her head. "You go. My work." She shooed Dulcie out of the kitchen.

Dulcie stifled her objections and promised she'd help with the chores that needed doing when she got back from town. As Dulcie left the kitchen, she wondered how the Engs had made their way to California and if they missed home as much as she did.

She found a bonnet of blue calico on the bench seat of the coat-rack in the hall. She tied it on. The soft fabric covered her neck, and the brim would keep the sun off her face.

When she looked into the square mirror set in the middle of the coatrack, she didn't recognize herself. She saw a soulful girl of eighteen looking back in a getup meant for a lady.

Her pa had called her pretty, but she suspected that was the sort of thing a pa would say. Tom and Ma had said the same, but they would, given she was company. She was plain to her way of thinking.

Had she set her sights too high, hoping Tom Walker would take a second look at her? He'd resisted enough when they'd left the claim yesterday. Except last night, when he'd brushed tears from her face, when she'd thought her heart would break, he'd seemed genuinely concerned about her welfare.

Mrs. Walker came down the stairs, pulling on a pair of white knitted gloves. She handed Dulcie a second pair. "I want you to meet my friends."

"I would like that just fine."

Dulcie put on the gloves, her nerves getting the best of her. What would the ladies of Hangtown think of her? Pa's hanging would be fresh in their minds. Would there be hard feelings about Pa's murdering a man or how he died in such a disgraceful fashion?

Mrs. Walker had only kind words and hadn't mentioned her pa's sinful behavior. She hoped the other ladies of Hangtown would be as understanding. Would they be generous in their forgiveness? Or would they turn away in disgust?

Mrs. Walker opened up the door, and the sun poured in.

Mr. Eng had hitched up the dun-colored horse to the high-society carriage and adjusted the traces. Mrs. Walker climbed aboard, and he handed the reins over to her.

"Come on, Dulcie," Mrs. Walker said.

"Forgot the shotgun. Pa warned me never to go anywhere without a firearm."

She ran inside and found the shotgun propped up in the corner of her bedroom where she'd left it the night before. She came out the door carrying the weapon.

"Do you know how to use a shotgun?" Mrs. Walker asked from her seat in the buggy.

"I reckon. Pa always said knowledge of weapons was necessary with so many varmints around. Both the four-legged and two-legged kind."

Mrs. Walker opened her dainty satin reticule and showed her a tiny, pearl-handled pistol tucked inside. "Looks like we'll be ready if need be."

Dulcie smiled so wide, her cheeks hurt. She took a seat next to this woman who was full of surprises.

Mrs. Walker released the brake, gave the reins a good shake, and they started rolling.

The well-traveled road was bumpy from deep ruts carved by a slew of wagons wheels. Before long, Dulcie's mood improved. The day was too nice not to be grateful for it. The air was warmer down here in the valley, with hardly any snow left over at all, and she loved the fresh smell of cedar and newly budded wild rosemary.

"I love a spring day," Mrs. Walker said, as if reading her thoughts.

"Me too."

She remembered how much she had always watched for the first signs of spring back home in Ohio from the protection of their log cabin as the heavy rain fell from the sky. Sometimes the storms came quietly, but other times the wind howled and the ground shook from thunder. Either way didn't matter. Each spring the surrounding countryside greened up with a promise of abundance.

Coming to the El Dorado had changed her. She'd hated the cold and the bleakness of living up at the claim. She'd struggled with the sorry excuse for a shelter and the long days of panning for gold that wasn't there. Winter seemed to go on forever. She had despaired that spring would ever return.

Most of all she'd hated the isolation.

"I'd like to marry by planting time," Dulcie said.

"I wouldn't rush into a hasty marriage," Mrs. Walker cautioned her.

"Patience isn't my strongest feature, but I'll try my best."

Mrs. Walker nodded, no doubt satisfied that Dulcie would heed her advice.

"Have you lived around here long?" Dulcie asked.

"Since the first rush for gold back in '48. When Mr. Walker and I first arrived, the area was a terrible, lawless place. Bandits roamed the hills and ambushed many a prospector. Those desperadoes would slit a man's throat for his gold."

"I've heard such stories," Dulcie replied with a shudder. Her pa had told them around the campfire. She looked up at the hills on both sides of them. She couldn't help but be wary.

"My husband had a great deal to do with changing this town for the better. He brought many a criminal to justice."

"Is that how Hangtown came about its name?" Dulcie asked.

"We've had our share of hangings," Mrs. Walker confirmed.

"*Hangtown* doesn't seem a fitting name for a town that aims to be civilized," Dulcie said.

Mrs. Walker's laugh was halfhearted. "I suppose that's true."

"I'm sorry about what my pa did," Dulcie said.

Mrs. Walker winced. "Thomas told you."

"Last night."

"I didn't say anything because I wanted you to hear it from him."

"Tom said he had a fair trial. A guilty man must pay for what he's done." Dulcie didn't want Mrs. Walker to think she blamed anyone.

"I'm glad you're not vengeful."

Dulcie wondered why Mrs. Walker would think she could be vengeful. "No, ma'am, I'm not."

"Good. You'll be better off forgiving those who've brought harm against you than to hold on to a grudge."

"Seems to me, I'm the one who should be asking the citizens of this town for forgiveness."

The horse began to slow, and Mrs. Walker encouraged it along with a quick cluck of her tongue.

"Are there hard feelings against my pa?" Dulcie asked. She had to know what she was up against.

"There's bound to be some."

"Ezra Dixon, for one," she guessed.

"Don't fret about Ezra. He thinks he's more important than he is."

"A man who's so self-important shouldn't be sheriff," Dulcie replied.

Mrs. Walker was silent for a while.

"You don't like it much that Tom is doing his part to uphold the law," Dulcie said.

His ma looked at her. "He's all I have left."

"Most likely any job he took on out here in the El Dorado would be dangerous."

"Not like being sheriff. My husband was ambushed by a gang of outlaws who'd robbed the stage. He didn't stand a chance against so many. Thomas is playing the same odds. I won't bury my son. He can take up farming."

Dulcie understood what was required of her. "I don't think he'll give up running for the office of sheriff."

"He'll change his mind when the time comes, Dulcie."

Dulcie wasn't so sure. Tom Walker took his job more seriously than any man she'd ever met. She doubted anyone would be able to change his devotion to his duty as a lawman.

They arrived on the main street of Hangtown amid a bustle of activity. Townsfolk always seemed in a hurry to get where they were going.

A few did stop and stare at the buggy going by. Some waved at Mrs. Walker. Others turned their heads.

More than likely, they knew who Dulcie was, which put her at a disadvantage. But with Mrs. Walker's help, she'd make their acquaintance soon enough. Once they got to know her, hopefully they'd think better of her.

Election posters had been nailed to just about every tree and post on Main Street. She hadn't noticed them last night, but in the morning light they stood out like blisters.

One in particular caught her attention. She had no trouble picking out the words EZRA DIXON FOR SHERIFF in big black letters. It showed a sketch of a balding man sporting a bushy mustache and wearing a frown that was intended, no doubt, to scare any criminal who dared linger in the town.

"Mr. Dixon doesn't look all that pleased to be running for office," Dulcie said.

"He'll make a good enough sheriff," Mrs. Walker replied sharply.

Dulcie feared she'd irritated the lady. She didn't want to upset Mrs. Walker, who'd taken her in like she was kin. Dulcie would have to learn to keep her yap shut about any thoughts she might have about Mr. Dixon.

As they approached the sheriff's office, Dulcie decided she'd like first thing to stop by with a friendly hello. When Deputy Walker had left last night, she'd been too upset to express her gratitude for all he'd done for her.

She opened her mouth to make the request, but Mrs. Walker passed the office without a glance. Obviously, the woman had no need to greet her son that morning.

They pulled up alongside a tall building made of timber. She sounded out the words on the sign: "A. Paisley, Dry Goods and Notions."

"Very good, Dulcie," Mrs. Walker said.

Dulcie jumped down from her seat, feeling there was nothing she couldn't master, given time.

A short man wearing a black coat and a black bow tied around the collar of the whitest shirt Dulcie had ever seen hurried out of the store.

"Good morning," he said as he reached up to Mrs. Walker. Mrs. Walker grasped his hand, and he helped her down from her seat.

Dulcie knew Mrs. Walker was plenty able to get into and out of the buggy without help, but she seemed willing enough to let this man dressed up in his Sunday best assist her.

Mrs. Walker thanked him, and the man looked pleased with himself. She turned to Dulcie. "Mr. Paisley, I'd like you to meet Dulcie Crowder."

Dulcie joined them on a boardwalk made of new pine boards.

Mr. Paisley's eyes twinkled. "How do you do?"

"Good enough, I reckon," Dulcie answered.

"Dulcie's come to live with me. It's surely a blessing to have her."

Dulcie had never been called a blessing before, even by Pa, who'd never spent time counting his. Having Mrs. Walker say so, Dulcie blushed with pride.

"Please come in, ladies," Mr. Paisley said. He bowed and indicated with a sweep of an outstretched hand for the two women to enter his place of business.

Dulcie went inside to a brightly lit room. She stood slack-jawed as she looked around her. She'd never seen such abundance in one place. All kinds of dry goods and notions were stacked high on long shelves reaching to the ceiling—so high that Mr. Paisley needed a ladder to reach them.

Brightly colored penny candy filled glass jars on the counter next to a brass cash register. She'd like to buy some, but she needed to save her money for necessities.

Dulcie wondered how anybody earned enough money to pay for these wonderful things. Mr. Paisley must be the richest man in Hangtown, with all these goods to sell.

Her gaze went next to a bevy of women trying on new straw bonnets. They tried not to show they were curious about the new arrival by averting their eyes whenever Dulcie looked their way.

One of the prettiest came forward. Her blue bonnet with matching blue ruffles framed shiny brown curls. She'd tied that bonnet's ribbons under her right ear with a wide bow.

"Hello," she said. "My name is Maryanne Greenwood." She stuck out her gloved hand.

Dulcie shot a glance at Mrs. Walker, who'd taken up with Mr. Paisley over by the bolts of calico and gingham.

"I'm Dulcie Crowder." She shook the woman's hand.

"Willie Crowder's girl?" Maryanne asked.

"One and the same."

"We heard Tom had gone up to your claim to bring you to town."

"He's done it, and now I'm staying with Mrs. Walker."

"I'm sorry about what happened to your pa," Maryanne said.

Dulcie had no reason to doubt the sincerity of the offered condolences and accepted them gracefully. "What's done is done," she said.

Maryanne reclaimed Dulcie's hand and gave it a squeeze. Hardship and sorrow were shared, Maryanne seemed to be telling her.

"Seems you know more about me than I know about you," Dulcie said.

Maryanne laughed. "Spoken plainly. We're going to get along just fine."

"Dulcie, come here," Mrs. Walker said.

Dulcie pulled away.

"I hope we can be friends," Maryanne said.

"I'd like that," Dulcie replied.

"You'll come for a visit? We live off the road to Coloma. Mrs. Walker can tell you how to get there."

Dulcie wasn't sure how to answer.

"Please say you will. I'll tell you all about myself when you come."

"I'd like that," Dulcie said again.

Maryanne Greenwood, her new friend, excused herself and joined the other ladies.

Dulcie returned to Mrs. Walker, who sorted through a table filled with bolts of colorful cloth.

As Mrs. Walker explained what they needed for Dulcie's new dress, Dulcie cast glances at the younger women. They'd put their heads together and talked so softly that Dulcie couldn't hear what they said. One of them, a woman with dark hair and penetrating dark eyes, shot Dulcie a sour-faced look.

Dulcie turned away, taken aback by her rudeness, but she'd expected there'd be some who'd judge her harshly by what her pa had done.

All of a sudden, they put down the hats they'd been admiring and ambled to the door in a herd, laughing.

Dulcie smiled as she watched them leave. She wanted badly to be one of them. None of them looked her way or seemed to notice. Dulcie decided she would have to be patient with them as well.

Mrs. Walker decided on a lovely yellow calico and told Mr. Paisley she'd take two yards. Dulcie would've preferred the blue, but she didn't put up a fuss. Mrs. Walker knew more about dresses and what was proper than Dulcie ever would.

Mr. Paisley measured out a length of yellow cloth, set a notch in the fabric with shears, and tore it clean through.

"Anything else I can get you ladies?" he asked as he folded the piece of cloth into a neat bundle.

"I need a packet of needles and some yellow thread," Mrs. Walker said.

Mr. Paisley pulled out a drawer and showed Mrs. Walker all the different colors he had to offer.

Mrs. Walker took her time picking out a perfect match, so Dulcie wandered to one of the windows. The ladies were gone.

She liked Maryanne Greenwood. Maryanne had been willing to shake Dulcie's hand and express her condolences. Hers was a kindness Dulcie would never forget.

Mrs. Walker carried on with Mr. Paisley about the weather, namely the lack of rain and what that would do to this year's planting.

Dulcie decided Mrs. Walker didn't need her, so she'd take a walk over to the sheriff's office.

"I'm going outside," she called over to the two.

"All right, but don't be long," Mrs. Walker answered.

Dulcie opened the door and shut it behind her.

Chapter Nine

Dulcie felt exposed, walking alone, as folks cast sideways glances her way, but she couldn't hide out at Mrs. Walker's until memories faded. She intended to claim her place in Hangtown society as rightfully as the next person.

She started for the sheriff's office. Some men she passed tipped their hats, and a few of the ladies smiled politely, which relieved some of her anxiety.

Maybe they didn't know who she was. Maybe they didn't yet know her story. And maybe, and this was a big one, maybe that forgiveness Mrs. Walker spoke about had found its way into the hearts of some of these citizens already.

She crossed the street. Jasper Jenkins sat on a chair tipped back against the adobe wall of the jailhouse. He jumped up when he saw her and doffed his hat.

"Good morning," he said, bright-eyed as a possum. He settled his shock of hair with a quick combing of splayed fingers.

"Howdy to you," she replied.

"You look different," he said.

"Mrs. Walker lent me this dress and one of her bonnets," Dulcie explained.

"You sure are pretty," he said.

"It's the dress, I reckon."

Jasper grinned, showing all his teeth. The deputy surely was complimentary and easy to please. He knew how to treat a lady.

"I'm looking for Deputy Walker," she said.

Jasper hooked his thumbs in the waistband of his trousers. "He's out behind the hay yard practicing with his new Sharps rifle. Came in the U.S. Mail this morning."

"Will you point me in that direction?" she asked.

"I'll take you myself."

"No need. I'll find it."

Jasper stepped off the boardwalk and drew himself alongside Dulcie in a manner that was a little too familiar. Now, she didn't know what a lady would do, but Jasper was crowding her, and she stepped back.

Jasper didn't take unkindly to her putting some distance between them. He kept beaming.

"You go up this street and pass the bakery, Miss Dulcie," he said.

She looked in the direction he pointed.

"Best mince pies I ever tasted," he added. He rubbed his belly.

Dulcie just had to laugh.

"You'll see the Empire Theater. Now, that's a place for men only. Are you sure you don't want me to accompany you?"

"No, thank you. I just need directions," she replied.

"I thought that's what you'd say. You're not like the other ladies in this town."

"I reckon that's the truth," Dulcie said.

Jasper cracked his knuckles and gawked.

"Where do I go once I reach the Empire Theater?" she prompted.

"Just keep walking. There's a wagon shop and a couple of saloons. You'll see a big white oak next to the hay yard. That's the hanging tree. The livery's just beyond."

"The hanging tree?" Dulcie asked.

"Yes, ma'am." His jocular mood evaporated. He went red in the face as he realized what he'd said.

"Don't be mortified on my account," Dulcie replied. "The hanging tree is what it's called."

Her words seemed to relieve Jasper somewhat, but he avoided her gaze.

She thanked him for his help and left him standing in the street. She'd likely be the cause of many such embarrassing moments, but she wasn't one to dwell on what couldn't be changed. Jasper would understand that one of these days.

She found the bakery. Its sweet smells had miners lining up at the door. Some had washed up and combed their hair. Others were in need of a good scrubbing.

Dulcie greeted each of them. Every one of them pulled off his sweat-stained hat and replied with a hello.

There was a spring in her step as she continued down the boardwalk. The Empire Theater, the place Jasper had cautioned her about, stood tall and imposing. The theater was quiet at this time of day. She chanced a peek in a window and saw a blue velvet sofa and fancy chairs with curved legs. In the daylight, the Empire looked as cozy as a lady's parlor, but by nightfall, apparently, only men gathered here for stage and other entertainment.

Ladies weren't allowed? Dulcie snorted. She'd have something to say about changing that silly rule.

Just ahead, she saw the hanging tree. The oak didn't impress her much. The leafless limbs sagged. The bark was scarred and peeling.

She'd come across plenty of white oaks up in the foothills, some looking the worse for wear as this one did. She shivered as she thought of her pa swinging beneath one of the branches.

Fighting tears, she quickened her step. As she approached the hay yard, she heard gunfire coming from behind a wooden shed. She couldn't see who was shooting or what he was shooting at. That'd be Tom practicing, she decided. She dried her eyes with the back of her glove and stood tall before circling the shed.

Tom picked up cans and set them along the fence posts. He looked over his shoulder and saw her coming. His smile of recognition set her heart thumping.

He was freshly shaved, which made him look younger. Her insides tingled. He surely was a fine-looking man.

He put two fingers to the brim of his hat as a greeting. He was a man of few words, but he was a good man. She'd realized how good last night on his ma's front porch as he'd tried to comfort her.

Tom finished setting up the cans and picked up a firearm that rested against one of the posts. He took long strides to stand next to her.

She caught a whiff of gun oil and burning gunpowder. Wads of burned paper littered the ground.

"Are you all right?" he asked.

"I'm better than I was last night," she replied.

He shifted his weight. "I should've told you what happened to Willie up at the claim. There was no need to wait."

She wanted him to know she didn't hold any blame against him. "You did what you thought best."

She'd no doubt Tom's smile was sincere. He had a way about him, kindly when it came to womenfolk. She liked a man who could be considerate.

She heeded Mrs. Walker's advice and didn't blurt out how convinced she was in her feelings that he had the makings of a good husband. Yet such a declaration was there, ready to surface at a moment's notice.

"I didn't expect you in town today," he said.

"Your ma had some shopping to do. I left her at the A. Paisley Dry Goods and Notions. She's picked out a yellow calico to sew up a new dress for me."

"She's taken to you," he said.

"I'm happy to say the feeling is mutual."

She looked up into his dark eyes, eager to get the courting started.

He didn't take the hint.

She was disappointed but not discouraged. She'd seen more than a spark of interest.

Her gaze traveled to the rifle he held in his left hand. "Jasper told me you'd bought a new weapon."

"Arrived this morning from back East." He stroked the freshly oiled stock.

"You any good with it?" She looked at the row of empty cans. The tin cans were a far distance, maybe one hundred paces or more.

"Eight out of ten," he said with pride. "In under two minutes."

"All with this new rifle?"

"This here is a breech loader," he explained. "She uses cartridges." He pulled down on the trigger guard, which dropped the breech, and took a spent cartridge out. He fished a new one out of the pocket of his leather vest. He slipped it into the breech. Returning the trigger guard closed the breech.

"When I close the action, this strip of metal"—he pointed to a blade screwed to the front of the breech lock—"trims the paper and exposes the powder."

"May I hold her?" Dulcie asked, impressed with the quickness of loading this new type of rifle.

He handed it over. The barrel was still warm. It had a good weight and balance, lighter than her pa's muzzle-loading .36 or the double-barreled shotgun she used to hunt game, and it was much shorter.

"It'll give a lawman an advantage," Tom said.

"It will if the person you're after doesn't get the jump on you first." She winked.

"You got lucky at your claim yesterday," he said, still smarting, she decided, at how she'd surprised him when he'd arrived at the camp.

"I reckon I did," she replied with a smile.

She raised the rifle to her shoulder. "You suppose I could give it a try?"

"I don't see why not, although I'm just getting used to her myself. She's got quite a kick. You need to be careful."

Dulcie lowered the rifle and looked up at him. There was doubt in his voice. He'd underestimated her from the start. He was about to receive a lesson in Crowder capabilities.

He took great care to show her where to put her hands and how to position the stock against her shoulder.

"This elbow up," he said, lifting her left elbow level with the gun. Being this close to him was pleasurable, and she snuggled back against his broad chest, his arms around her.

Tom Walker was all business and didn't return her advances. Mr. Paisley had shown Mrs. Walker the same consideration helping her out of the buggy. The men of Hangtown sure liked being attentive to females, Dulcie decided, but she was after more than a man with good manners.

"You look to the sight blade and line it up where you want to shoot. There are two triggers. Give the front trigger a gentle squeeze." Tom took her hand and showed her where to place her fingers. His hand covered hers, and she felt a ripple of excitement.

This seemed as good a time as any to sneak a kiss, but Mrs. Walker had warned her to hold her horses. So she concentrated on his instructions instead, which was no easy feat, given how all she could think about was that kiss.

After he set the other trigger, he stood back.

"See if you can hit one of those cans yonder," he said.

Dulcie sighted on the closest can.

"Take your time," Tom said. He was an excellent teacher.

She pulled off a shot. The can blew up into the air, tumbled over and over, and dropped to the ground.

"Whoa," Tom said. He pushed his hat back on his head.

She lowered the gun and gave him a knowing smile. "How did I do?"

"You did just fine."

She removed the spent cartridge just as he'd shown her and held out her hand. Tom took out another from his pocket.

"I'll load her," he said.

"Let me give it a try." She removed what was left of the smelly cartridge, tossed it to the ground, and added the new one.

Without waiting for further instructions, she shut the breech and shouldered the gun. She fired at the next can. She continued until every last one had jumped off its perch and landed on the ground and the air stank from the gun smoke.

She lowered the weapon with satisfaction. Tom Walker narrowed his eyes into tiny slits.

"Ten out of ten," she said.

"So it appears," he growled.

"Pa claimed I was the best shot he'd ever seen."

Tom yanked the gun from her. "You're a better shot than most."

"I have Pa to thank. He taught me most of what I know using his buffalo gun. But I've never shot with a brand-new firearm, and I appreciate your instruction. You can teach me how to shoot any day of the week."

His face colored up. "You shouldn't go fooling a man like that."

With those words of warning, he turned and headed back toward the hay yard shed.

What had gotten into her? Why had she seen fit to show Tom up like that? She should run after him and apologize. After all he'd done for her, she didn't want to seem ungrateful.

Instead, she let him go off in a lather. Hopefully, he'd calm down when he realized that what she'd done had taken skill.

A person needed skill and a whole lot of gumption to survive in the El Dorado. There was no use in pretending otherwise.

Chapter Ten

Dulcie strolled in the direction of A. Paisley's Dry Goods and Notions in no particular hurry. A freighter hauling wagon wheels drove down the middle of the road, hollering at his team, which was struggling with the load. His whip cracked, and the horses strained against the harness.

She jumped up onto the boardwalk to give them plenty of room. A woman came out of the door of a rooming house and threw a bucket of dirty water out into the street. She wore a red velvet dress trimmed in black lace and a string of black stones around her creamy white neck. Her copper-colored hair was drawn up and pinned on top of her head. At her ears dangled gold nuggets the size of wren's eggs.

"Howdy," Dulcie said.

The woman scanned her from head to toe but showed no signs of recognition or curiosity. Instead, she retreated into the building.

Dulcie didn't take offense. She reckoned some folks were friendlier than others. She vowed never to be so busy or so tired that she wouldn't greet a fellow citizen.

She continued down the boardwalk and heard shouting and cheering coming from behind the row of buildings. She hurried down to the end of a long alley to see what had brought on the commotion.

She spotted a crowd of men gathered around a stockade. Some of them were dressed as gentlemen, while others wore the animals they'd trapped and skinned. They gave a cheer at a bellowing cry that sent chills up her spine.

Dulcie elbowed her way to the front to get a closer look.

The men threw stones at a young grizzly imprisoned in the stockade. The bear pulled against an iron chain clamped around his back paw and staked in the ground.

A stone smacked the bear right between the eyes. He clawed at the air as he yelped in pain. The man who'd thrown the stone slapped his thigh and laughed. As the bear's fury grew, the men cheered louder.

"Why are you tormenting that animal?" she asked the nearest man.

The man spat on the ground. "To see how riled he gets."

"Don't you find that unfair, him being staked out like he is?"

The man picked up another stone, this time a large chunk of granite. "Why should I care? That bear is just a big ol' dumb animal."

He hurled the rock and struck the bear in the shoulder.

The bear twisted around and let out a cry. The man stepped back and hooted. The others laughed so hard, they had to hold on to their sides.

Dulcie had seen enough. She pushed her way out of the crowd and ran back to Mrs. Walker's buggy. She pulled out her shotgun from underneath the seat and checked to make sure both barrels were loaded.

She carried the weapon back to the stockade. Nobody paid her any mind, their concentration fixed on that bear. She pointed the shotgun skyward and fired. The blast of black powder shattered the air.

The laughing stopped abruptly, and she aimed the second barrel at the next man ready to hurl a rock.

"Drop it," she said. "The rest of you put up your hands so I can see them."

The men muttered and seemed unsure what to do. Dulcie thumbed back the second hammer and leveled the shotgun at the man's thick belly. He tossed the rock aside. Every hand went up.

"We were just having a little fun," one of the men said.

"That's right. No harm done," another added.

Dulcie wasn't listening to excuses. "Now, real slow, throw your shooters to the ground."

Several of the men took pistols out of their waistbands and dropped them at their feet. Others stacked their rifles and shotguns against the stockade.

She eased the hammer of her weapon back into place. She'd made her druthers known, and the men had complied.

"Which one of you locked up this animal?" she asked.

"What business is it of yours?" a man with a black hat asked.

She aimed the shotgun at his belly. "I'm making it my business."

"Let's not argue," the man pleaded. Sweat beaded up on his brow.

"With your left hand, toss me the key to the stockade," she said.

He did what she asked him. He was plenty mean-spirited, shackling a wild animal like he'd done, but luckily he wasn't stupid.

A large iron key fell into the dirt at her feet. The men exchanged glances. Kneeling, she scooped up the key. Nobody moved. She kept the shotgun pointed their way as she opened the padlock and threw the gate wide.

The bear rose to his feet. He was a good six feet and would maul her to shreds if she came within reach.

"Look," the man with the black hat said. "That's a dangerous animal. You'd better stay back."

"Shut your yap," Dulcie replied. "I know he's dangerous, and I know he's scared."

"What are you going to do?"

"Let him go."

"You can't do that. Nobody can."

Dulcie didn't listen. These men had tormented an animal that couldn't fight back, and she wasn't going to ignore an unfair fight.

"How'd you get that shackle on him?" she asked.

"Four men and a length of sailing canvas," he said with foolish pride.

She shook her head. The bear would never let her get close enough to unlock the shackle. She aimed at the cotter pin and then stopped. Scattered shot from her shotgun could hit the grizzly and injure him. She set the shotgun down against the stockade and picked up one of the muzzle loaders.

"This thing loaded?" she asked.

"Yes, ma'am," came a voice from the crowd.

She wiped one hand and then the other on her skirt. The bear dropped to all fours and growled a warning. Dulcie sighted on the cotter pin, mindful if she successfully blew it to pieces, the bear would be free, and she'd be standing in his way.

It was a risk she was willing to take.

She eased back on the hammer. A trickle of sweat ran down her forehead and into her eyes. The stinging made her eyes water even more. She blinked rapidly. Her vision cleared, and she sighted on the pin. Holding her breath, she pulled the trigger. The hammer struck flint. Gunpowder exploded. The muzzle loader bucked. The iron shackle split apart amid a shower of sparks.

The bear paused for a second and then lunged at Dulcie. The men scattered. She threw the weapon down, scampered behind the stockade door, and pulled it back as a barrier. She crouched down, hoping the bear wouldn't see her as enough of a meal to bother with.

Thankfully, the beast ignored her as he lumbered out of his prison. He started for his tormentors. The men scrambled up the nearest tree.

Those men looked a spectacle, sitting two by two on the branches as the bear watched from below.

Dulcie snatched up her shotgun, ready to fire a warning shot if the bear got any ideas about climbing the tree.

After a few minutes, the bear gave up on the men and lumbered off into the hills, bellowing as he went.

Dulcie shut the stockade gate, feeling satisfied.

Someone behind Dulcie reached over and grabbed her weapon. Dulcie spun around. Tom Walker stood over her.

"What do you think you're doing?" the Hangtown deputy asked.

"I can't abide anybody mistreating an animal," she said. She stuck out her hand. "Give back my shotgun."

"No, ma'am. This shotgun is now town property."

"On what account?"

"On account the law doesn't allow a weapon to be discharged within the city limits."

The men climbed down from the tree and surrounded them.

"I had good cause." She lunged at him, but he held the weapon out of reach. "You've no right to my property."

"I'm not going to let you violate the law," Tom said.

"I demand you arrest her, Deputy," the man in the black hat said.

"If I arrest anybody, Orville, it'll be you," Tom replied in his bossy way.

"Me?" The man in the black hat looked angry. "Nobody got hurt."

"Somebody would have if that bear had had any say." Tom's dark eyes flashed a warning.

"I realize the lady doesn't appreciate our kind of Hangtown entertainment," the black-hatted man said.

Dulcie planted her hands firmly on her hips. "I reckon I don't. It's time townsfolk found another form of amusement."

"You men go about your business," Tom said, "before I arrest you."

Dulcie nodded vigorously.

The man in the black hat sputtered. "On what grounds?"

"Subjecting the citizens of this town to a dangerous animal."

"You wouldn't dare."

"I'll include resisting arrest to the charge if I have to," Tom answered forcefully.

The man in the black hat backed down. He faced Tom with his upper lip curled into a frightful snarl. "I demand compensation. That bear was valuable. I stood to gain by holding fighting matches with that bear."

The other men added a chorus of agreement.

"Consider yourself lucky the bear hightailed it out of here instead of having you for dinner," Tom said forcefully.

Dulcie realized that the Hangtown citizenry was sore at Tom, even though it was all her fault.

"You men turn your backs," she said.

"What's she up to?" one of them said.

"Just do as I say."

They turned around, shaking their heads.

"You too, Deputy."

Tom looked at her as if to say he wasn't about to tolerate any nonsense, but he turned around when her hand dove down the front of her skirt. She retrieved the leather pouch and opened it. She shook out the few gold coins her pa had left her.

"Here you are," she said.

The man in the black hat turned and looked at the coins in her hand.

"I aim to compensate you for your loss," she said.

He took the money but didn't look her in the eye. He was ashamed, she reckoned, to take money from a woman, but after all the protest he'd made, he couldn't refuse either.

Tom started down the street.

After a half dozen paces, Dulcie caught up.

"How long are you going to confiscate my firearm?" she asked.

"The law says ten days."

"Ten whole days? That weapon belongs to me."

"Now it's the property of the Sheriff of El Dorado County."

Clearly, her objections met a pair of deaf ears. Tom Walker didn't make exceptions where the law was concerned.

"It's worth the inconvenience," Dulcie said finally. "Did you see the look on Orville's face when that bear ran off?"

"If he or anybody else in this town needs to be taught a lesson," Tom replied, "the law will be the one to do it."

She followed close on his heels. She intended to give him both barrels of her rightful opinion, and, by golly, he'd listen.

"When did you reckon the law intended to get involved?" she asked.

Tom slowed a mite. "I had other things to attend to this morning."

Dulcie huffed. "You could ask the sheriff to deputize me. Someone with my skills would be a valuable person to have at your side."

Tom climbed the steps of the boardwalk. "I'll do no such thing."

"I could've arrested those men, quick as you please."

He opened the door and turned. "Stay away from those men."

"I'm not afraid of them, if that's what you're thinking," she said.

"You should be."

"You sound just like my pa," she answered, and she followed him inside.

He set her shotgun in a corner and dropped his hat onto a peg.

"Your pa had plenty of reason to warn you off some kinds of men," he said.

"Believe you me, he kept them away," she replied, "which is why I'm eighteen going on nineteen and still not hitched."

Tom scowled.

"Promise you'll stay away from Orville and the rest," he said, keeping to the subject at hand.

"I'll make no such promise."

"The shotgun stays here," he said.

"No matter. I've got my pa's .36 to take care of my defensive needs."

"Discharge that old muzzle loader in town, and I'll confiscate it too." He sat down behind his big desk and picked up a newspaper.

"Is that all you've got to say?" she asked.

"Yes, ma'am."

"Then I'm leaving."

"Suit yourself."

With one last, longing look at her shotgun, she pushed through the door and stomped out. He surely could be a stubborn man.

Her sharp spike of anger quickly cooled. Tom couldn't play favorites, and he couldn't waver when it came to upholding the laws these citizens had made for their town. He stuck to the rules, fair and simple. Come election time, the people of Hangtown could rest assured that Tom Walker was a lawman they could depend on.

Dulcie shook her head. She could be a big help to him if only he'd let her.

She spotted Mrs. Walker waiting on the boardwalk and looking down the street in both directions. She hurried. She hadn't meant to be gone so long.

"Where have you been?" Mrs. Walker asked when Dulcie reached her.

"Talking with Tom," she said, nearly out of breath. Would Mrs. Walker consider what she'd done about the bear unladylike?

Thankfully, Mrs. Walker didn't ask any more questions and

didn't notice that Dulcie's shotgun was missing. She handed Dulcie a package wrapped in brown paper. "I've got what we need for your new dress. We'd better be going. There's work to be done at home."

Dulcie tucked the parcel under one arm. "Thank you, ma'am. I'm obliged."

Mrs. Walker dismissed the notion with a wave of a hand.

"I'm glad to have met Maryanne Greenwood," Dulcie told her as they climbed into the buggy.

"The Greenwoods are fine people," Mrs. Walker said as she untied the reins.

"Maryanne invited me to her house," Dulcie said.

"I'm glad you're making friends," Mrs. Walker replied as she settled in. Mrs. Walker seemed sure, but Dulcie had her doubts. She'd been in town the better part of the morning, and only Maryanne Greenwood had come forward to welcome her.

Mrs. Walker released the brake, and the buggy rolled forward. Dulcie grasped the back of the seat. With a shake of the reins, they started on home.

"I enjoyed meeting Mr. Paisley," Dulcie said. "I should include him on my list of new acquaintances."

"He liked you as well."

"Do you think he'd give me a job working in his store?"

"What do you need a job for?" Mrs. Walker sounded alarmed.

"To earn some money. I want to pay my way."

"You do more than enough around my place to earn your keep."

"You've gone ahead and spent money on dress material. I can't let you spend money that you could be spending on yourself."

"Now, what gave you the idea I need anything?" Mrs. Walker asked.

"I only thought . . ."

"There'll be no talk of taking a job. A lady doesn't work outside of her home."

Dulcie listened to the mare clopping along on the hardpan. She hadn't thought of it like that. Again, Mrs. Walker seemed so sure.

"I don't mean to be nosy, but didn't your pa leave you any money?" Mrs. Walker asked.

"Yes, a hanky full, but I spent it." Dulcie had no choice but to tell her about the man in the black hat and what she'd done about the bear. She glanced over at Mrs. Walker, sure of a scolding. The lady started laughing until big tears rolled down her cheeks.

"Dulcie, you surely are a caution." Mrs. Walker took a hanky out from under her sleeve and gave her nose a good blow.

"Yes, ma'am. Tom wasn't too pleased. He took away my shotgun. I'll have to rely on my pa's buffalo gun from now on."

"You don't need to carry any kind of weapon," Mrs. Walker said with a hiccup. "You'll soon have a husband to take care of you."

Dulcie would like that fine, although she believed a husband and wife were a team, like two oxen yoked together, pulling the same load. She didn't explain her views to Mrs. Walker.

The lady would probably think that was funny too.

Chapter Eleven

Tom chewed on a forkful of homemade apple pie, watching his ma rolling out another piecrust. The woman hadn't been this industrious in a long while.

"There's no quit in her," Ma said. "She was up before me, scrubbing the wood floors. I don't think I've ever seen them so clean."

Ma hadn't stopped crowing about Dulcie Crowder since the minute he'd arrived. He knew what his ma was after. The fire in him didn't need stoking.

He'd done a lot of thinking about Dulcie. He recognized her virtues as well as any man would. He must keep his distance for practical reasons. A woman was a distraction, and in his line of work, a distraction could prove fatal.

This morning he'd no choice but to pay a call. A stranger had ridden into Hangtown asking about her. Tom decided to give his ma and Dulcie fair warning they were about to have company.

"What do you think he wants?" Ma asked as she wiped her hands on her apron.

Tom speared the last bite. "Don't know, and he wasn't saying. He did say he came from Sacramento." He popped the morsel into his mouth.

Ma took the coffeepot from the back of the stove and poured him another cup. "He's from the new capital. Is he a government man?"

"No, he would've said."

"You don't suppose she's got kin?"

"That'd be my guess," Tom said, scraping his plate with the side of his fork.

"She didn't mention anybody to me," Ma said as she set the cup in front of him.

"Maybe she doesn't know of any family," Tom said. "Willie didn't talk about his people. Said Dulcie was his only living kin." He frowned. He should've asked Willie more questions about his background.

"He kept his daughter isolated up on his claim," Ma said. "Maybe he'd kin he didn't want Dulcie to know about."

"Could be," Tom answered.

Dulcie came into the kitchen from the back door carrying a basket of eggs on her hip. Her gaze lit on him, but she didn't falter.

"Well, if it ain't the deputy come calling."

"*Isn't,*" Ma corrected.

Dulcie's eyes widened. "Sorry, Mrs. Walker. If it *isn't* the deputy."

Tom tried to keep a straight face, but it was a struggle.

She turned a playful gaze on him. "Did you bring me my firearm?"

"I confiscated that weapon for your own good." His voice broke. He realized she was getting under his skin. To let her could prove dangerous to them both.

"So you've said," she answered.

He wiped his mouth with a cloth napkin. "I'm here on another matter."

She looked inquiringly at Ma.

"Thomas has brought some news," Ma said.

Dulcie set the eggs on the table and brushed off her hands. Fixing him with a piercing gaze, she said, "I guess I'm ready to hear what you have to say."

"Sit down," his ma said. Dulcie pulled out a kitchen chair and sat next to him. Ma took the seat opposite.

"Do you have any kin that you know of?" he asked.

Dulcie looked puzzled. "None that Pa ever spoke about. Not any living in the States anyway. Why do you ask?"

"There's a fella riding out here to see you."

"Did he give a name?"

Tom fished the card the man had given him out of his vest pocket and gave it to her.

Ma leaned over and read the card out loud. "R.J. Buchanan," Ma said. "Sacramento."

"Does the name mean anything to you?" Tom asked.

Dulcie handed the card back. "No, I can't say I ever heard the name Buchanan before."

"He'll be here shortly, no doubt," Tom said. "You want me to stay and see what this is all about?"

"Only if you want to," Dulcie said. She turned to Ma. "I'd better go and wash up."

Ma nodded. Dulcie headed outside.

"I don't like the sound of this," Ma said.

"Me neither," Tom agreed. He'd expected that Dulcie would ask for his help. He'd thought she'd rely on him when the stranger arrived and made his business known.

She didn't seem to care one way or the other if he stuck around or not. Her quick dismissal left him smarting.

"Let's hope his visit is a friendly one," Tom said. He'd no reason to be optimistic, but he didn't want his ma to fret unnecessarily. He picked up his cup and took a gulp.

"What did he look like?" Ma asked.

"Dressed in a store-bought suit," Tom said.

"No doubt a gentleman. You don't suppose he wants to take Dulcie back to Sacramento with him, do you?" Ma's voice took on an urgency Tom had heard in the many arguments they'd had since he'd become deputy.

Tom smiled to quell her growing alarm. "You think Dulcie would go?"

His ma worried a button at her throat. The thought of Dulcie leaving clearly distressed her. To be honest, he didn't like the idea either.

"I don't rightly know," Ma said. "She's taken to town life quickly enough. She talks about Hangtown as if it was home."

"There you go. I don't think she'll run off with a stranger."

"I hope you're right. The town needs her."

Ma was singing Dulcie's praises again.

Tom couldn't say he blamed her, even though he knew what she was after. Marrying and settling down wasn't in the cards for him.

He'd once believed he would settle down with Maryanne one day, but Maryanne had married a New Yorker named Stuart Greenwood who'd come out to the El Dorado to take up ranching.

There was a time when he'd believed Greenwood would turn tail and go back to city life. That'd been two years ago this spring. Tom had to say that the man had done fine by Maryanne and their sprout, young George Arthur. Tom was proud to call Stuart his friend.

"Thomas?" His ma's voice broke into his reverie.

He straightened.

"You all right?"

"Yes, ma'am. I was just thinking how some things turn out for the best."

"You'll stay, won't you?" Ma asked.

"I'd better," he replied, knowing the presence of his badge would keep the stranger from pulling any shenanigans.

Ma patted his hand and rose from the table. "Good. You help yourself to another piece of pie. I'll go see what's keeping Dulcie."

As it turned out, the stranger wasn't far behind Tom, arriving on a sorrel gelding. Tom saw him from the window and gulped down the last of his coffee as he pushed away from the kitchen table.

He met the man at the front porch.

"Deputy," the man said as a greeting. If he was surprised to see Tom, he kept it to himself.

The man was friendly enough, and Tom could've let down his guard. He didn't. Something about the man caused the short hairs on the back of his neck to quiver.

The two women joined him. Dulcie had scrubbed her face and put on a fresh apron. Her brown hair had been freshly braided with a green ribbon.

Tom was struck by how lovely she looked. He saw that the stranger appreciated what he was seeing as well. Tom felt protective of her. R.J. Buchanan had better mind his manners.

"I'm Dulcie Crowder," she said in a voice edged with a wariness that Tom was happy to hear. "This is Mrs. Walker."

"Pleased to meet you." The man tipped his tall hat at the ladies.

"Likewise," Dulcie said.

"Name's R.J. Buchanan."

"They know who you are," Tom replied.

"Then you know I've come from Sacramento to speak to Miss Crowder."

"I reckon anything you have to say can be said in front of the Walkers," Dulcie said.

Tom was thankful she'd said so.

Mr. Buchanan removed his hat and held it against his chest. "I was sorry to hear about your father. Please accept my deepest sympathies."

"Thank you, Mr. Buchanan," Dulcie answered.

"State your business," Tom said flatly, knowing the man wasn't here to pay a sympathy call.

R.J. Buchanan shifted in his saddle. From the surprised look on his face, he hadn't expected Tom to speak so harshly.

Dulcie's eyes narrowed. Had she also seen something to dislike about this man?

"I represent interests looking to buy some land." Buchanan spoke directly to Dulcie. "I heard you might have some land to sell."

"Land?" Dulcie said. "You must be mistaken."

"Your family worked a claim over by Twin Pines?"

"We did."

R.J. Buchanan patted his thick mustache. "Your pa owned a sizable piece of land up there."

"I think you're mistaken. My pa never owned any land," Dulcie corrected the man. "Where we come from, owning land isn't the privilege of a workingman."

"Perhaps he never got the chance to tell you," R.J. said.

Dulcie shook her head. "He would've said something if he'd bought any land."

"I assure you, he did. There's a deed recorded at the Land Registry Office."

"A deed registered to Willie Crowder?"

"That's right."

"Free and clear?" she asked.

"Exactly." R.J. looked over at Tom. "You can check."

"And you'd like to buy what he owned?" Dulcie asked.

R.J. turned greedy eyes on Dulcie. "I'm prepared to make you, his only heir, a generous offer."

"You'd better come inside," Ma said. She turned and led the way. Tom waited for R.J. to dismount and tie up his horse. He held the door open for Mr. Buchanan and let it slam shut behind them.

They sat down in Ma's spotless parlor. Tom remained standing. Ma offered lemonade but was refused with polite thank-yous.

Mr. R.J. Buchanan pulled out a sheet of paper from his coat pocket.

Dulcie folded her hands in her lap. She looked young and innocent in that getup, but Tom wasn't fooled. He knew she'd the heart of a cougar and would make short work of R.J. if he was up to no good.

Tom shifted his feet. The man looked prosperous, and he'd come prepared. He knew about the property Willie had bought, going so far as to look up the recording of the deed. Something about R.J. Buchanan didn't hold water. Why would he need that piece of land? From what Tom had observed, all the property amounted to was a pile of rocks and a stand of trees fit for nothing more than firewood.

"Let me tell you straight up, Mr. Buchanan," Dulcie said. "Me and my pa worked the claim for a good long while and never found any gold."

"I appreciate your honesty, Miss Crowder." He looked at all of them in turn. "In this day and age, honest folk are a rare breed."

"Thank you," Dulcie replied as sweetly as a Sunday school teacher.

He handed Dulcie the piece of paper. "I took the liberty of drawing up a bill of sale. As you will see written on this paper, your pa invested wisely. He owned eighty acres."

Dulcie took the bill of sale and laid it in her lap.

"Like I said, you being the only kin, the land belongs to you," R.J. continued. "I represent interests that would like to buy you out."

Tom straightened. R.J. Buchanan had traveled a two days' ride to buy the Crowder land, and Tom was mighty curious what kind of offer he intended to make.

"An offer?" she asked. She hadn't looked over the paper. No doubt the legal language confounded her.

Buchanan smiled indulgently. "I'm prepared to offer you one dollar an acre."

Tom looked at Dulcie. She remained unruffled.

"My pa was a good man," Dulcie said. "I didn't know he was a rich one."

"You will be a wealthy woman," R.J. replied.

"Mr. Buchanan, I'll consider your offer, but I need to look over this bill of sale first," Dulcie said.

"Of course." The man stood. "I've taken up enough of your time. Thank you, Mrs. Walker, for your hospitality."

"We're pleased that you came," Ma replied agreeably.

R.J. picked up his hat and bowed to the ladies. "I hope to hear from you soon, Miss Crowder. I'm staying at Mary's Hotel in town if you have any questions or concerns."

"I'll see you out," Tom said. He was proud of Dulcie. A dollar an acre was a mighty hefty sum, but she hadn't been swayed into making a hasty decision. Most likely R.J. had counted on her not having any book learning, so she wouldn't be able to read the bill of sale he'd brought. Dulcie knew enough to have someone look over the paperwork before she gave the man her answer.

If Tom was a gambling man, he'd wager that R.J. Buchanan was holding back valuable information. A man didn't offer that much for a parcel of rocks without a good reason.

"You didn't say who you represented," Tom said when they'd reached the porch.

"No, I didn't. The buyer wishes to remain anonymous."

Tom didn't like it. "Can you tell me if he's local?"

Mr. Buchanan put on his hat. "I can tell you he isn't. He's a successful businessman from Sacramento."

"What does a successful businessman want with Willie Crowder's land? Dulcie told you there's no gold up there."

"My client isn't interested in mining," R.J. said.

"There's plenty of good land to be bought in the El Dorado," Tom replied. "Why the Crowder claim?"

Mr. Buchanan picked up his reins. "My client owns a great deal of property. He considers land in this area a prime investment."

Tom wasn't satisfied, but R.J. was tight-lipped about giving out any more information than he had to.

R.J. put a shiny boot into a stirrup and mounted his horse. "Good day, Deputy," he said. "No doubt we'll be seeing each other again."

He looked at Tom full of confidence and good will. Tom didn't trust him an inch.

Even though Tom had been happy that Dulcie had bought some time to find out what Buchanan was really after, he suspected R.J. wouldn't leave until he got what he wanted.

As soon as Tom got back to town, he'd send a telegram to the sheriff in Coloma. If R.J. was a scoundrel and up to no good, there was nobody better than a lawman to know about it.

Dulcie was flabbergasted to learn that her pa owned so much land. It'd always been Pa's dream to own the land he worked. And he'd done it. By all the Crowders living and dead, he surely had.

Where'd he get the money? Crowders had been tenant farmers for generations. There'd been little money and never a chance to own a bit of God's green earth.

The hills around Hangtown ran with gold, and men made fortunes there. Pa hadn't been one of them. He'd picked out the sorriest scrap of real estate to lay his claim to—had probably bought it dirt cheap.

She smiled. *Dirt cheap.* Pa's luck had finally changed.

"Looks like Pa made a good investment," Dulcie said.

Mrs. Walker beamed like a ray of sunshine. "Mr. Buchanan was right. You're going to be a wealthy woman."

"I'll be glad to have the money," Dulcie admitted. "I'd like to have a house as grand as yours and a buggy with a pretty mare to pull it."

Mrs. Walker laughed. "You'll have enough and more, by my account."

Dulcie couldn't imagine having more money than she knew what to do with.

"What do you suppose Tom is saying to Mr. Buchanan?" Dulcie asked.

"I imagine he's asking some questions about his credentials."

"Credentials?"

"To see if Mr. Buchanan is who he says he is."

Naturally Tom would be suspicious of a stranger making big promises. Dulcie liked that Tom saw fit to check out the man's credentials. That was something she'd have no idea how to do.

"Do you think that'll take long?" Dulcie asked.

"There will be others to ask," Mrs. Walker replied.

"Who?"

"Hangtown has a telegraph now," Mrs. Walker said. "Thomas will send inquiries to people in Sacramento. Most likely he'll send word to the sheriff in Coloma as well. He'll have an answer in a day or two."

"That's good. I don't want to keep Mr. Buchanan waiting. He might change his mind or find a better piece of property to buy."

She picked up the piece of paper Mr. Buchanan had left. Mrs. Walker patted the cushion next to her.

"Let's take a look," she said. "After we've read through the paperwork, we'll go into town and talk to a lawyer."

Dulcie sat next to Mrs. Walker. That was a good plan, to her way of thinking. When Tom came inside, she'd tell him. He didn't like Mr. Buchanan; she'd seen the scowl on his face, although Tom seemed mistrustful of just about everybody.

She heard Mr. Buchanan leaving. She was anxious to hear what Tom had found out.

At the sound of another horse clopping up the road, Dulcie jumped to her feet and went to the window. She saw Tom riding Star and heading for town.

A sigh escaped her.

"Better he sends those telegrams right away," Mrs. Walker said.

Dulcie turned away from the window. "I suppose."

She wished Tom would've told her what he'd found out about the man.

"How do you suppose a businessman from Sacramento came to know about my pa's land?" she asked.

"He must've been looking for a parcel in the land office and came across your pa's name," Mrs. Walker answered. "Then someone in town told him about you."

Mrs. Walker must be right. What other explanation could there be?

"Thomas will tell us when he's got news," Mrs. Walker said encouragingly.

Dulcie settled next to Mrs. Walker, and they waded through the four-dollar words on the bill of sale. Despite her excitement, for the windfall couldn't have come at a better time, Dulcie decided to heed Mrs. Walker's advice and wait on the telegrams. Although she didn't know what difference it would make. If the papers were legal and proper according to the lawyer from town, she couldn't think of any reason for keeping the land. She'd no use for acreage that couldn't be cultivated, and the money would be all she'd ever need.

After they'd gone to town and consulted with the lawyer, she'd keep her promise and pay a call on Maryanne Greenwood. She had a powerful need to share good news with her new friend.

Chapter Twelve

Dulcie could ride a mule—or a horse, for that matter—as well as any man, but Mrs. Walker wouldn't hear of Dulcie saddling up Chester. She said it wasn't proper for a lady to sit astride a mule, insisting Dulcie take the buggy to pay her social call.

She heard no argument from Dulcie. The fancy carriage pulled by the dun-colored mare would do fine.

Dulcie changed into her town dress and presented herself in the kitchen.

Mrs. Walker gave her a nod of approval, then slowly lowered herself into a chair and grimaced.

"Are you all right?" Dulcie asked.

"My rheumatiz is acting up," she explained.

"I should stay and help with the chores," Dulcie said.

"I'll be fine. You go on now. It'll do you good to have a woman your own age to converse with."

Dulcie thought the same and appreciated that Mrs. Walker could spare her.

"I won't be long," Dulcie said, putting on her bonnet and tying the ribbons under her left ear. "I'll be back in time to do my supper chores."

Mrs. Walker picked a needle and spool of thread out of her sewing box. "I'll work on your new dress while you're gone."

Dulcie reckoned one dress was enough for any woman, but Mrs. Walker was determined she should have another.

Dulcie would soon be rich, and rich ladies had as many dresses as they wanted.

She found Mr. Eng mending a harness.

"Good day," Mr. Eng said, carefully pronouncing each word.

"Howdy." Dulcie smiled. "I'm going over to the Greenwood place. I'm taking the buggy."

Mr. Eng put down the harness, seeming to understand what she needed.

She turned in the direction of the stable. The dun-colored mare greeted her from one of the stalls with a soft whinny and stuck her head over the Dutch door. When the mare saw Mr. Eng lift the tack off the wooden peg, she retreated.

"Don't be shy," Dulcie said. "A walk will do you good."

She reached out with a lump of brown sugar, and the mare came around to nibble out of her hand. She patted its soft neck, and the mare's hide rippled under her touch. She did so love the smell of horseflesh, which was preferable to a mule's stink any day.

Mr. Eng showed her, without words, how to hitch the mare up to the buggy. He was a patient man, and his skillful fingers worked quickly on the harness. Dulcie was full of gratitude by the time he finished.

Dulcie stowed her pa's muzzle loader underneath the seat. The smoothbore could do the job as well as her shotgun, she reckoned, which Tom wasn't inclined to give back to her anytime soon. She climbed aboard.

"Thank you, Mr. Eng." He handed over the reins. "Don't you worry about me. I've driven a wagon. A buggy can't be much different."

Mr. Eng smiled ever so slightly, and Dulcie needed no translation.

The mare looked back at her. Dulcie released the brake and gave the reins a confident shake. She didn't want the horse to think Dulcie was new to driving a buggy. A horse was prone to take advantage if you didn't show her who was boss.

The buggy lurched forward, and she was on her way.

Mrs. Walker didn't come out onto the porch to wave good-bye. Dulcie felt pangs of guilt that she'd left Mrs. Walker hurting, but a rest off her feet would ease the pain, and she had Mrs. Eng to help.

The road toward Coloma was smooth and the mare steady. Dulcie tried to quash any natural misgivings she might have about Mr. Buchanan. The bill of sale he'd given her had panned out as he'd described. The lawyer in Hangtown, who'd charged a silver dollar for his services, had agreed.

Who would've thought the claim would finally be worth something? Even thinking about the amount of money R.J. had offered started butterflies to fluttering inside her.

It didn't take long to get where she was going. The Greenwood ranch was nestled in a pretty valley like a newborn chick in a nest.

Dulcie hollered a greeting as she drove up to the farmhouse. Maryanne came out of the log house carrying a babe. She wore a simple cap, the same as Mrs. Walker. Her hair, escaping from the bun at the back of her head, curled in pretty tendrils around her face. She greeted Dulcie with a kindhearted smile and a one-armed hug as if they were old friends.

"This is George Arthur, but his pa wants to shorten his name. Don't ask me why." She laughed and pulled down on the nightshirt that reached to his toes.

Dulcie cooed at the lively baby. "The name's a mouthful, but he looks like a George Arthur to me."

Maryanne's eyes sparkled with delight at the young'un. A bolt of envy shot through Dulcie.

"Come out to the barn and meet my husband," Maryanne said in her sweet way.

They crossed the courtyard, where chickens pecked at the insects hopping on the ground. An old dog lay asleep underneath an empty corncrib. He lifted his head an inch, barked a couple of times, and then went back to sleep.

Mr. Greenwood was deep in pig muck, shoveling dirt into the holes the sow dug with her snout. The piglets, herded over to one corner, watched from behind their ma, who glared at the intruder with open hostility.

Stuart Greenwood wore a wide-brimmed hat of woven straw and a long-sleeved shirt. He'd rolled up his pant legs, and his sun-freckled legs were heavily spattered with dirt.

"Stuart, say hello to Dulcie Crowder."

Stuart Greenwood quit his shoveling, leaned on his shovel, and grinned. "Howdy, Dulcie. I'm pleased to meet you."

"Thank you," Dulcie replied. "Same here."

Stuart Greenwood had a long face and was so thin, a strong wind would most likely blow him into the next county, given half a chance.

Dulcie saw how lovingly he gazed at his wife and son. Maryanne was a lucky woman.

The baby began to fuss.

"We'd better go," Maryanne said as she jostled her boy. "The straw dust blowing around isn't good for George Arthur's lungs."

She turned back to Stuart and cast him a playful look. "Supper will be on the table in an hour. Don't you keep us waiting."

Stuart kept on grinning. "No, ma'am, I won't."

The affection between them was a wonder to see, in Dulcie's opinion. Those two were in love and not shy to show it.

Unlike Deputy Sheriff Walker, who kept his distance. Why he did so remained a mystery to Dulcie.

Maryanne showed off the rest of their homestead: the fenced-in paddock with a fat mare ready to foal, the corncrib, empty after a long winter, and a chicken coop standing on stilts to keep varmints from stealing eggs.

She pointed out the boundaries of their spread, to the hills behind them. Their homestead wasn't big, but Dulcie was struck by Maryanne's pride in what they owned and how she didn't seem to find pride a failing.

Dulcie smiled. Having a spread such as this one would do just fine, except she couldn't picture Tom as a farmer. His job as the deputy sheriff of Hangtown suited him. If he ran for the office of sheriff, she'd no doubt he'd win.

Most likely, Mrs. Walker wanted Dulcie and Tom to get hitched so Dulcie would persuade Tom to quit the law. She realized it was something she couldn't do.

The inside of the farmhouse was neat and cozy, and Dulcie smelled a stew cooking. The furniture was plain, and Maryanne's kitchen was an open fire in a stone fireplace. She put her baby down in a cradle for a nap and then tended to Stuart's supper, which had bubbled down the sides of the Dutch oven. Using a long-handled fork, she lifted the pot away from the fire and set it on the hearth.

Dulcie noticed a daguerreotype sitting on the mantel over the fireplace of Maryanne and Stuart in their wedding finery.

"Stuart and I sat for our photograph in San Francisco," Maryanne explained, picking up the picture and giving it a quick dusting with her apron.

"I like it," Dulcie said. "It says this is a home built on a lasting bond."

Maryanne nodded and returned the picture to its place. There were happy tears in her eyes.

"Let's go out to the porch where we can talk," she said, her voice thick with emotion.

Dulcie didn't know what she'd said to bring on a fit of weeping, but she guessed some ladies must cry from sheer happiness.

Maryanne poured lemonade into two tall glasses. Dulcie held the door open for her.

They sat on a swinging chair in the shade of the house, drinking lemonade and chattering like two birds.

Maryanne was full of plans for her farm. "Stuart is real good with woodworking. He built this swinging chair for me."

"And your baby's cradle."

"Yes, as soon as I found out I was in a family way." Maryanne sat back in the swing chair, content in a way Dulcie could only imagine.

Dulcie listened with growing envy. She pictured herself in her own swing chair, on her own porch, much like this one.

She looked out in the direction Maryanne looked. The land around them was dry and bare from a winter short on snowfall, surrounded by trees that needed clearing.

Maryanne and her husband had a long way to go before this homestead would prosper, but Maryanne didn't seem to worry about what lay ahead for her and her family.

Dulcie leaned back and started to rock. She reckoned that was one of love's rewards, faith in a future together.

"All we've talked about is me," Maryanne said with a girlish giggle. "What do you have to say for yourself?"

"What do you want to know?" Dulcie asked, enjoying the swaying of the swing chair.

"How are you getting along with Mrs. Walker?" she asked.

"She's a fine lady."

"Oh, I couldn't agree more. Since Mr. Walker passed, she'd been lonely."

"She has Tom."

"Those two argue over the smallest things," Maryanne said, shaking her head.

"She doesn't want Tom to take over for his pa."

"She doesn't want him to get killed."

"Mrs. Walker's stubborn," Dulcie said, remembering the fight after dinner the first night she'd come. "But Tom's just as hardheaded about being a lawman."

"I know. He won't change his mind even if it's for his own good."

"You seem to know a lot about him," Dulcie said.

"We courted for two years," Maryanne said. "Nobody told you?"

Dulcie stopped rocking. "I guess nobody saw a need to."

Maryanne shrugged. "I can't claim Tom Walker's affections anymore. I married Stuart."

Dulcie considered what Maryanne had told her. Two years was a long time to be courting and still not tie the knot.

"You're telling me Tom's not the marrying kind?"

Maryanne laughed lightheartedly. "The subject of marriage never came up, even though I hinted strongly enough. So did my family."

"Tom can't make a mistake," Dulcie said. "Even if he did, he wouldn't admit it."

"Some men are born that way," Maryanne said. No doubt she'd given Tom's disposition considerable thought.

"In my opinion, he's skittish because his pa was ambushed. Makes a man jumpy if he can't see what's coming."

Maryanne tilted her head to one side. "You sure have a different way of talking."

Dulcie took that as a compliment. "Although why he's jumpy

with me, I'd like to know. I've been honest with him from the start about my intentions."

"You're sweet on him."

"I am. I need a husband, and I picked him the first time I laid eyes on him."

"Why did you decide on Tom? You may have noticed there aren't a lot of women in Hangtown. Most have already been spoken for. You can have your pick of any man you want."

"My heart's set on Tom. He's a good man—I saw that in him right away—and not hard on the eyes either. In fact, I'd have to say he's the handsomest man I've ever come across. Stuart being a close second, of course," she added so as not to sound ill-mannered.

Maryanne sat back. "I couldn't be happier for you. You just might be the woman to get Tom Walker to the preacher."

Dulcie was relieved that Maryanne had faith in her abilities, but she had a question that needed asking. "What if he still has tender feelings for you?"

"I don't think you need worry. We weren't meant for each other, and Tom knew it before I did."

Dulcie wasn't so sure that Tom didn't hold on to more than a friendship with Maryanne Greenwood. Even the possibility made her heart ache.

"I'm glad to hear you say so," Dulcie replied, so there wouldn't be any misunderstanding. Maryanne had convinced Dulcie she'd made her choice and had no regrets. "I welcome any suggestions you might have to convince him we should get married. I can't wait two years."

"The man's devoted to his work. He'll need some persuading," Maryanne said with a deep sigh.

"How do I go about persuading him?"

Maryanne sat up and clapped her hands together. Her eyes were bright and shiny, like two copper pennies. "There's a town social on Saturday night. Tom is sure to be there."

"Mrs. Walker already told me. I intend to go."

"There'll be dancing."

Dulcie understood what Maryanne was getting at and saw the flaw right away. "I can't dance."

"I'll teach you."

Dulcie choked on her gratitude. She'd been shown so many kindnesses since she arrived. A lesson would surely be a cure for her clumsy feet.

Right there on the Greenwood porch, with Maryanne humming a tune, they danced. Dulcie picked up the steps quickly, and Maryanne praised her for being a good student.

Being held by a man would be a different matter, and the thought of being in Tom Walker's arms gave Dulcie gooseflesh. She flushed with anticipation.

If Maryanne noticed, she didn't let on. She came to the end of her tune, and they stopped.

Dulcie would have liked to stay longer, but she didn't dare. "I'd best be going. Mrs. Walker will need me to help with chores."

"You just got here," Maryanne said.

Dulcie hated to disappoint Maryanne. She'd enjoyed Maryanne's company and believed her new friend had enjoyed hers. Dulcie reckoned there was plenty of loneliness living out here, even with a husband and baby.

Dulcie smiled. "We'll get together again real soon."

Maryanne nodded. "Of course we will. I'll see you Saturday night."

Dulcie smiled even more broadly.

"You stay one more minute. I've got something for Mrs. Walker."

Dulcie waited outside, anxious to be on her way.

Maryanne returned with a jar with a strip of calico wrapped around the top for a lid.

"Wildflower honey," she said as she handed it over.

Dulcie thanked her, and they hugged as good friends do. She climbed aboard the buggy and set the honey snugly between her feet.

"You take care now," Maryanne said.

"I will," Dulcie replied.

She shook the reins and headed down the road. When she looked back, Maryanne was waving.

Dulcie realized she'd forgotten to tell Maryanne her good news.

* * *

Less than forty-eight hours after R.J. Buchanan arrived in Hangtown, Tom received a telegram from the sheriff in Coloma. He left the telegraph office with a purposeful stride. The telegram had confirmed his suspicion. R.J. Buchanan was up to no good.

The land Willie Crowder had owned was going to be bought up by the railroad people at a considerably better price than a dollar an acre. They needed the trees to make railroad ties for a set of tracks coming over the Sierra Nevada Mountains. Tom had heard talk that the railroad men intended to build tracks that would span the entire continent one day. It didn't seem possible, but it looked like they were getting ready to do just that.

Who R.J. represented remained a secret. Why, Tom would like to know. In Tom's estimation, the buyer had sent a representative to make an offer who hadn't presented his interest in the land fairly. Someone intended to hornswoggle Dulcie out of her inheritance and make a tidy profit that wasn't rightly his.

He'd put R.J. in jail, except he had no call to arrest the man. Offering Dulcie money for her land wasn't a violation of any law, even if R.J. had tried to take advantage of her.

When Dulcie found out, and he was the man to tell her, there'd be no way she'd sell that land cheap. R.J.'d have no choice but to inform his buyer that the law in Hangtown was wise to their scheme and wouldn't tolerate how they conducted business here.

By the time Tom reached Mary's Hotel, he had a sizable burr under his collar. The sooner Tom saw the back of R.J. Buchanan, the better off the town and other unsuspecting citizens would be.

The front room of the hotel was empty, but Tom heard voices in the back. He pushed opened the swinging door into the kitchen. Mary stirred a pot on the cookstove she'd had freighted out here all the way from Mobile. The Littman girl kneaded dough on a floured board. They both stopped what they were doing and looked up at him.

"Morning Mary, Alice." He took off his hat.

"Morning, Tom. What can I do for you?" Mary asked. She knocked the wooden spoon against the lip of the tin pot and set it alongside.

"A city man calling himself R.J. Buchanan has taken a room here."

"That's right." Mary brushed a limp hank of hair off her face. "He came in day before yesterday."

"I'd like to talk to him."

"He's in number eight, top of the stairs."

Tom thanked her.

"Is there anything wrong?" Mary asked.

"No, ma'am." He adjusted his hat on his head. "Nothing to concern yourself with."

He took the steps two at a time. The brass number eight on the door was as shiny as a gold tooth. He rapped on the door.

There was no reason to be in a temper, but Tom wasn't in a hospitable mood either.

R.J. opened the door a few inches. When he recognized Tom, he opened it wide.

His case was open on the bed.

"Morning, Deputy."

"Looks like you saved me the trouble of asking you to leave."

R.J. licked his thick lips. "My business is done in Hangtown."

"What business are you talking about?"

"The land purchase, of course."

"You can't buy Dulcie's land. It isn't for sale."

"You're too late, Deputy. Miss Crowder signed the papers this morning." He showed Tom the bill of sale with Dulcie's carefully written name on the bottom. "I rode out to Mrs. Walker's house first thing."

Tom was steaming mad, but he kept his anger under control. "You took advantage of that girl."

"The sale is legal and proper." R.J. tossed the paper inside his case and closed it. He put on his hat. "If you'll excuse me, I've a stagecoach to catch."

Tom caught him by the arm. He wanted to shake the life out of him. The man shrugged away and picked up his case.

"I'd advise you to be careful, Deputy. The law is on my side."

Tom watched in stunned silence as R.J. walked out of the room as pleased with himself as a man could be.

"What's Mr. Buchanan done?" Mary asked when Tom came down the stairs. "He sure was in a hurry."

"Pulled a fast one."

Mary frowned.

"He bought Dulcie Crowder's property dirt cheap," Tom explained. "The railroad is buying up timberland and for a better price than R.J. gave her. I received a telegram from the sheriff warning me."

"Why was she so eager to sell her land?" Mary asked.

Tom shrugged. "I guess Dulcie is used to making do with little, and the big sum of money tempted her beyond her ability to resist."

Mary nodded. "I guess that's a good enough reason. What will you do now?"

"There's nothing more to do. R.J. has a signed bill of sale, and Dulcie has her money."

Tom left it at that. It wasn't the best deal she could've gotten, but she had received a fair enough price. He wasn't about to rob her of her sense of accomplishment.

He had a bad feeling there'd be others who'd take advantage of Dulcie. Without a doubt, R.J. Buchanan wouldn't be the only scoundrel to seek her out, especially after word got around that she had a pocketful of money.

He'd warn her, but would she listen?

Obviously Dulcie was set on doing things her own way. It was something they had in common. Tom smiled.

Chapter Thirteen

Dulcie counted out the smooth paper currency for the third time. Mr. Buchanan's offer had been a good one, and she'd no regrets. She had no cause to hold on to land where she had no intention of living.

There were eight crisp ten-dollar bills. Mr. Buchanan paid her in U.S. currency instead of gold dust, as was the custom in these parts, but he'd assured her the paper bills were as good as gold.

Still, she had trouble believing all this money was real and that it belonged to her.

Tom didn't trust Mr. Buchanan, but Tom needn't worry so much about her. She'd learned how to take care of herself from an early age. She'd seen no reason to wait on those telegrams.

Mrs. Walker had advised Dulcie to open an account in the bank, where the money would be safe, but she wouldn't part with her newly found wealth. Instead, she stuffed the bills into the leather pouch and tied it around her waist. She hid the stash underneath the waistband of her skirt the way she'd done with the money her pa had left her.

She was no longer a homeless stray to be felt sorry for, but a lady with a grubstake. Now Tom would have to give her serious consideration as a woman of independent means.

Mrs. Walker was taking a pie out of the oven when Dulcie joined her. She felt guilty for taking so long with Mr. Buchanan. He'd taken his time explaining the bill of sale. He wanted everything legal and proper, he'd assured her, and she'd been grateful.

R.J. Buchanan was a bit too prissy for her liking. There wasn't a speck of dirt under his fingernails. His knuckles weren't scabbed

106

and cratered from hard work. He wouldn't be the kind of man who'd kill a deer to put meat on the table or build a satisfactory house for his family to live in with the sweat of his brow.

Still, he'd been patient and, as far as she could tell, honest. He'd shaken her hand when they'd finished as if she were the finest lady in the El Dorado.

"What do you intend to do with all that money?" Mrs. Walker asked as she set the steaming apple pie on the table.

Dulcie's mouth watered. She'd grown partial to those brown cubes of sugar since she started living with Mrs. Walker. The pie smelled full of their goodness.

"Pay off my debts," she announced with some pride. "Including my room and board."

"You earn your keep around here and then some," Mrs. Walker explained. "I don't want any of your money."

"I'd be pleased if you'd take it anyway. I don't like being obliged to anyone."

"Don't talk nonsense." Mrs. Walker went back to the range oven. "You're welcome in my house, and I'll not hear another word about paying for hospitality."

Dulcie hadn't expected Mrs. Walker to accept payment for a kindness. She'd offered anyway. Cash money, Pa'd told her, was the best currency for satisfying an obligation. It was tougher repaying a kindness with a kindness.

There'd come a time when Dulcie would repay Mrs. Walker. She always paid her debts.

Mrs. Walker opened the oven door and took out another pie.

"Are you expecting company?" Dulcie asked.

"No, I'm baking for Saturday night," she said as she set the pie next to the first one and inspected them.

"I'm looking forward to the social," Dulcie said.

"So am I. We always have such a good time."

Dulcie grinned. "I intend to show Tom how much I've learned about being a lady."

"You've grown fond of my boy."

"More than fond."

Mrs. Walker's eyes sparkled. "I had my suspicions."

"He's the man I intend to marry."

"Don't try too hard."

"What do you mean?" Dulcie asked, confused. Did Mrs. Walker disapprove of Dulcie's plans for matrimony?

"A lady must act as if she's not interested," Mrs. Walker explained.

"What good will that do?"

"A man likes a challenge."

Dulcie deliberated a minute or two on what Mrs. Walker had said. This courting business was more complicated than she'd first thought. Luckily, Mrs. Walker was willing to give her pointers.

"You mean Tom likes to think he's in charge."

Mrs. Walker smirked. "That's exactly what I mean."

Dulcie realized why she'd given Tom the jitters. She'd been in too much of a hurry to allow for considering his male sensibilities.

"You talk with every man who's there," Mrs. Walker said. "See if Thomas doesn't come around."

"I reckon I have a lot to learn about catching a man," Dulcie said with a short laugh.

Mrs. Walker sighed.

Dulcie reached for a clean apron and tied the strings behind her back. "Now, what can I do to help?"

Tom checked the load in his six-shooter, then shucked it into his holster, buckled his gun belt, and adjusted it on his hip.

The folks of Hangtown depended on him to keep the peace. Nobody was going to spoil their evening get-together.

He'd taken a bath over at Mary's Hotel and had a shave at the barbershop. His Sunday best shirt was pressed and his boots polished to a shine.

At a quarter to six by his pa's watch, he stood outside the Union Hotel waiting for Dulcie and his mother to arrive.

He hadn't seen Dulcie since R.J. made his offer for her land, and he was looking forward to her company.

He tipped his hat to a bevy of ladies who carried baskets covered with red and green checked cloths. He greeted the sour-faced Mr. Beechum, who toted a violin case under his arm. The man fiddled like a sweet angel, and folks traveled for miles to hear him play.

There were bunches of girls giggling and boys hanging around the hitching posts pretending not to notice. Tom caught a whiff of hair oil and an abundance of rose-scented toilet water, reminding him of his younger days.

Tom felt old. He leaned against the porch railing, wondering where the time had flown.

He saw his ma's buggy and the mare she prized coming down the street. He straightened. Dulcie drove, and his ma hung on to her best hat.

Seconds later, Dulcie pulled back on the reins, and the mare slowed and stopped, bringing up dust.

Tom strode across the street. Dulcie's hair poked and curled out from beneath a straw hat decorated with silk daisies. Her dress was the color of freshly churned butter and fit to within an inch of her life. He recognized the knitted shawl she'd tied around her shoulders as one of his ma's.

He'd never seen a finer sight than Dulcie Crowder come to town in her finery.

Tom pulled off his hat. He wouldn't have thought she could make such a transformation in less than a week, but she had. Dulcie Crowder was a lady, and he'd challenge anyone who said different.

Tom felt a twinge of male possessiveness when she acknowledged his gaze. She'd turn heads tonight, and who could blame the young men of Hangtown for looking?

"Ladies," he said.

"Evening, Deputy," Dulcie answered.

He squashed his hat onto his head and offered her his hand.

"I reckon I got up here all right, and I can get myself down," Dulcie said.

"Oh, let him think you're too feeble to do it yourself," his ma said, laughing.

He put his hands around her waist. Dulcie opened her mouth, but he didn't give her any time to argue. He lifted her up. She was as light as a feather.

"I declare, Tom Walker," she said as he swung her to the ground. Surprisingly, she pulled away.

"I'll thank you kindly to keep your hands to yourself," she said. She pinched her mouth into a proper pout.

He didn't know what he'd done to make her so sore, but he reckoned she'd let him know soon enough.

Folks gathered around them and started laughing.

"You heard her, Tom," someone said from behind him.

Dulcie lifted her nose and marched in the direction of the doorway.

"What's she so mad about?" he asked his ma.

His ma brushed off her skirt and looked up. There was laughter in her, but she kept a straight face.

"Bring in those baskets, Thomas."

Tom scratched his head. What had gotten into those two? Why did a woman flirt one minute and go ornery the next?

Dulcie's attitude set him off balance. She'd been only too eager to have him court her. Now she seemed to have changed her tune. For the life of him, he couldn't think what he'd done to get her so riled.

Wondering at the fickle nature of the female of the species, Tom lifted the baskets out of the back of the wagon and carried them to the door.

"Aren't you coming inside?" his ma asked.

"No, ma'am. Not just yet. I have some business to attend to." He'd seen Ezra Dixon watching Dulcie just now from across the street. He meant to have a few words with Ezra before the man did something they'd both regret.

Dulcie returned to take the baskets from him, her brown eyes full of mischief. "You'll be sorry if you miss out on a piece of your ma's apple pie," she said.

"I won't miss out," he said as his gaze slid to those puckered lips. He tipped his hat.

She spun around and marched inside.

Dulcie looked behind her. Tom was gone. She'd been caught in his gaze like a fly in bear grease, and tearing herself away took a heap of doing. She'd not mistaken his interest in the new dress and straw bonnet. The fancy duds had worked wonders on the man.

As much as she wished he'd come in with them, she understood he put sheriffing before socializing, and that was his way.

"Set that basket down over there," Mrs. Walker said, pointing to one of two long tables covered with snowy white cloths.

Dulcie carried the heavy basket to the table loaded with crockery heaped with chicken and baking-powder biscuits, smoked beef and legs of venison, and crowded with taters, turnips, and rutabagas piled high. Some mashed and some fried. Some baked in a roaster with corn bread steaming on top.

The smell alone gave her stomach a rumble. She set out her plate of fried chicken and removed the checked cloth.

She'd never seen so much food set down in one place. Where she'd come from, such abundance, especially at this time of year, was rare.

She joined Mrs. Walker and her friends. The ladies started talking about the election.

"Do you think Tom will stand for sheriff?" one of the ladies asked Mrs. Walker.

Mrs. Walker shook her head and smiled at Dulcie. "He may have considered such a notion, but I think he'll change his mind."

"Tom won't change his mind," Dulcie said.

Each woman standing there registered surprise on her face.

"Run along, Dulcie," Mrs. Walker said, her voice as cold as the north wind blowing, and she turned her back.

There was a strained silence among the rest of the ladies.

When Dulcie was out of hearing range, they started chattering like ducks in a pond. She should've kept quiet, except there was no use in saying Tom wasn't going to run for sheriff when Dulcie knew full well he would.

Without a doubt that's what Mrs. Walker expected Dulcie to do. Shift Tom's ambition away from the law. Dulcie shook her head. Mrs. Walker had too much faith in Dulcie's abilities.

She removed her hat and gloves and stowed them in a corner of the room where the other ladies had done the same. She draped the borrowed shawl across the back of a chair.

Everyone seemed busy catching up with old friends and setting out their fixings. Mrs. Walker set out her pies next to Dulcie's plate of fried chicken and was accepting compliments.

Dulcie looked around for Maryanne and Stuart, but they hadn't arrived. She grasped her hands behind her. She wished Tom was here to take his place among family and friends. The social seemed empty without him.

Whenever a lady glanced her way, she smiled. But then another lady would claim the first one's attention, and they would start yammering. So she wandered around, looking for something to do, but nobody she asked seemed to need her help.

Tom had said he'd return. She'd acted unfriendly, maybe a mite too unfriendly. Mrs. Walker had assured her a chilly reception would give him a challenge he wouldn't likely shy from. She'd accepted her advice quickly enough, but now she wasn't so sure she'd done right by him.

A fella her age, his hair slicked down and parted in the middle, sidled up to her. He smiled widely and bobbed his head in greeting.

"How do you do? My name is Elias Steptow."

Mr. Steptow didn't talk English as well as the rest of them, but his smile beat all others' hands down.

"Pleased to meet you. I'm Dulcie Crowder."

"You are new in town?" he asked.

"I lived up in the hills working a claim with my pa, and now I live here."

"I am new in Hangtown as well." He bowed his head. The name Crowder didn't seem to warn him off. "I am from Polska. My people live under the oppression of a Russian czar. Here in America, I am free man."

"I don't know where that is, but I reckon you're welcome."

"We have seen the elephant," he said, standing taller.

"I guess that's true," Dulcie said. She didn't much understand the expression, forged in the early days of the gold rush, but there was no denying that arriving in California was bigger than the imagination allowed.

Elias shifted his feet.

"What kind of work are you in?" she asked after a lengthy pause.

He hooked his thumbs in the waistband of his britches. "I am a placer miner working a claim along a creek bed that runs into the American. I intend to be very rich one day and live in San Francisco."

"I've never been to San Francisco," she had to admit.

"You should go one day. It is a magnificent city with many things to see."

He was trying to impress her with his worldly ways, and she didn't mind. She liked Elias Steptow. He was pleasant to converse with and didn't have a bossy disposition, like some men she could mention.

"Well, Elias, looks like there's going to be some dinner served at this shindig. Would you like to sit with me?"

The boy's eyes lit up. "I surely would, Dulcie."

They were joined by two fellas who looked closely alike. Their hair, too, was slicked down flat. They wore collarless shirts and were clean shaven.

"Who have you got there?" one of them asked.

"This is Dulcie Crowder," Elias replied.

Those two looked ready to shove Elias aside, so Dulcie slid her hand around the crook of Elias' elbow.

"Name's Riley Gibbs. This here is my brother, Casey."

"I'm happy to make your acquaintance," Dulcie said.

All three began to talk at once. Dulcie put up both hands, and they stopped. Much as she liked being the center of attention, she could answer only one question at a time.

Luckily, at that very moment, Maryanne and Stuart came waltzing through the door. Maryanne carried little George Arthur on her hip, and Stuart hefted a basket covered with a red-checkered cloth. Dulcie excused herself and made a beeline toward Maryanne.

"Don't forget dinner," Elias said from behind her.

Dulcie turned and smiled. "I won't."

Elias put his hand on his heart and bowed the most touching bow she'd ever been the recipient of.

Dulcie couldn't help but smile wider. She left the gawking men and met Maryanne and Stuart at the front door.

"Am I glad to see you," Dulcie said to Maryanne. She took George Arthur and gave him a cuddle. He wore a white cotton dress that reached down to his knees, and an adorable bonnet framed his face. Thankfully, the square of cotton hugging his lower half was dry.

He smelled like warm milk, and she gave him an extra hug. She did so love the smell of a baby.

Maryanne told Stuart to take the basket over to the table. He went on ahead and set it down. The ladies of Hangtown swarmed around him and began unpacking what Maryanne had brought, a huge pan of corn bread.

Stuart broke off a piece and crammed it into his mouth. He joined a group of men conversing over by the cut-glass punch bowl.

"We almost didn't come," Maryanne said. "Our dairy cow is sick. She's not given any milk since the day before yesterday. Stuart is real worried we'll lose her."

"What's the matter with her?" Dulcie asked as she jostled George Arthur until he started giggling.

"He doesn't know. He's here to ask the other farmers about the symptoms and what he should do." Maryanne chewed her lower lip.

Dulcie wished there was something she could do.

"I don't know how we'll manage if she doesn't get better," Maryanne continued. "We depend on the milk she gives for George Arthur. We won't be able to afford to buy another until this fall's harvest."

Dulcie stopped playing with George Arthur and settled him on her hip. He looked at her with his big eyes and popped his thumb into his mouth.

"Isn't there an animal doctor hereabouts?" Dulcie asked.

"There's one in Sacramento City, I'm told."

"You'd better send one of those telegrams and have him come and take a look at her."

Maryanne looked over at Stuart. Dulcie saw desperation and fear in her expression.

"If it's a question of money . . . ," Dulcie started. She knew

Maryanne would be too proud to ask. "I've got a few dollars put by."

Maryanne didn't look Dulcie in the eye. "Thank you, Dulcie. We couldn't ask you for any money. I'm sure the local men will know what to do."

"I hope you're right," Dulcie said, "but the offer stands."

They walked over to the table. Dulcie sat on the nearest chair with George Arthur while Maryanne cut up her corn bread. The other women beamed with satisfaction at what they'd made, and the men rubbed their hands together, eager to dig in.

Dulcie chattered to George Arthur, making baby sounds. He looked at her with watchful eyes and gurgled. A bubble of spit emerged from the corner of his mouth. Dulcie wiped it away with her thumb.

She was going to have four or five, maybe even six, youngsters, the good Lord willing. They'd all live on the homestead she intended to buy. That dream had seemed so far away only a few weeks ago. Now all she needed to do was convince Tom Walker.

Mrs. Walker called the stragglers to the table. They bowed their heads and gave thanks.

A small community but growing, Mrs. Walker had said of Hangtown.

Dulcie watched as every one of the good people of Hangtown helped themselves to supper. They were a community, and they shared what they had. She was glad to be here among them.

Acceptance would come in time.

Elias hung back, waiting for her at the end of the line. He and the others hadn't heard of the name Crowder, or if they had, they were too polite to mention her pa. She supposed that was the way life here was meant to be. Folks moved on from disappointment and death.

Otherwise you'd go crazy thinking about how things could be different if only other choices had been made.

Chapter Fourteen

Tom found Ezra Dixon where he'd last seen him, standing on the boardwalk across the street from the Empire Theater, smoking a clay pipe. He'd a suspicion it was Ezra who'd paid a call to Dulcie in his ma's stable the other night and given her a fright she wouldn't soon recover from.

Ezra and some other Hangtown citizens had started the Vigilance Committee to keep those deemed undesirable out of Hangtown. It was an impossible task. Talk of mountains of gold and instant wealth for those willing to mine it drew newcomers from all parts of the world. Nobody would be able to stop anyone who wanted to from coming.

Tom had no reason, except if someone broke the law, to keep anybody away.

"Evening, Deputy," Ezra said, his face partially hidden by the shadows.

"Ezra." Tom climbed the steps to the boardwalk.

Dixon took out his pipe and pointed at the front door of the hotel. "I see Willie Crowder's girl is still in town."

"Yes, sir, and that's who I've come to talk to you about. She's done you no harm, and I want you to stay clear of her."

Ezra stepped out of the shadows. His beady eyes smoldered with a hatred deep and potent. What Tom saw convinced him Ezra could be a dangerous man.

"We don't need her kind in our town," Ezra said.

"Willie paid for what he did. Justice has been served. You leave Miss Crowder alone."

Ezra frowned. He didn't seem satisfied with Tom's answer. Men like him never were.

Ezra knocked his pipe against the post and ground out the ash with the toe of his boot. "There's a meeting of the Vigilance Committee after the prayer meeting tomorrow morning. Will you be there?"

"No, sir, I won't."

"Your pa never missed a meeting."

"I'm sure my pa had his reasons."

"He was a heck of a sheriff."

"That he was, Ezra."

"You'd do well to follow his example."

Tom looked Ezra square in the eye. He admired what his pa had done for this town, but he'd take no part in a group of men bent on frontier justice.

"I took an oath to uphold the law, and that's what I intend to do," he said.

"The Vigilance Committee only means to be helpful."

"If you ask me, the Vigilance Committee has outlived its usefulness," Tom replied.

"Well, nobody's asking." Ezra jabbed a finger into Tom's chest. "Some of these newcomers don't even speak English. Who knows what they're up to?"

Tom kept his stance. "As long as they abide by the law, Ezra, I've got no quarrel with any of them."

"Think of the disease they bring to the town," Ezra continued. "And their foreign ways ain't right."

Tom had heard these complaints before. "Ezra, you know better than to spread such tales."

"They're no good, I tell you, especially the Crowder woman," Ezra said defiantly. "I heard she held a shotgun on a group of citizens."

"I've confiscated the weapon," Tom said. "It won't happen again. Now, you go about your business."

Ezra shook his head. "Some say you're too tender-hearted for this job."

"I guess folks are entitled to their opinions." A slow burn started in Tom's gut, but it'd do no good to pick a fight.

Ezra stuffed his pipe into his coat pocket. "Come election time, there will be some changes made around here." He turned and headed in the direction of the Blue Stocking.

Tom watched until he disappeared around the corner.

Ezra Dixon had been one of his pa's closest friends and, by most accounts, a good man. Tom had spoken strong words to him, and he'd been unwilling to listen.

Why Ezra held a grudge against folks he didn't even know was beyond Tom's understanding. His kind of hatred could only lead to violence.

Tom wouldn't back down. As long as he wore the badge, Ezra Dixon and men like him would do as the law said. He started up Thompson Way.

Tom heard the music begin, the sound of Mr. Beechum's fiddle rise and fall.

Confident Ezra would leave Dulcie alone, he headed back to the social, to find out what Dulcie was riled about.

"You have not touched your food," Elias said.

Dulcie didn't have much of an appetite. "To tell you the truth, I'm not hungry."

"I will get you some punch," Elias said, rising to his feet.

"Let me," both Gibbs brothers sang out in unison.

The three men scrambled for the punch bowl, leaving Dulcie in a quandary. She liked everyone she'd met tonight. They all seemed like nice fellas. She tried not to favor one over the other, but of course they expected her to.

They came back, each with pink-colored punch served in a fancy cut-glass cup.

Each man looked at her with expectations she drink the cup of punch he'd brought over.

"I'm thirsty enough to drink all three," she said so nobody's feelings would be hurt. She was dry enough, but Mrs. Walker cautioned it was unladylike to eat and drink like a half-starved mule skinner.

She accepted the cup of the closest Gibbs brother and took a sip.

"I hope the fiddler don't quit," Elias said. He'd plenty more gumption in him, Dulcie was delighted to see, than when he'd introduced himself.

Dulcie looked over at the fiddler drinking his own cup of pink punch. He'd been playing for a time and had a good shine to him.

She'd noticed the other ladies lowered their eyes and flapped their lashes at the menfolk. She'd been waiting for an opportunity to try this feminine wile out.

"He just needs a rest," Dulcie said to Elias. She batted her lashes.

"Something in your eye?"

Dulcie whirled around.

Tom Walker stood over her with his arms crossed.

"Why, Tom Walker." She gulped. "What a surprise."

Tom crowded out those boys without so much as a "pardon me."

"I reckon you know Elias Steptow and Riley and Casey Gibbs?"

"Evening, Tom," they all said.

She sashayed over to Elias and threaded her hand around his arm.

Elias lit up like a sunrise.

"I've come for a dance," Tom said to her. "Would you oblige me?"

"I'm taken, Tom Walker, as you can see. In fact, I've promised each one of these men a dance as soon as the fiddler is done with his refreshment."

The boys looked at one another.

Tom's gaze never left hers. "They can wait."

"That'd be impolite. You'll just have to take your turn." She gave Elias' arm a tug.

Elias' gaze darted to Tom and then back at Dulcie.

Tom snorted much like Chester was prone to do, but he didn't argue. "I'll take myself over to the punch bowl and have some of Mrs. Paisley's fine punch while I'm waiting."

"Makes no difference to me," Dulcie said, and she pulled Elias closer.

Tom was as good as his word. He ambled in the direction of the punch bowl and was quickly surrounded by a gaggle of women vying for his attention.

Tom greeted his neighbors cordially, but now he was the one who was riled. He hadn't expected Dulcie to turn him down. She was making a fool of herself, encouraging every young buck in the county.

"She's the most popular woman here tonight, don't you agree?" Ma said from behind him.

A crowd of boys surrounded Dulcie, and he could only see the top of her head. There was no mistaking the sound of her voice.

"You'd better go rescue her," she said.

"Dulcie can handle the Gibbs brothers and the others," he replied gruffly. He didn't like them taking up Dulcie's time, but she'd made her choice.

"I'm sure that's true," Ma said. "Any one of those boys would make a fine beau for Dulcie."

The music started up amid hearty applause. Mr. Beechum, long-faced and scowling at them all, played a waltz. The dancers gathered in the middle of the room, including Dulcie and that Elias fella.

Tom turned away.

"Where are you going?" his ma asked.

"Need some male company."

He was intercepted by Maryanne Greenwood, a fine figure of a woman. She offered him a square of corn bread from a nearly empty plate.

"Hello, Mrs. Greenwood," he said, taking one.

"Tom. Lovely evening for a dance."

They both looked at Dulcie as she twirled by in the arms of Elias Steptow.

"She's the belle of the ball," Maryanne said.

"So I see."

"And a wonderful dancer."

Tom shook his head. The women weren't going to give him any peace. "I have a feeling you had a hand in showing her how."

"Why, Tom, you remembered how I love to dance."

"I recall you were light on your feet."

"Seems like ages ago."

"That it does."

"Why don't you ask Dulcie to dance? She loves to waltz."

Tom stuffed a bite of corn bread into his mouth. "I already did."

"She turned you down? That's hard to believe."

She was joshing, but Tom didn't mind.

"You must ask her again," Maryanne said.

"I just might." Tom finished the last morsel of corn bread and brushed off his hands.

"I'm glad to hear you say so. You're a fine lawman, but at some things you're slow on the draw."

Tom began to choke. Maryanne thumped him on the back.

He recovered quickly enough, but Maryanne's gentle teasing stung—he wouldn't deny it.

His gaze lit on Dulcie Crowder. She sure did smile a lot this evening. The fiddler was playing up a storm, and she looked like she enjoyed being flung around the room.

Those boys she was with were beginning to annoy him. What that woman needed was a man's firm guidance.

"My feet have never been so tired," Dulcie said to Maryanne. "How do ladies hold up in these fancy shoes?"

"They're not very practical, I must admit," Maryanne answered.

The fiddler had popped a string and was repairing it as they spoke. She and Maryanne took up chairs at the far end of the room. Little George Arthur had fallen asleep in his ma's arms, and Maryanne looked more relaxed than when she had arrived.

Dulcie was happy to see that, despite all of her friend's troubles, she seemed to be having a good time.

"Why haven't you danced with Tom yet?" Maryanne asked.

"I had to refuse his offer when he asked."

"What on earth for?"

Dulcie shrugged. "I didn't want to look too eager."

"That doesn't sound like you," Maryanne said.

"It's not, only I aim to be a lady, and that's how a lady behaves herself in the company of a gentleman."

Maryanne laughed. "A lady doesn't give a gentleman the wrong message either."

She'd made a good point.

Dulcie searched the crowd and found Tom talking with a group of men. "What if he doesn't ask me again?"

"I expect he will."

The music started up again, and a group of fellas crowded around Dulcie, asking her to dance.

She shook her head. "I'm all worn out. I need to sit this one out. Why don't you fellas have some pie? There's plenty of good ones over at that table."

They all agreed it was a fine idea and left her alone.

Tom strode over. His gaze seemed to look into her heart.

"That fiddler's about to play a waltz," he said.

Dulcie sighed. She did love the waltz. "How would you know, Tom Walker?"

"I made a request."

Dulcie jumped to her feet.

"I'll take that as a yes, you'll dance with me," Tom said.

"Are you denying you ordered up a waltz just for me?" she answered, about bursting with pride.

Mr. Beecham began his fiddling, and the floor crowded up with dancers.

Tom put one big hand around her waist and grasped her right hand in his other one. She started off.

"Are you going to let me lead?" he asked.

She looked up into those brooding eyes, but she saw a flicker of amusement and something more. "I guess I'd better."

He steered her to the middle of the room and started in. His footwork wasn't as good as Maryanne's, but what did it matter? She was where she wanted to be, in his arms.

He held her steadily, guiding her with a firm hand on her back. They glided around the room. She'd never known a more perfect moment.

"I do declare, you're a fine dancer, Tom Walker."

"I'm no dancer at all."

"You're determined to resist my compliments," she said.

"You make a poor liar," he said.

"I suppose I should be happy you're saying so?"

"That's up to you." He pulled her closer to avoid colliding with another couple. The heat of his body seared her. She didn't pull away.

"What's got you acting so strange tonight?" he asked, looking down at her.

"I'm practicing being a lady," she confessed.

"You fit in well with the rest of the Hangtown ladies." Tom knew how to give a compliment.

"You could court me if you'd a notion to."

He smiled a slow, lopsided smile. Dulcie would likely melt into a puddle before long. "I'd like that."

She squelched back a landslide of emotion. "I'd hoped you would."

"Are you sure you want to step out with the likes of me? There are plenty of other good men in this town."

"I already know that's so."

"I'll never be rich."

"I've got enough money for both of us."

"A sheriff's woman has to be tough as hide," he continued. "The work is dangerous. There may be times when my life will be on the line."

"Are you saying I'm not sturdy enough?"

His mouth curved into a smile with the most scrumptious lips a woman ever could lay eyes on.

"What I'm saying is—"

"How long is this courting going to take?" she interrupted. There was no doubt in her mind he was the man for her, and she hated hearing the doubt in his voice.

"Not long, unless I miss my guess."

"Good, 'cause I'm as ready as I'll ever be."

The music stopped, and the dancers started clapping. He held her a moment longer than need be. She looked up at him and felt his breathing. His gaze embraced her. Her heart was likely to stop beating.

She'd a notion he'd like to kiss her. She was ready to let him.

His hand slid away from her waist, and he held on to her hand. They stood side by side in the noisy room. The dancers laughed and begged for another tune, and she and Tom joined them. They were a couple, all right, enjoying a Hangtown dance among good friends and neighbors.

Dulcie looked over at Mrs. Walker. Tom's ma watched them like a hawk watches her patch. When she caught Dulcie's gaze, and a smile intended as a thanks, she smiled back.

A course of excitement raced through Dulcie, so strong she could hardly contain it. She squeezed Tom's hand, to make sure the moment was real. He was flesh and blood. She'd like to ask him if he'd take her outside so they could do some courting in earnest, but she remembered Mrs. Walker's words. A man liked to do the asking, and so she put a damper on her desire and a lock on her lips.

The fiddler agreed to one more tune, a lively ditty that had the men stomping their feet and slapping their thighs.

Jasper Jenkins was the first to take the floor, leading a pretty girl dressed in pink gingham with matching pink ribbons woven into her straw-colored hair. Jasper twirled her under his arm, and the girl knew exactly what to do. Dulcie got dizzy watching.

Dulcie turned to Tom. He was laughing. Even his eyes were bright with laughter. She liked seeing him so.

They joined the circle surrounding Jasper and his partner, clapping and shouting out encouragement. Jasper didn't need any. He lifted that girl off the ground like she was a sack of feed. She squealed, but there was no fright in her.

When he put her down, she pushed him away. Jasper fell backward, exaggerating the force of her push, and a group of men behind him caught him and shoved him back toward the girl. Jasper caught her around the waist, and she planted a kiss on his cheek.

Dulcie laughed so hard, her sides ached. She wiped hot tears from her eyes with the kerchief Mrs. Walker had given her and that she'd stowed in the sleeve of her dress.

The rest of the circle joined in, making such a ruckus that the sawdust jumped.

Tom stayed put, his gaze on the dancers.

Dulcie gave him a nudge.

"I'd better go do my rounds," he said without looking at her.

"Again?" She immediately regretted the question. Of course he had to. He was a lawman. This was his town.

Tom shifted his gaze to her. He held a magic kind of power over her that no other man ever would.

"It needs to be done," he said. "There's nobody minding the streets of Hangtown."

"I'll go with you," she said. She wanted to be by his side.

"No, Dulcie."

Dulcie stifled a protest with difficulty. "Will I see you later?"

"I'll be back in time to take you and Ma home," he said. "Unless you don't want me to."

She squeezed his arm. Her whole body tingled with anticipation. "That'll be just fine, Tom Walker."

She watched him leave, tall and broad-shouldered, decked out in his best shirt and boots shining. She wanted to run after him, to tell him all that was in her heart.

She didn't. Tonight he'd laid out what he needed from a wife, from her, and she would show him she could be that woman.

Chapter Fifteen

Maryanne kept glancing behind her. Dulcie followed her gaze and saw Stuart talking with a group of men. He got his point across with sharp jabs of his finger to the chest of a man Dulcie hadn't met. The man was short and stocky. His arms were as thick as fence posts, and he'd planted his feet wide apart. To Dulcie's way of thinking, that showed aggression, like a bull ready to charge.

Stuart's face had gone as red as his flannel shirt as he carried on the one-sided conversation.

"What's that all about?" Dulcie asked, rubbing her stocking feet. She'd had enough of the tight lace-up shoes and had peeled them off. She'd strip off her stockings and garters except it would cause a scandal Mrs. Walker would most likely not recover from.

Maryanne bit her lower lip. "Stuart put a fence up along our back boundary. Our new neighbor's steers wander free range and will trample our crops once they start to come in."

"Let me guess. The fence didn't keep out those steers."

"I think they had some help. A steer won't pull down a fence with barbed wire."

"Stuart thinks your neighbor had some part in knocking down the fence?" Dulcie asked, even though she'd guessed the answer.

"He's sure enough to ask him."

They watched the two men arguing, drawing a crowd.

Their voices became louder, and words of denial were shouted out. The men in the crowd added their two cents.

"What's your neighbor's name?" Dulcie asked.

Maryanne frowned. If she didn't stop fretting, she'd look like

126

an old woman way before her time. "His name is Judson Chase. He and his brother just bought the homestead over the ridge from us. They've made threats from the first day they moved in. They even warned Stuart they'd keep water from flowing into our creek."

"Why would they do something so mean?"

"I don't know. I guess some men don't know how to be good neighbors."

Dulcie agreed with Maryanne's assessment of the two brothers. Whatever their reason for keeping the water all to themselves, it wasn't a neighborly thing to do.

"Maybe that's why your cow is sick," Dulcie said. The notion needed saying.

Maryanne's eyes widened. "Wouldn't that be a shame?"

Judson Chase pushed Stuart's hand away. Stuart hunkered down and put up his fists.

Maryanne rose to her feet so sharply, she woke George Arthur. The baby began to fuss.

Dulcie looked around the room for Jasper Jenkins but couldn't find him. The men had taken sides and were spoiling for a fight. Some shook their fists and called out their opinions on the matter. They ignored the pleas of the ladies in the room to calm down and remember why they were there.

"Somebody'd better go get Tom," Dulcie said.

"Please, Dulcie, you go," Maryanne said, patting the baby's back.

Dulcie tucked her shoes under her chair and stood. She wouldn't waste time lacing them up.

If anyone could put a stop to a fight, Tom Walker could. She skirted around the men who by this time had been whipped into a frenzy.

Dulcie was tempted to remind them to mind their manners. Ladies were present. The men weren't likely to listen, so heated was their arguing.

When she reached the front door, Mrs. Walker was there.

"Where are you going in your stocking feet?" she asked.

"I'm going to fetch Tom before somebody gets hurt."

Mrs. Walker looked over at the men and frowned. "Riley Gibbs has been deputized. Let him take care of it."

Dulcie saw Riley hanging back from the crowd.

"I'd better find Tom all the same. Riley may need help."

Dulcie opened the door and scrambled down the dusty street. When she turned the corner and climbed onto the boardwalk, she caught a stocking in one of the boards. She yelped loudly enough to raise the dead. A splinter had lodged in her heel. She didn't spare the time to remove it—the light was too dim anyway—so she ran on tiptoe. As she turned the corner, she saw Tom checking to make sure the doors of Mr. Paisley's dry goods store were locked.

"Tom!" she shouted, and she crossed the street toward him.

He turned around. "What's wrong?"

"Stuart Greenwood and another fella are disputing Stuart's fence across their common border," she said between breaths. "They aim to use their fists."

"I'd better break them up."

Tom walked with long strides, and Dulcie was determined to keep up. He took no notice of her stocking feet or her strange way of walking, and if he did, he made no comment.

She saw in the flickering light the hard glare of a man who didn't tolerate lawlessness. She was beginning to understand how necessary his disposition was in a place where tempers flared easily and disputes could be deadly.

They rounded the corner side by side. The shouting and yelling from the social had died down.

"Sounds like those two resolved their differences," Dulcie said hopefully.

They crossed the street. Another sound ripped through the night. Dulcie's insides tightened. The unmistakable sound of sobs and wailing came from the hotel.

"Oh," she said as she exhaled. She looked up at Tom. He showed no emotion, but his hand was on his six-shooter.

"Wait here," Tom said.

He opened the door and disappeared inside.

Dulcie wasn't about to stand out on the street biding her time. She had to see why women were crying and men were silent.

No one looked up when she came in, their gazes stuck on a man lying on the floor. When Dulcie got a closer look, she saw it was the man Stuart had been arguing with.

Tom knelt beside the man and loosened the bandanna from around the man's throat.

"Doc's on his way," somebody said.

Tom laid two fingers against the man's neck. "Too late. This man is dead."

A hushed silence followed.

Dulcie couldn't help but stare at the body. The dead man's eyes were open, and he looked at nothing in particular. His lips had lost their color. A trickle of blood, almost black, escaped from the corner of his mouth. More blood pooled on the floor.

Dulcie wrinkled her nose. He smelled like yesterday's breakfast.

Tom closed the dead man's eyes. "What's his name?"

Riley Gibbs stepped forward. "Jud Chase."

Tom rose to his feet. "What happened?"

"Jud pulled a knife, Tom," Riley Gibbs said. "Stuart Greenwood was only defending himself."

"That's the truth," old Mr. Paisley chimed in. "I was standing right here and saw the whole thing."

Tom searched the crowd until his gaze fixed on Stuart Greenwood, supporting a shaken Maryanne. Stuart stroked Maryanne's hair as she clung to his shoulder. The front of his shirt was spotted with dark stains. His right hand was wrapped in a checkered kitchen towel that had turned crimson.

"How did it come to this?" Tom asked.

Stuart looked up. There was no defiance in him, only misery. "We were having words over what he'd done to my fence. He pulled a knife and cut me. I don't know what happened after that. I must've lost my temper."

"Jud cut Stuart bad," Riley said. "Stuart knocked his feet out from underneath him, and he fell hard. Jud went wild. He jumped to his feet and lunged at Stuart. Before he could do any damage, Stuart caught him by the wrist. Those two struggled until the man dropped his knife."

"That's right, Tom," Mr. Paisley said. "Yes, sir, that's what happened all right."

"Stuart picked up the knife," Riley continued, "and Jud charged at him. The knife went clean through him."

Dulcie's gaze returned to the victim. Stuart had bested a man twice his size. Now, that was more luck than you could shake a stick at.

"That's not how I saw it."

Dulcie turned to see a short, muscular man push his way through the crowd. He stopped to face Tom.

"Who might you be?" Tom leveled his dark gaze at the stranger.

"Name's Bert Chase. Judson was my older brother."

"You'd better start planning a funeral," Tom said.

Bert stepped closer. He glared at the rest of the townsfolk and then turned burning eyes to Tom. "You're going to arrest this man, aren't you?"

Everybody looked at Tom.

"Appears this was an accident," Tom said.

"What kind of lawman are you?" the man growled.

"The kind who knows an unfair fight when he sees one."

Bert Chase colored. "Greenwood's a murderer, sure as I'm standing."

"Now, see here," Dulcie said. Calling Stuart a murderer set her afire. "Your brother did a foolish thing pulling a knife. Stuart Greenwood was unarmed and only defending himself. He did what any man would've done."

Everyone in the room stared at Dulcie.

"Come along, Dulcie." Mrs. Walker tugged on her sleeve.

Dulcie looked at Tom. He nodded in agreement.

"Let the men take care of this," Mrs. Walker said.

Dulcie glared at Bert Chase, giving the devil his due, and then yielded. Clearly, her help wasn't needed. Mrs. Walker led her away.

"Your brother's death was an accident," Tom said after the women had retreated to the tables and the rumble of angry voices had died down. Dulcie had spoken the truth of the matter. This wasn't a murder. Jud Chase had brought this on himself. Stuart had had every right to defend himself.

There were murmurs of agreement.

"On who's say-so?" Bert asked.

"I've plenty of witnesses."

"You can't take the word of these folks," Bert said. "They're all friends of this murderer."

"Are you calling me a liar?" Mr. Paisley stepped between Tom and Bert Chase, ready to give as good as he got.

"Alistair, calm yourself," Tom said evenly, and he rested his hand on the old man's shoulder. "This man has just lost his brother and is liable to say anything."

Mr. Paisley backed away. "You're right, Tom. I'm sorry."

Tobacco-colored spit dribbled down Bert's whiskered chin. He made no effort to wipe it away. The man lived hard and rough and obviously didn't care where he was or whom he offended. "Deputy, I demand you arrest Stuart Greenwood and put him behind bars."

"I don't think that's necessary," Tom said, but he was losing ground.

"If you don't, I'll find a lawman who will."

Tom knew Bert was within his rights to do so.

"Come on, Stuart," Tom said.

"You can't be serious," Riley said.

"For his protection," Tom told the crowd. He didn't know what Bert Chase was capable of, or if he'd take the law into his own hands.

Stuart kissed Maryanne on the forehead as she clung to his shirt, refusing to let him go. She held on to him with such desperation, Tom regretted he had to make this arrest.

"It's for his own good," he said gently. "A man has died, and a thorough investigation is needed."

Dulcie marched to Maryanne's side and took the baby. Tom was about to voice his appreciation, but he held off. Whereas Maryanne looked frightened, Dulcie looked ready to skin him alive.

"Stuart will be staying at the sheriff's office until the law is satisfied," he said. It wasn't an apology. Everyone in the room knew he was doing his job. Bert Chase had challenged him, and Tom had no choice. Stuart needed the safety of a jail cell. Tom didn't doubt that protecting Stuart from Bert Chase and his kind was a matter of life or death.

Stuart looked at Tom. He was beaten and knew it.

He detached himself from his distraught wife and kissed her trembling hand.

Stuart's concern for his wife's distress made him a decent man in Tom's book.

"Let's go," Tom said.

There were shouts of protest. Tom hated that it had come to this.

"Aren't you going to put me in handcuffs?" Stuart asked.

"Don't make this harder than it has to be," Tom said.

Maryanne wouldn't release Stuart's hand. The crowd was restless, mumbling angry words.

They stared at Tom with open hostility.

Tom was aware that it would only take one irate citizen, one stray bullet shot in frustration, to start a bloodbath.

Tom searched the room for Dulcie. She'd be a comfort to Maryanne just now, and he could rely on her to take the grief-stricken lady home.

He caught Dulcie's gaze. She didn't need an explanation. She pushed through the crowd.

Dulcie put an arm around Maryanne's shoulders and gently pried her away from Stuart. She talked as if she was gentling a high-strung horse, and Maryanne came away but looked close to bolting.

George Arthur began to cry full bore, which brought Maryanne out of her shock. She took the baby from Dulcie.

"You go on and take Maryanne and my boy home," Stuart said.

Dulcie's gaze softened for a moment as she surveyed Stuart Greenwood. She fixed Tom with a fire-eating, man-branding glare.

"Come on," she said to Maryanne, without a second glance his way. The crowd parted, and the two women and a crying baby left.

Tom pushed Stuart ahead of him. Stuart stumbled and fell to one knee. He'd no fight left in him.

Tom hauled him to his feet. Stuart raised his shoulders in defiance or self-defense—which, Tom wasn't sure. He'd no more strike Stuart than Maryanne, but Stuart saw him as the enemy.

"What should we do?" An anxious voice stirred up the crowd. Others repeated the question.

A sea of fearful faces looked at him.

"You all go home," Tom told them. "There's nothing more that can be done right now."

Ezra Dixon pushed his bulk into the aisle. "This is surely a miscarriage of justice. Ask anyone in Hangtown if we wouldn't be better off with the Vigilance Committee in charge."

"Ezra, don't go jumping the gun."

"You can't expect this town to stand idle while Stuart Greenwood hangs."

"There won't be any hanging," Tom replied. He believed in the law. The days of frontier justice were behind them.

The sure-as-certain words seemed to be enough, at least for now. The men cleared the aisle. He walked Stuart out the front door, the crowd swarming behind them.

Stuart turned in the direction of the jailhouse. He walked with rounded shoulders and head bowed. Not out of guilt for what he'd done, Tom decided, but because no man liked being humiliated in front of his wife and friends.

Tom trailed behind with his hand on his six-shooter, flanked by the two deputies holding shotguns. The boardwalk on both sides of the street was crowded with men, women, and curious children. News of the killing had spread like wildfire.

Time they all went home. It'd make his job easier.

They'd all come to their senses eventually and figure out the arrest was purely a formality. A man had been killed in a fight. Bert Chase demanded the law look into the matter. Justice would be served.

For Stuart Greenwood and all citizens of Hangtown, the well-oiled wheels of justice were already turning.

When they reached the sheriff's office, Bert Chase and his men were waiting.

Bert stood in front of the door, legs apart, arms crossed over his wide chest. His eyes glowed with hatred. Tom's gaze fell on Bert's six-shooter stowed in the waistband of his pants.

"You've got a big responsibility there," Bert said, nodding at Stuart.

Bert surely was a different man now than the one Tom had questioned, a man who'd just lost a brother. He'd convinced a roomful of Hangtown citizens of his indignation and his grievous loss.

Tom never doubted Bert Chase was out for revenge, and a vengeful man was a dangerous man.

He put himself between Stuart and Bert Chase. "Out of my way," he said to Bert.

Bert didn't budge. "Maybe we should send for the sheriff," he said. "Just in case you decide to interfere with the prisoner, Greenwood and his missus being your friends and all."

Tom kept his anger in check. One day Bert Chase would goad the wrong man.

"Chase, step aside, or I'll arrest you too."

"On what charge?" Bert cried out so all would hear.

"Obstruction of justice, for starters," Tom replied. He stared at the man long and hard, wanting him to know he wouldn't back down if an arrest was necessary.

Jasper Jenkins and Riley Gibbs stood shoulder to shoulder with Tom, shotguns at the ready.

"Jasper, show Mr. Chase and those with him to the street."

Jasper raised his shotgun to eye level and sighted on Bert's chest.

Bert Chase shifted his feet. "Let's not be hasty. We're law-abiding citizens here, ain't we, boys? We'll move on."

He stepped down from the boardwalk.

"You go on home," Tom said.

"You can't keep me and the boys out of town," he said. "We have a right to be here, just like any other citizen."

Tom had to admit Bert was right. Tom opened the door, and Stuart shuffled inside.

"We'll be back," Bert Chase said from behind him.

Tom turned and met his gaze. "As long as you and your men mind your manners, I've got no reason to stop you from coming to town."

"You can count on us being here, making sure you do your job," Bert Chase replied, his mouth twisted into a self-satisfied smirk. He took a place among the nervous crowd. His men followed, grumbling. No doubt they'd been spoiling for a fight.

Tom wasn't about to give them one.

"Jasper, you come inside with me," Tom said. "Riley, you stay out here and arrest any man who as much as spits on the sidewalk."

"Sure thing," Riley said.

Tom kicked the door shut behind him.

He opened the middle drawer in his desk and removed the iron ring with two keys on it.

Stuart headed for the cell. "Do you think Chase will be back?"

"Don't know."

"Maryanne can't be left alone out at the farm."

"Dulcie won't leave her. The entire town will look after her." Tom pushed open the door to the cell, regretting what he had to do next.

Stuart fell onto the cot, stretched out, and covered his eyes with his arm. Tom inserted one of the keys on the iron ring in the door and turned it.

"Do you think that's necessary?" Jasper asked.

"Yes," Tom replied. "Like it or not, he's a prisoner."

"Prisoner?" Jasper scratched the back of his neck.

"I'm afraid that's the way it has to be."

He checked Stuart for a reaction, but Stuart hadn't been listening.

"You need anything?" he asked Stuart.

Stuart didn't respond.

He tossed the ring to Jasper. "Don't let anybody in here."

Jasper caught it. "Where you going?"

"I'll take first watch and let Riley get some shut-eye."

Tom looked out the window. The crowd had thinned, but he knew trouble was brewing. Stuart was well liked, and Maryanne's roots went deep in the community. The Chase brothers had made themselves a nuisance. No man interfered with another man's property. What had Jud Chase expected to accomplish by pulling out a knife?

Bert Chase and his friends were no longer around, fomenting trouble. They were itching for a hanging, but Tom would make sure that didn't happen.

Tom opened the door, expecting a crush of questions from the good citizens of Hangtown who still lingered on the boardwalk. He walked out of the office, ready to answer them.

Chapter Sixteen

Maryanne protested as Dulcie walked her to her wagon, believing her place was with her husband.

"There's nothing we can do tonight," Dulcie said, "and you know Tom won't let anything happen to Stuart."

Even though Dulcie understood that it wasn't Tom's job to decide if laws had been broken, only to give the law a chance to work, she had been furious, same as everyone, when Tom arrested Stuart.

Now she realized the wisdom in keeping Stuart behind bars. No telling what Bert Chase might do. Hopefully, in the light of a new day, he'd come to his senses.

Maryanne was as limp as a dishrag and, thankfully, too worn out to argue any further.

Elias Steptow volunteered to come out to the Greenwood place first thing in the morning and take care of their stock. It was a neighborly thing to do, and Dulcie smiled at him with gratitude.

Dulcie knew there was another reason Elias had offered. Nobody trusted Bert Chase a lick. His place was just over the ridge from the Greenwoods' spread and too close for anybody's comfort.

The townsfolk meant to do right by Maryanne. They loaded up the Greenwood wagon with Maryanne's basket and a crate of leftover food the women had put together. Dulcie took up the reins. She was glad to do her part.

Bert Chase had surely done wrong by Stuart Greenwood. He'd stood next to his brother when Judson Chase pulled a knife. He must have seen Stuart cut. How could he believe Stuart could've done anything other than what he had done?

Maryanne didn't say a word all the ride home. The shock of leaving Stuart behind was too much for her.

The stars were so bright, it seemed as if Dulcie could touch them. They rattled down the dark road, the horses' hooves clopping on the hardpan and the jingle of the harness the only sounds.

Dulcie was relieved when the farmhouse came into sight. She pulled the horses to a stop at the front porch. Maryanne got down slowly and stood in her own front yard as if she was lost, a concern for Dulcie. Maryanne's fight had just begun.

"You go light a lantern," Dulcie said. "I'll be right in."

Maryanne nodded and climbed up the porch steps. She opened the door and carried George Arthur into the house.

Dulcie set the basket and crate of food next to the swinging chair she was so fond of. She unhitched the horses from the wagon and walked them to the corral.

No doubt, the stabbing had been an ugly thing to witness. She'd no dispute with the accuracy of Mr. Paisley or Riley Gibbs' account of the matter. Those two could be relied on when the truth needed to be told. Judson Chase didn't deserve to die, but he'd brought on his own demise when he pulled out his knife.

Stuart had acted in self-defense, and no other conclusion could be drawn.

She unbuckled the harness, stripped the leather off the horses, and hung the gear over a fence post. She shut the gate behind her.

There was a lot she could do around here to help out, but most of all she could be Maryanne's friend.

Tom would clear the matter with the law. He'd called it an accident. He wouldn't find anybody to contradict him.

After tempers cooled and the dead man's brother had been satisfied that the law had done its work, Tom would set Stuart free.

They all could go back to the way things were before this terrible tragedy happened.

Early the next morning Dulcie sat on the swing chair on Maryanne's front porch picking splinters out of her feet with a sewing needle. Her stockings were in shreds and beyond repair, but they were the least of her worries.

She'd tried to sleep, but she hadn't been able to stop thinking about the stabbing.

She wondered why neighbors couldn't be helpful instead of fighting over every little thing. It seemed to her there was more to gain by cooperating.

Elias Steptow came up the road riding a dappled mare. He'd changed his outfit into sturdier clothes and wore a sober expression.

"Glad to see you!" Dulcie shouted when he came within earshot.

"Reckoned the chores could not wait," he replied, tipping his wide-brimmed hat.

"You reckoned correctly," she answered. She finished the last painful extraction and smoothed bee balm onto her wounds.

Elias dismounted and walked his mount the rest of the way to the house. There were dark patches under his eyes. Nobody had slept, Dulcie realized. They all were on edge.

To Dulcie's surprise, Maryanne came out of her house dressed and pulling on lacy gloves.

"Morning, Elias."

Elias shucked off his hat and held it to his chest. "Morning."

"Would you be so kind as to fetch my team and harness them to the wagon?"

He shot a look at Dulcie.

"It's Sunday," Maryanne said. "I'm going to church."

"Do you think that's wise?" Dulcie asked.

"Why wouldn't you think so?"

"What happened last night is still fresh in everybody's mind. Emotions will be running high."

"All the more reason for a Sunday service," Maryanne replied.

Dulcie understood Maryanne's reasoning, but she shuddered to think how folks would react when they saw her in town.

"Do as she says," Dulcie told Elias, a trifle uneasy. She tried to hide her misgivings from them both.

It didn't take long for Elias to bring the team around. By then Dulcie had had just enough time to change into her good dress.

She didn't bother with Mrs. Walker's fancy button shoes. The loan of a pair of Maryanne's boots would have to do.

Dulcie drove. Marianne was lost in her thoughts, so Dulcie kept silent, even though she had plenty on her mind.

The town residents gathered at the church, their teams waiting alongside the road. Dulcie drove up to the front door and set the brake. Mr. Paisley lent a hand with Maryanne and the baby. Dulcie climbed down and joined them.

Dulcie saw Mrs. Walker sitting in the first row of the church, where sun streamed in from every window. The lady smiled, worry showing in her face, and Dulcie smiled back.

Tom was noticeably absent. She wasn't surprised, but she would've liked to have seen him there.

The congregation moved aside to give Maryanne, carrying her baby, some room. George Arthur looked at them, wide-eyed, from beneath his sunbonnet.

They took seats next to Mrs. Walker.

Mr. Paisley stood and said a few words of greeting.

Mrs. Paisley led them in "Beautiful Redeemer," a song Dulcie hadn't heard since childhood. She was struck by how the sweet music brought back a wealth of memories. How fond she'd been of the green hills back home, and how she missed their neighbors and friends.

During the prayers, Dulcie bowed her head and asked forgiveness for any hard feelings she may have had toward others since arriving in Hangtown and for being slow in showing her appreciation for all her blessings.

She had a sense of relief and accomplishment when she'd finished. She promised to be more diligent about her prayers in the future.

The preacher man must've been thinking about last night's social when he talked about loving your neighbor. The congregation responded with a hearty "Amen."

Again the crowd gave way to Maryanne. Dulcie followed her outside.

Mr. Paisley stretched out his hand to help her into the wagon.

"I want to see my husband," Maryanne said, refusing to get into the wagon.

"Tom won't let anyone in the jail," Mr. Paisley told her. His voice was raspy.

"He'll let me in," Maryanne replied.

Dulcie waited by the wagon as Maryanne hurried down the street. Dulcie feared she'd stumble and fall going at that pace. When Maryanne reached the sheriff's office, Dulcie let out her breath.

"I wish this was over," Mr. Paisley said.

"Me too," Dulcie replied.

She realized she'd been treating Tom too harshly. He could be ornery at times, and more than often tight-lipped, but she'd come to know him. He was a decent man. He was a man who could be depended on to know that fair was fair.

The way was clear. Tom Walker would make this right, but he couldn't do it alone. She would do what she could to make sure Stuart went home where he belonged.

Dulcie took a deep, restoring breath. There was no more time for wallowing in misery. She said good-bye to Mr. Paisley, telling him to bring the wagon around to the sheriff's office when the other wagons had cleared the way.

She retied her bonnet as she hurried up the dusty street, the wind kicking up grit into her eyes. The weather had turned frightful, with big black clouds looming in the northeastern sky. The air crackled with anticipation and danger. It put her nerves on edge.

She climbed the steps to the boardwalk. Citizens greeted her with a doff of a hat and the bob of a head. Every last one of them looked uncertain and afraid.

Riley Gibbs stood by the door of the sheriff's office gobbling his breakfast. A shotgun was propped up against the wall within easy reach.

"Hello," he said as he touched the brim of his hat.

"Afternoon, Riley. Is Tom here?"

Riley scooped up another forkful. "You just missed him, Miss Dulcie."

"Where'd he go?"

"Over to the telegraph office. Said he'd important business."

"What kind of business?" Dulcie couldn't help but wonder.

"Sheriffing business, I reckon."

She heard Maryanne's voice coming from inside the office and opened the door.

"You can't go in there," Riley said. "Tom left specific instructions that nobody be allowed inside the sheriff's office."

Surely Tom hadn't meant her. Dulcie went inside.

Maryanne had drawn up a chair in front of the cell and was talking to Stuart.

Jasper said hello from behind the big desk. His empty plate sat on top next to his shotgun. He'd tipped his chair backward and rocked on the back legs.

Maryanne turned to see who'd come in. Her eyes were red and puffy. She clutched a hanky to her bosom.

"Oh, Dulcie, what can we do?"

Dulcie took her friend's greeting to heart.

"I'll help however I can," Dulcie said.

"Dulcie, take my wife and son home," Stuart said.

"No," Maryanne cried.

Dulcie knew Stuart was done in by his wife's misery, and she saw the wisdom in removing Maryanne.

"Come with me," Dulcie said. "Mr. Paisley is bringing the wagon around to fetch us."

Maryanne kissed Stuart fiercely, desperately. She rose from her chair. She'd been dealt a terrible blow but kept a fragile dignity about her.

Dulcie hooked her arm around Maryanne's. There was no resistance. They left the men.

Dulcie wished she could've seen Tom that morning. She needed to hear his calming voice. She needed to hear him say that everything would be all right.

All the way back to Maryanne's house Dulcie couldn't help but think about how Bert and Judson Chase had done wrong by the Greenwoods, taking down their fence and threatening to hold back their water supply. No one could deny that those two had a nasty streak in them. Now Jud Chase was dead, and Bert was calling Stuart a murderer, even when everyone who'd been at the social disagreed.

Bert lived on the other side of the hill off yonder. Dulcie decided to pay him a neighborly visit. She wouldn't tell Maryanne what she intended to do. Her friend would only worry, and Dulcie didn't want to add to her already heavy burden.

The man could use some comforting words too. Being a newcomer to Hangtown, and unfriendly as he was, he'd most likely not received any neighborly consolation for the death of his brother. Nobody'd told him what a good brother Judson Chase had been or other kind words to soothe his troubled soul.

Bert was alone in his grief, and she understood how that felt. She'd remind him he wasn't alone.

She worked hard and finished her chores. She found Maryanne nursing George Arthur. Dulcie admired her friend's resilience. It was a testament to Maryanne's strength and gumption that she didn't let Stuart's arrest paralyze her.

Dulcie told Maryanne she was going for a walk unless she needed help.

Maryanne shook her head. "You've done more than your share."

Dulcie started up a path worn down by livestock, which wound its way up the hill. Before long, she came across a half dozen steers wandering on the Greenwoods' property. A row of fence posts had been yanked out of their holes, and barbed wire lay on the ground. Stuart had plenty of cause to be angry with the Chase brothers.

When she reached the top, she could see the Chase homestead below. The clapboard house was nestled in the only flat part of the spread. She climbed down the path and followed the road carved by last year's rain so it looked like a washboard. As she walked, she thought about what she would say to Bert.

Hopefully, by this time, he'd reined in his temper. Would he listen to what she had to say?

She found Bert chopping firewood behind his house. He'd been at it for a while. A stack of firewood stood as high as a buckboard.

Bert had worked up a sweat, and he'd unbuttoned his flannel shirt despite the frosty temperature. He looked up when he heard Dulcie clopping along the hardpan but went back to his work.

Dulcie was clearly unwelcome, but she didn't let Bert's poor manners stop her. She had something to say, and Bert would have no choice but to listen.

He tapped an awl into a length of wood with the backside of the ax. With a powerful swing, the ax came down and split the log in two.

Dulcie sat down on a nearby stump and watched.

"What do you want?" Bert growled. He planted the ax into the chopping block and pulled off his gloves. She should fear him. If the man was like his brother, he'd be in possession of a fighting nature.

She hadn't brought a weapon. He'd be able to overpower her if he fell into a rage, but she'd come to speak her mind, and she wasn't about to back down.

"You and me have some words to say to each other," she told him.

He scowled as he wiped his wide face and thick neck with his shirttail. "Who are you?"

"I'm Dulcie Crowder."

Bert spat on the ground. "I recognize the name. A fella named Crowder killed a man over at the Blue Stocking and was hanged for it."

"He was my pa."

Bert's upper lip curled disagreeably. Clearly, his social skills needed work.

"State your business," Bert said. "I haven't got all day."

"I've come from the Greenwood farm. I'm proud to say I'm doing what I can to help that lady while her husband's in the jailhouse."

"Is that what you've come to tell me?"

"No, sir." Dulcie took a softer tone. "I wanted you to know I'm sorry for your loss. I truly am."

He buttoned his shirt, thinking on what she'd said. The anger that had boiled up so easily seemed to ease.

"I reckon you want me to be grateful to you for coming out here offering sympathy," he said, sour-faced. She suspected his temper got the best of him at times.

"Did I ask you for gratitude?" Dulcie said.

Bert blinked his sleep-deprived eyes. Unless she missed her guess, his grief was deeper than even he was willing to admit.

Dulcie straightened her skirt and sat up as prim as a school-marm.

"Seems to me the law is meant to protect us citizens," she said. "For it to work, it has to be fair."

She paused to let her meaning sink in.

"Your brother shares the blame in what happened to him. By all accounts, he pulled a knife and cut Stuart."

Bert slapped his gloves against his hip. "That's not how I saw it."

"A man has a right to defend himself," she continued. "Stuart didn't mean to kill Judson. You know that as well as I do."

"A judge and jury will decide," Bert said.

"Maybe so, but no judge and jury will convict him."

"I wouldn't be so sure."

Now she was truly peeved with the man. "What good has picking a fight ever done you?"

Bert clenched his jaw so tightly, his eyes looked ready to pop. "Don't come preaching to me. Jud and I never did the Greenwoods any harm."

"That's a lie, and you know it."

"If you weren't a woman, I'd thrash you for talking so much."

"I'm a lady," she corrected. "I'm entitled to my say."

Bert shook his head. "How come you're speaking up for Stuart Greenwood anyway?"

"Because the Greenwoods are my friends."

Bert frowned. "You tell me how this killing is any different than the one your old man did over at the Blue Stocking."

"Speak plainly, Bert. I've got no patience with riddles."

"The law out here don't pay no mind to the circumstances. A killing is a killing." He pulled on his gloves, looking sure of him-self. "After the law is done with Stuart Greenwood, he'll meet the same fate as your pa."

Dulcie stood and brushed off her skirt. She wasn't about to let Bert Chase rile her.

"Time folks stopped relying on the hanging tree," she said, "but since you're too mule-headed to listen to reason, I've got nothing more to say."

"About time," Bert replied. He picked up his ax and let it rest across his broad shoulders.

She turned and retreated. The climb up the hill left her huffing and puffing. When she reached the top, she looked back.

Bert Chase was setting another log on the chopping block. His hurt ran deep, and he'd needed to lash out. He'd said those mean things to upset her because she supported Stuart.

Pa had murdered a man. The law said so. She'd absolute faith Tom Walker had made sure the law treated her pa fairly.

Judson Chase's death had been an accident. Nobody except Bert thought otherwise.

She started down the other side of the hill. She'd said what she'd come to say.

Had it done any good?

Whether Bert Chase would come around to her way of thinking was up to Bert. Some folks, in her opinion, were just too stubborn to admit when they were wrong.

Chapter Seventeen

Tom crossed Main Street, on his way to the sheriff's office. He'd sent off a telegram first thing that morning to the sheriff in Coloma, explaining the circumstances of Judson Chase's stabbing and his arrest of Stuart Greenwood. He'd added that Stuart and Maryanne were friends of his. How he'd understand if the sheriff wanted to take custody of the prisoner and relieve Tom of his duties.

Now all he could do was wait for an answer.

Tom found Riley with his nose in a book, Jasper winning at solitaire, and Stuart hunched over on the cot, his hands on his knees. "Everything quiet?" Tom asked.

"Yes, sir," Jasper said. He shuffled the deck expertly and started a new hand.

Tom pulled off his hat and set it on a peg.

"Mrs. Greenwood stopped by," Jasper said. "I didn't think you'd care if she spoke to Stuart, her being family and all."

Tom scowled. He'd left specific instructions that nobody be let into the sheriff's office except the barmaid from the Blue Stocking bringing breakfast.

"Dulcie was here too," Jasper said.

"Where'd she go?"

"She took Maryanne home."

Tom was relieved. He didn't want the women in town with tempers running so high. He took his new rifle down from the rack and checked the breech. He loaded a cartridge into the chamber.

"Time I went on my rounds. Do you think you can keep visitors out of the office while I'm gone?"

Jasper looked up from his game. "I reckon that's what I'm here for."

Tom opened the door, his new rifle in hand. One day soon he'd have a talk with Jasper about taking his responsibilities more seriously.

He saw Oscar Smalley, bareheaded and without a coat, headed his way. Tom held the door open as Oscar stepped up onto the boardwalk.

"Good to see you," Tom said, and he followed the man inside. The light from the kerosene lantern wavered as he shut the door.

Oscar headed for the potbelly stove and rubbed his hands together. "I came as soon as I got word from Coloma." He drew a sheet of lined paper out of his vest pocket and handed it over.

Tom braced himself. "Is the sheriff on his way?"

Oscar blew on his hands. "You'd better see for yourself."

The message was short and to the point. *Trial set for this Tuesday. District Judge Hennessy presiding. You handle this.*

Tom appreciated that the sheriff had such faith in him, but a trial wasn't welcome news. He tossed the scrap of paper onto the desk.

"What's this all about?" Stuart asked.

Tom turned. Stuart clung to the iron bars and regarded him with arched eyebrows and his mouth twisted.

Tom had meant to explain everything to Stuart but had held back until he had something hopeful to tell him. "There's going to be a trial day after tomorrow. The sheriff has sent for the district judge."

Stuart collapsed onto the cot, the weight of the news, no doubt, unbearable. "This is a disaster."

"Don't think the worst," Tom answered.

"Maryanne might as well sell out. She can't keep up the place by herself."

"What kind of talk is that?" Jasper asked.

"Now, you see here," Tom said. "Your woman isn't about to give up on you, and you shouldn't either."

"What chance does a dirt farmer have against a judge?" Stuart replied.

Stuart's doubts were unfair.

"The law treats every man the same," Tom said.

Stuart scoffed. "You really think so?"

Tom stood his ground, even though he recognized a man who thought he'd lost everything. "Look here, Stuart. Judge Hennessy runs a fair courtroom."

Stuart laughed. "I've heard he's called a hanging judge. Seems to me a hanging judge has already made up his mind as to my guilt."

"There'll be a jury of twelve able men from the area," Tom assured him. "They'll listen to the testimony and come to the same conclusion the rest of us have."

Stuart shook his head and stared at the floor.

Tom didn't argue anymore, even though Stuart's doubts about the legal system stung. The law had let Stuart down. It was up to the law to make this right.

"I'd better get back to the telegraph office," Oscar said.

"Send off an answer to the sheriff to let him know we're obliged," Tom said.

"I'll get right on it," Oscar said eagerly. He turned to Stuart. "You keep your spirits up, boy. There's plenty to fight for. You've got a wife and boy to look after."

"Believe me," Stuart said, looking up, his eyes brimming with tears, "I think of nothing else."

Tom dreaded riding out to the Greenwood place to tell Maryanne the news, but he didn't want her to hear it from somebody else.

The sheriff's decision would make him mighty unpopular in the community as word spread.

Adding to his concern, the circuit court judge coming to hear this trial was the judge who'd presided over Willie Crowder's trial. He was called a hanging judge for a good reason. He had more convictions than any other judge sitting the bench, and every one of those defendants had received the sentence of death by hanging.

Besides telling Maryanne this sorry news, Tom needed to see Dulcie. She held him responsible for arresting Stuart. She needed to understand how he couldn't be partial. An officer of the law who took sides was no use to the community he was sworn to serve.

He'd warned her that a lawman's job wasn't easy.

Tom hadn't ever been out to the Greenwood place. The house and barn were small, he saw now, but there was room to grow. Stuart had some big ideas. He'd been telling folks how he planned to raise pigs and grow corn. Tilling this rocky land would take some doing. Tom believed Stuart and men like him were the future of their community. He along with Maryanne and his youngster would give Hangtown stability.

Tom didn't doubt Stuart had a future.

Young Elias Steptow sat on the top step of the Greenwoods' porch. He scrambled to his feet when he saw Tom approaching.

Having a man around the place was a necessity for Maryanne and Dulcie, especially with Bert Chase only a stone's throw away.

Dulcie came out of the farmhouse pushing a straw broom. Her face lit up for a second, but only for a second. Her expression then took on the severity of quick anger and blame. She was still sore at him, he could plainly see, and his news would only add kerosene to the fire.

He remembered the first time he'd laid eyes on her. She'd been pointing a double-barreled shotgun at him, scared and not wanting him to know it.

He'd come to know her better since then. She never flinched when others needed her and didn't back down when faced with injustice.

He'd no doubt she had enough gumption to be a Hangtown resident, but could she deal with being a deputy's wife? He'd need her to support him, to stand by his side when trouble blew their way and not take sides even when friends were involved.

He touched two fingers to the brim of his hat. She looked away. The wind whipped a loose strand of her hair across her face as she continued to sweep. She didn't stop to tuck it behind her ear.

Tom dismounted and gathered up his reins.

"Howdy," Elias said, and he extended his hand.

They shook. "How's Maryanne holding up?"

The boy grimaced. "As well as can be expected."

"I need to speak to her," Tom said.

"She is inside," Elias replied. His gaze shifted uneasily to Dulcie.

Dulcie stood with the broom in front of her like a sentry with a rifle.

"I will water your horse," Elias said nervously.

Tom handed over the reins. Elias led Star away, leaving Tom alone with an angry woman. He searched for words that wouldn't set off a powder keg.

"Looks like you two have kept the place up," he said, turning back to Dulcie.

"You've brought bad news, haven't you?" she asked.

"Yes."

She made no move to fetch Maryanne.

"Could you call her to come out here on the porch?" he asked with authority in his voice. He could easily shout out to Maryanne. He would if Dulcie didn't cooperate.

"I will as soon as you tell me whose side you're on," she said, her anger flaring.

Tom shifted his feet. "I'm not on anybody's side. Can't be, and you know it."

"I also know that Stuart isn't guilty."

"A man died at his hand."

"The man pulled a knife," she shot back.

"That's the way most folks who were there saw it, but there are two sides to any argument."

She gave those words consideration. "There's no truth to what Bert Chase is saying."

"The majority of folks agree with you, but it's not up to me to decide who's right and who's wrong."

The door opened, and Maryanne stood there. Her eyes were weary and bloodshot. Her complexion was gray. He'd known her a couple of years, and he knew she was terrified.

Tom pulled off his hat. He hated that he had to break this news to her, but he couldn't avoid telling her. He owed her that much.

"Tom has something to say to you," Dulcie told her.

Maryanne's eyes widened.

"I received a telegram from the sheriff. There's gonna be a trial," Tom said. "The district judge will be here shortly."

Maryanne clutched the doorjamb. "A trial?"

"Come Tuesday morning."

Dulcie dropped the broom and hurried to her friend's side. She put an arm around Maryanne's shoulders and helped her inside. Tom followed.

Maryanne fell into the nearest chair. Her youngster was sitting on a quilt spread out on the floor, sucking his fist.

Dulcie poured water out of a brown jug into a glass and set it in front of Maryanne. Dulcie glared at him. Her message was clear.

See what you've done?

Tom attempted some soothing words. "Stuart is keeping his spirits up," he said, "for you and your young'un."

"Tell Stuart I'm coming back to town this evening," Maryanne said.

"Whenever you like," he said. "You have Dulcie or Elias drive you into town."

Maryanne stared at the glass of water. "Can I bring him some food?"

"You sure can," Tom said.

Dulcie stood by the open door, her arms crossed.

"It was kind of you to tell me in person, Tom," Maryanne said, dismissing him.

"I'll see you two later," he said.

He hurried out the door, glad to be out of there. He could handle the meanest, orneriest desperado to ever roam these hills, but Dulcie with her dander up was more than he could manage.

She was fast on his heels. "Isn't there anything you can do?"

Tom turned and faced her. "I'm doing all I can."

She planted her hands on her hips.

"I need you to believe that justice will prevail," he said.

"Will it?" she challenged him.

Tom wished she trusted him. If she doubted the law, then she doubted what he stood for. He didn't know how to convince her. With a shake of his head, he headed over to where Elias had tied up his horse.

"I believe he's about the most infuriating man I've ever met," Dulcie said, sputtering, as she watched Tom ride away.

The news Tom had brought was worse than she'd imagined. A trial, of all things, and for what reason?

"Don't blame Tom." Maryanne had come outside to join her. She managed a smile. It was the first time she'd smiled since Dulcie had been with her at her farm.

"He's letting Bert Chase have too big a say," Dulcie said.

"Tom has to be fair," Maryanne answered with more generosity than Dulcie would have.

"We could bust Stuart out of jail," Dulcie said.

"We'll do no such thing," Maryanne replied.

"You're not giving up, are you?"

"Of course not," Maryanne said. She looked back to check on George Arthur.

"We'll hire a lawyer," Dulcie assured her. "I talked to a lawyer in town when I sold my land."

Maryanne faced her and frowned. "What do you think a lawyer will cost?"

"I don't know what they charge for a trial, but don't you worry. I've got plenty of cash, and you can have all you need."

"I couldn't take your money."

"I'd be offended if you didn't."

Maryanne pressed her hanky to her cheek, catching the tears. "What's going to happen to us?"

"I don't know," Dulcie said. She couldn't tell Maryanne that everything would be all right for her and her family. She honestly didn't know. "One thing I'm certain of is, we're not doing Stuart any good sitting around fretting."

Maryanne seemed to take heart from Dulcie's advice. She stowed her hanky in the sleeve of her dress and took a deep, restoring breath.

"I'll go tell Elias about the trial." Dulcie tied her bonnet.

"Yes, he should be told. He'll need to stay on a little while longer."

"No doubt he will."

"I must see Stuart," she said. "I need to talk this over with him."

"It'll be dark soon," Dulcie said.

"This can't wait."

"I'll bring around the wagon," Dulcie said. "We can leave as soon as you're ready."

"Thank you, Dulcie." Maryanne's damp eyes showed appreciation. Dulcie was humbled by her friend's gratitude.

Maryanne went back inside, and Dulcie shut the door behind her. There was a nip in the air. The sun had dipped behind a string of clouds.

A trial was all Bert Chase's doing, setting the law on Stuart to avenge his loss. Obviously, her words that morning had fallen on deaf ears.

Why did some men find a vengeful nature to be more satisfying than a forgiving one?

She shaded her eyes and searched for Elias. She saw him in the paddock forking dirty straw into a pile.

"Stuart is not home yet?" Elias asked when he saw her coming his way.

"No." Dulcie sputtered. "Tom Walker was just here. There's going to be a trial."

"No fooling?" Elias gasped.

"Do I look like I'm fooling?"

Elias hung his head like a dog who'd been spoken harshly to.

"My apologies," she said. "I'm out of sorts after hearing that Stuart must stand before a judge."

"I am sorry also. Maryanne must be crushed."

"She's taken a blow, that's for sure."

"I will stay on as long as the Greenwoods need me."

"You're a good neighbor," Dulcie replied.

He stuck out his chest. "You know you can count on me."

Elias was only too eager to help her hitch up Stuart's team of horses to the wagon. Dulcie climbed aboard, and he handed her the reins.

"You be careful," he said. "There's bound to be hard feelings."

She nodded. "Don't you worry. I can take care of the three of us."

Chapter Eighteen

Maryanne had wrapped George Arthur up in a fringed shawl and was waiting on the porch. She handed him to Dulcie and set a basket in the back of the buggy.

As she climbed into the box, George Arthur cooed at her.

They both laughed at the boy's antics. The tension that seemed so unbearable loosened a mite.

Dulcie gave the baby to Maryanne and picked up the reins. She smelled fried ham and corn bread. Feeling hopeful, she let off the brake, and they started off to town.

"I'm frightened, Dulcie."

"That'd be natural."

"I'm so frightened, I can't breath sometimes."

Dulcie shook her head. "You oughtn't work yourself into such a state. What would George Arthur do without you?"

"What if Stuart's found guilty?"

"Now, don't go thinking the worst," Dulcie said. "Besides, Tom won't let that happen."

Maryanne cheered up a little, attempting a weak smile. They all believed Tom Walker wouldn't let harm come to Stuart.

Dulcie spotted a deep rut in the road ahead and guided the horses around it.

"What'll I say to Stuart?" Maryanne asked.

"You tell him he has a powerful number of friends willing to help."

"I'm very thankful."

Dulcie smiled. "If you don't mind my asking, where're your kin?"

"Ma and Pa went back to Illinois. There was nothing for them here."

"What about Stuart's people?"

"He lost them to the fever. He's been on his own since he was sixteen."

Maryanne had to dig deep for her strength, but it was there. Her husband needed her. That baby needed her. The farm and all it represented, home and life, depended on her holding up until this mistake could be made right.

Dulcie pulled the horses to a stop in front of the sheriff's office. Tom Walker came out, carrying his hat.

Her poor heart did a little hop, skip, and jump as usual. That much hadn't changed.

"Ladies," he said, as if it'd been a long time since he'd seen them.

Maryanne didn't waste time with pleasantries. She grabbed hold of the wood slat of the seat. Tom rushed to help her down.

He offered Maryanne and her baby a sturdy hand. Maryanne stepped down out of the wagon.

"There's food in the buckboard," Maryanne said sweetly. "Would you bring it in?"

Tom was only too willing. He fetched the basket and followed her inside.

Dulcie waited in the wagon so Maryanne and her man could talk in private.

To her surprise, Tom came back out and shut the door behind him.

"Do you think it wise to leave a dangerous criminal alone with her?" Dulcie asked.

Tom scowled. "Now, Dulcie, don't you start again. You know I'm doing what needs to be done."

"No one is saying any different," she replied.

He leaned against the hitching rail and shoved his hands into his pockets. What was wrong with her? Instead of showing gratitude for his consideration to Maryanne, she'd found fault.

They all were hurting, but Tom was doing everything he could, and Dulcie would be wrong to believe otherwise.

"I'm sorry," she said. "I didn't mean to snap your head off."

He smiled, but weakly.

"I can't wait for all of this to be over. I reckon I'm not alone in that." Dulcie shifted on the wood seat.

"You want help down?" Tom asked. He'd seen her discomfort.

"I'll manage," she said, knowing his hands around her waist would be her undoing.

She climbed down from the Greenwood wagon. She was about to take his arm and ask him to walk with her, when two elderly ladies came out of the dry goods store carrying baskets. When they saw Dulcie, they scooted her way.

"Yoo-hoo!" they shouted out.

Dulcie stretched her lips into a semblance of a smile.

Tom tipped his hat, but the ladies ignored him.

"How are things going out at the Greenwood place?" one of the ladies asked. Her tiny birdlike face peered out from her eggshell blue bonnet.

"As well as can be expected," Dulcie said.

"Is there anything we can do?" the other lady asked. "Anything at all?"

"Maryanne and her baby need their friends now more than ever," Dulcie replied.

The two ladies looked at each other. There was a kinship among the women of the town, Mrs. Walker had explained, a bond that grew tighter during hard times. These ladies now included her in their bond. Even though she hated the circumstances, she welcomed the change in their attitude toward her.

"Stuart Greenwood doesn't deserve to be in that jail," the birdlike lady said. "He should be home taking care of his family."

It was an attitude Dulcie shared.

Tom squirmed like a schoolboy caught throwing spitballs.

The other lady nodded. "That's what they're all saying around Hangtown."

"Yes, dear," the other lady replied quickly. "What's become of our town when a stranger's word has more sway than a decent, respectable citizen's?"

"It isn't right," her companion agreed.

They peered at the deputy with pinched faces.

Tom looked grim. He stood alone, and those two ladies wanted him to know it.

"I suppose you're satisfied by what you're doing," Mrs. Blue Bonnet said with a spark of anger. It wasn't a question.

"No, ma'am, this part of my job doesn't give me any satisfaction at all."

Dulcie cringed. He'd become an outsider in the community he belonged to as much as any other man did. They'd taken sides against him and treated him with public scorn. No telling what was being said behind his back.

And yet he'd protect them with his life.

"Ladies," he said. He tipped his hat and went back inside the sheriff's office.

"I'll send out some of last year's pickles," one of the ladies said to Dulcie.

"My Amos caught a mess of plump trout this morning. I'll bring some over for Maryanne and her baby."

"Thank you kindly," Dulcie said, politeness itself. "I'm sure Maryanne will appreciate your thinking of her."

The ladies nodded, satisfied they'd done enough. Dulcie watched them retreat, chatting with their heads together.

Dulcie had missed her chance to speak up, to point out to the ladies how Stuart's trial hadn't been Tom's decision, and how he couldn't take sides, and all the other things he'd tried to explain to her about the law, but for the first time in her life she'd kept silent.

She realized she'd made a terrible blunder.

Dulcie was still thinking about how she must stand by Tom's side and give him the support he needed right now, and how she'd let him down, when Maryanne came out of the sheriff's office carrying George Arthur. She looked paler than before, if that was possible, and was close to tears. She sniffed as she wiped at her nose with her frilly lace handkerchief.

George Arthur rubbed his eyes with his chubby fists. His lower lip trembled as if he might start wailing at any moment.

Dulcie wanted to confide in Maryanne, to tell her how she'd let Tom down, but this wasn't the time or place. Saving Stuart had to be their number one concern.

Maryanne waved a piece of paper in her hand. "Stuart says I should send for a lawyer from Marysville. He's a lawyer who is good with this kind of charge."

Dulcie noticed she didn't say *murder* charge. *Murder* was the kind of word that wasn't suitable in polite company.

"We'll send him a telegram right away," Dulcie replied. "The trial is the day after tomorrow."

"I don't know how a telegram works," Maryanne replied.

"Me either, but Tom sends them all the time."

"What if the telegram doesn't go through?"

Maryanne was working herself into a state of panic, which would only paralyze her.

"We'll send off a telegram and follow up with a letter on tomorrow's stage," Dulcie said reassuringly. "If we don't get word back, we'll send Elias off to fetch him. We're bound to reach this lawyer fella one way or the other. Now let's not waste any more time with worry."

Maryanne stiffened her spine. "You're right, Dulcie. We'd better get over to the telegraph office and send for the lawyer right away."

They had no trouble finding the place. A large sign painted in red letters hung above the front door of the brick building.

"California State Telegraph Company," Maryanne read aloud.

"That's a mouthful," Dulcie replied, struggling to make out the words in the growing darkness.

"They've just completed the lines between here and Marysville. I'm told you can send a telegram as far as San Francisco," Maryanne explained.

"A sign of progress," Dulcie answered, welcoming a new way to communicate.

They shaded their eyes to look in the window. The room was dark.

"The office is closed," Maryanne said with heavy disappointment.

"It can't be," Dulcie replied.

Maryanne slumped. "What do we do now?"

"How about looking around in back? Maybe the operator lives here."

They stepped off the boardwalk and hurried down an alley. Dulcie saw a light on inside and rapped on the door. A short man with a round face and thinning hair opened the door.

"My name is Dulcie Crowder, and this is my friend Maryanne Greenwood. Are you the telegraph man?"

"Howdy to you, ladies. I'm Oscar Smalley, telegraph operator, at your service."

"We've an urgent need to send a telegram," she continued.

Mr. Smalley grabbed his hat. "Come this way."

They followed him to the front door. He opened the door with a key and bade them enter.

"I want to send a telegram to a lawyer in Marysville," Maryanne said. She gave Mr. Smalley the piece of paper with the name.

Dulcie was gratified to see that Maryanne's resolve was getting stronger. Her friend needed to gather up all the grit she could muster to withstand the days ahead.

"What's this lawyer fella's address?" Mr. Smalley asked.

"Oh, dear, I don't have an address," Maryanne replied.

"Never you mind," Mr. Smalley said with a gentle smile. "I'm sure the telegraph operator in Marysville will have no trouble finding the man."

He started tapping. The telegraph machine was nothing more than a block of wood with two strips of metal held down with screws. Mr. Smalley tapped the two pieces of metal together to produce a series of clicks. He stopped after producing only a few. A minute later, the telegraph machine started tapping on its own.

Dulcie and Maryanne looked at each other.

"Good," Mr. Smalley said. "The operator in Marysville is in his office."

Dulcie watched as Mr. Smalley hunkered down and tapped out the message Maryanne had given him. When he finished, he sat back and looked pleased.

"Is that all there is to it?" Dulcie asked.

"Yes, Miss Crowder," Mr. Smalley replied.

"How long does it take?"

"The operator in Marysville has already received it."

She marveled at the speed with which he'd sent Maryanne's message flying off to Marysville.

"How does that contraption work?" she asked.

He explained that each letter in the alphabet had a number of short clicks or long clicks, called Morse code, and that the telegraph operator at the other end of the line received the clicks on a similar apparatus.

It was a marvel, this telegraph machine. No wonder Tom had sung its praises.

Fascinated, Dulcie had a hundred more questions, but she didn't want to keep Maryanne any longer than necessary.

Maryanne shifted George Arthur in her lap and opened the small bag dangling from her wrist. "How much do I owe you?"

"That'll be a quarter of a dollar," Mr. Smalley replied.

Maryanne fished out the eight-sided coin and laid it on Mr. Smalley's desk.

"How long before I receive my reply?" Maryanne asked.

"Couldn't say," Mr. Smalley said. "I'll send somebody out to your place when an answer arrives."

Mr. Smalley inclined his head. "If there's anything else I can do for you ladies, you let me know."

Maryanne stowed the receipt in her bag and rose from the chair. "You've been a big help. Good day, Mr. Smalley."

Dulcie stood. "Thank you for explaining how the telegraph machine works."

"Anytime, Miss Crowder."

Mr. Smalley opened the door. Without further ado, they exited.

"We'd better start for home," Maryanne said, looking up at the stars.

Those were welcome words to Dulcie.

They climbed aboard the wagon and headed back. The baby squalled the entire trip.

Elias was sprawled out on the swing chair and jumped to his feet when he heard them coming. Dulcie pulled the horses to a stop in front of the house. Elias reached up and helped Maryanne and the baby down from her perch.

"Thank you," Maryanne said. She carried George Arthur into the house.

"I'd better go in and help Maryanne," Dulcie said.

"I will take care of the rig," Elias said.

"Thank you," Dulcie replied, and she realized how bone weary she was.

Inside the farmhouse, Elias had built up a fire and brought in more firewood. The room was cozy and warm and smelled of oak.

As Maryanne settled the baby in his cradle, Dulcie looked around. She had dishes soaking in the wood tub where they'd been left that afternoon. More water needed to be hauled in from the well.

Weary as she was, she couldn't rest until the chores were done.

Chapter Nineteen

Come first thing Monday morning, Maryanne got her reply, and darned if it wasn't Jasper Jenkins who volunteered to bring the telegram out to the Greenwood homestead.

Dulcie was glad to see him.

Maryanne invited Jasper into the house for refreshments. He came inside, hat in hand.

Dulcie poured him a cup of clean water out of a stone pitcher. He thanked her and took a long drink.

Maryanne read the telegram a couple of times before she said a word. She looked up at Dulcie with tears glistening in her eyes. "Looks like we have a lawyer."

Dulcie felt such relief, she was close to tears herself. Lord knew she'd shed enough in the past week, and no doubt there'd be more forthcoming.

"His fee is fifty dollars," Maryanne said.

"I know you feel uneasy taking my money," Dulcie said, "but there's no better use for it in my estimation. Stuart needs a lawyer, and this fella from Marysville is a good one."

Dulcie hadn't wished to cause her friend any embarrassment, but Maryanne's need was too great to ignore.

"Fifty dollars is such a large sum," Maryanne said.

"His price is high, but it's results we're after," Dulcie said.

Maryanne regarded her with soulful eyes. "What about you? That money is for the home you want to build, for your future."

"I'll have money left over," Dulcie said, "and plenty of opportunities to earn the rest."

"Thank you, Dulcie," Maryanne said. The relief in her expression was more than enough thanks. She sank into her rocker like a wounded sparrow.

Jasper opened his mouth to speak, but Dulcie caught his arm.

"She has a powerful need to do some cogitating. Let's go sit on the porch." Dulcie picked up a shawl and went outside.

Jasper followed her to the swing chair and sat down. She plopped down beside him. She started to rock, hoping the swinging would relax her, but she was as jittery as a mare with a newborn foal, seeing danger from all sides and wishing to protect the innocent from harm.

The morning breeze chilled her quickly. The wind rattled the tree branches newly budded out. She smelled rain in the air.

She'd like to go back inside, but she didn't suggest it. Maryanne needed some time to sort through all that had occurred.

Jasper leaned forward and clasped his big hands. They were full of cuts, bumps, and bruises.

"Looks like you've been hard at work," she said.

He turned his palms up and showed her a spread of blisters the size of beans. "I have."

"You'd better put some salve on those blisters. They're apt to get infected if you don't."

"I bought a tin of Dr. James' Everyday All Purpose Ointment from Mr. Paisley over at the Dry Goods and Notions. He told me it would work wonders. I'll tend to these blisters come bedtime. Although I'd like it better if I had a wife to care for me."

Dulcie didn't have an opinion about his prospects for marriage. She hoped she hadn't given him any false hope about her availability.

"How'd you come by so many blisters?"

Jasper cleared his throat. "I've been helping to build sluices for a gentleman over by the American. He means to cut me in for a share of the gold. If the claim is as rich as he thinks it is, I'll be a wealthy man."

"That's a fine ambition," Dulcie said. "What will you do with so much wealth?"

"Once I get me enough savings, I intend to buy a place in the El Dorado and settle down."

"What about your job as deputy?"

"My heart's not in being a lawman. Not like Tom."

She sighed. "He sure is devoted to his job."

"Yes, ma'am. I don't reckon I'll ever be the lawman he is."

It pleased Dulcie to hear he had such a high regard for Tom Walker. She'd ridden Tom hard when he came out to the farm with the news about the trial. She was sorry she'd let her temper get the best of her and would tell him so the first chance she got.

"Sounds like we share the same ambition," Dulcie said.

"Do you think so?" he asked.

"Know so. I intend to marry Tom Walker, and you'll find a pretty gal, I've no doubt. Maybe we'll be neighbors."

He sat back in the chair.

She hoped she hadn't hurt his sensibilities, but she believed in plain speaking.

"I hope this lawyer fella Maryanne has sent for is a good one," Jasper said.

"He'd better be, for the amount of money he's charging."

"The judge that's coming is tough." Jasper stopped the chair from rocking. "He's called the hanging judge."

The cold felt even sharper. Dulcie drew the shawl closer.

"Was he the judge who sentenced my pa?" she asked.

"I'm sorry to tell you, he was," Jasper said.

"I wonder what kind of man calls himself a hanging judge," Dulcie said.

"One who's sentenced a number of men to the noose, I reckon."

"Are you saying Stuart doesn't stand a chance?"

"Stuart's luckier than most. He's got a heap of friends and a fifty-dollar lawyer on his side."

Dulcie's heart ached as she thought of her pa.

"I'd better see to the chores." She stood.

Jasper stood also. "Did I say something wrong?"

"No, Jasper, and thank you for coming out," she said, unable and unwilling to explain further.

*   *   *

Dulcie picked up a basket hanging outside the chicken coop and began gathering the eggs. Jasper had reminded her that Pa had been alone when he faced the judge and alone when he died. He hadn't any friends to speak of, but he'd had kin. She decided it was high time she paid her pa a visit.

She carried the basket into the house. From the look of her, Maryanne had been crying. Her eyes were swollen, and her nose was red. The joy for living that Dulcie had envied in her friend from the first time they'd met had vanished.

"There's something I've got to do, someone I've neglected," Dulcie said. She took out her britches from her saddlebag and hiked them up underneath her calico dress.

Maryanne stared at her. "Dressed like that?"

"I can't sit astride a saddle dressed as a lady," Dulcie explained.

"Why don't you take the wagon?" Maryanne asked, looking with dismay at Dulcie's clothing.

"No, a ride will do me good."

"I guess those pants will keep you respectable," Maryanne said.

"Where I'm going, it won't matter."

Dulcie stepped outside. She headed for the barn. Elias was emptying slops into the pig trough.

"Howdy, Dulcie," he said. He tossed the bucket aside and shucked off his leather gloves.

"Morning."

"Going somewhere?" He swept a shock of hair out of his eyes and smiled in the most appealing way.

"I'm taking one of the Greenwoods' horses for a ride."

"I'll go saddle one."

"No, I'll do it." She took the bridle off a wooden peg.

Elias wiped the sweat out of his eyes with the back of his hand. "How is Maryanne this morning?"

"Not well at all." There was no way to say it better.

Elias frowned. "Sorry to hear it."

"I've left a hot breakfast waiting for you in the Dutch oven," Dulcie said.

Elias' face lit up. "Much obliged."

"I'll be back to help you with your chores in an hour or so."

"Where you off to?"

"The cemetery in town. Time I paid my pa a visit."

Elias' smile faded. "I heard your pa isn't buried in the Hangtown cemetery."

"Where can I find him?"

"There's another place. You need to travel the road that goes to Diamond Spring," Elias said apologetically. "You'll come upon a stone fence a mile or so after the turnoff for town. You'll see a path big enough for the undertaker's buckboard. It's not easy to find unless you know where to look."

"I'll find it," she said.

Dulcie shouldered the tack and headed for the paddock. Maryanne hadn't mentioned where Pa had been buried, nor had Mrs. Walker. Dulcie reckoned ladies didn't talk about places where the criminal element was buried.

Of course, she shouldn't be surprised that her pa hadn't been included in the graveyard for respectable folks. He'd been strung up for killing another man. The citizens of Hangtown hadn't wanted the likes of Willie Crowder laid to rest next to their kin.

But, good or bad, he was her pa.

The two horses chewed hay in a fenced-in paddock behind the barn. They lifted their heads and nickered a greeting.

She decided on the roan. He was of no mind for a bit in his mouth and turned away when he saw what Dulcie was after.

"The day's going to be a long one," she told him. "We'd better get started."

The horse's ears flicked as he listened.

"Good," Dulcie said. "I'm glad we've learned to communicate."

She saddled up the gelding in no time. She pulled herself up into the saddle and took up the reins. With a second look at the dark clouds gathering in the north, she headed toward Diamond Spring and the vagrants' cemetery where her pa had been buried.

When she came to a stone fence, she turned off the road onto a path that led to a hill choked with gooseberry bushes. The horse needed urging, and she sang to him all four verses of "Beautiful Redeemer," which calmed him. Halfway up the hill, her mount stopped and wouldn't budge.

Nothing she said would change his mind. She dismounted and tied the flighty animal to the nearest sapling.

She walked the rest of the way. The graveyard was an untended patch at the crest of the hill. Some graves were marked with wooden crosses; others were nothing more than a mound of stones.

She searched the crosses. They'd been inscribed with first names—Lucie, Bessie, and Maud—but no last names. There was a cross marked UNKNOWN. She mourned for the person buried there, away from home and with nobody to mourn his passing.

She saw a freshly dug grave, the earth mounded and crusted over. The wooden cross, tipped to one side, read WILLIE C., B. 1812, D. 1854. This was her pa's final resting place, as humble as he'd been in life.

She took a deep breath. She wished they'd had a chance to say good-bye.

"I'm sorry you had to face a judge and jury by your lonesome. Doesn't seem right, and if I'd known, I would've been there."

Knowing Pa, he wouldn't have wanted her to see how he'd left this life.

"I'm here now, and there's no disputing I should've come sooner," she said. "I'm truly ashamed for neglecting you."

Saying so didn't seem to be enough and didn't relieve her heavy heart. She didn't offer an explanation either. Pa could never abide excuses.

Tears rolled down her cheeks, and she wiped them away. "Look at me, bawling like a baby."

She told herself that enough tears had been shed, but they seemed to come without any bidding. She gave in to despair and heartache and sobbed until her whole body shook.

She covered her eyes with a trembling hand. She hadn't grieved properly, but the grief had always been with her, ready to surface. It wasn't only for her pa that she wept. She cried for the women whose last names hadn't been asked for and for the stranger who'd been buried under the cross marked UNKNOWN. She cried because they'd been set out here with nobody to remember them.

Finally, after the tears wouldn't come anymore, she wiped off her face and blew her nose into the hanky Mrs. Walker insisted she carry. The tiny square of cloth soaked through quickly, so she used her sleeve to dry what tears were left.

She straightened Pa's cross and set rocks around the base to keep it upright.

"I'm well looked after," she said, brushing off her hands. She thought he'd want to know.

She suspected her pa knew how lonely it'd been for her. "Tom Walker brought me down from the claim like you asked. I'm grateful you sent him. I'm not a solitary creature like some."

She heard rumbling and looked up at the sky. The dark clouds were closer. The storm was coming fast. She'd better hurry.

"We came out here to have a better life. It's up to me now. I sold the land you worked so hard for. Mining just isn't in my blood."

She paused. She suspected Pa had known that too.

"I aim to marry Tom Walker and settle in Hangtown. We'll buy a place in town and raise a family. I'll be a respected citizen, someone everybody will be proud to know.

"No offense intended," she added.

The sky lit up, and a crack of thunder followed. A gust of cold wind about blew her over.

She stood tall, having said all she'd wanted to say for now and believing Pa would understand and approve of the decisions she'd made.

"I'll come see you again," she said. "Don't think I won't."

She headed down the hill. By the time she reached the horse, fat raindrops pelted them. She untied the gelding and jumped into the saddle. With one last look at where she'd come from, she turned the horse's head and started back.

Chapter Twenty

Dulcie had picked up the straw broom and begun to sweep where Elias had tracked in dirt when she heard a horse approaching at a trot. Hoping Tom had returned, she opened the front door. To her surprise, R.J. Buchanan came riding onto the Greenwood place as jaunty as you please.

"Oh, no," she said under her breath, thinking how R.J. Buchanan was like a buzzard circling wounded prey.

Maryanne was hanging out laundry and must've not noticed his arrival. Dulcie didn't disturb her and went outside to meet Mr. Buchanan by herself.

Mr. Buchanan climbed down from the big horse.

"Miss Crowder," he said, sweet as one of Mrs. Walker's pies. He doffed his tall hat like a gentleman. The wind blew his hair to one side, showing a considerable bald spot.

Dulcie wondered why he'd stopped by. She'd some powerful words saved up if he was here for any reason except being neighborly.

"Good afternoon," she said. It took effort to keep the misgivings out of her voice.

He brushed the trail dust off his hat. "Mrs. Greenwood home?"

"Where else would she be?" Dulcie said.

Anger flashed from his beady eyes. Then he smiled a smile that nobody except his ma would've found endearing.

"I'd like to speak to her." He put one of his twenty-dollar boots on the first step.

"What about?" she replied. She swept dust his way.

"Business," Mr. Buchanan said, scowling. He wisely removed his foot from Maryanne's porch step.

The door creaked behind Dulcie. She whirled around. Maryanne stood there.

"I heard voices," Maryanne said.

Mr. Buchanan bowed. "Ma'am, I'm R.J. Buchanan out of Sacramento. I've traveled a fair distance to see you."

Maryanne came outside and shut the door behind her. "I've heard of you," she said as she adjusted her shawl.

Elias came out of the barn, tucking his shirttail into his pants. There was straw in his hair and hostility burning in his eyes.

"Dulcie," Maryanne said urgently. She nodded in Elias' direction.

Dulcie was torn between letting Elias have a swing at R.J. or settling him down. R.J. was company, and leveling him wouldn't get them anywhere.

"Excuse me," she said as she passed him. She met Elias halfway.

"I recognize that man," Elias said. "He is a land agent."

"Don't work yourself into a state. I know him too."

"I do not like him going anywhere near Maryanne," Elias said. He was breathing heavily.

"Me either, but since he's here, we've got no choice but to treat him politely."

Elias put up both fists. "I would like to punch him."

"That'd be a fool thing to do."

Elias glared as R.J. climbed the porch steps and disappeared inside the farmhouse, but he didn't try to follow.

Dulcie was relieved he'd seen the sense in what she'd said. Elias lowered his fists.

"What does Maryanne want with him anyway?" Elias asked.

"Nothing, as far as I can tell."

"She'd better be careful."

"She will be," Dulcie assured him. "When we find out what he wants, we'll send him on his way."

"See that you do," Elias said.

"Just stay within hollering distance," she said.

"I will." Elias turned on his heel and headed back for the barn.

He was protective of Maryanne and didn't like the looks of R.J. any more than Dulcie did, but he'd heed Dulcie's warning for Maryanne's sake.

Elias wasn't alone in his opinion. R.J. was going to provoke a multitude of hard feelings in Hangtown when word got around he was out here at the Greenwood homestead.

Dulcie returned to the house. She didn't want to leave Maryanne alone with that rascal any longer than need be.

R.J. was sitting in Stuart's chair as if he owned the place. Maryanne had poured him a cup of coffee.

"I'm the man who bought Miss Crowder's land," he told Maryanne. "I'd like to think she was pleased with the deal."

Dulcie squelched a reply. She'd taken his money and had no one to blame but herself if she'd made a mistake in doing so.

"What can I do for you?" Maryanne asked, all sweet and ladylike.

"As you may know"—he shot an indulgent look at Dulcie—"I represent interests in Sacramento."

"Is that a fact?" Maryanne said.

He took time to clear his throat. "I apologize for the timing—these things are never easy. I'd like to make you an offer for your homestead."

Maryanne grasped her hands in front of her. Dulcie held her breath.

"Why do you think our place is for sale?" Maryanne asked.

R.J. Buchanan bowed his head slightly. "I heard about your misfortune. I thought extra money would come in handy."

Maryanne turned as gray as a goose.

"Especially with Stuart facing a hanging judge," Dulcie blurted out.

"Dulcie!" Maryanne said, sharp as a thorn.

Dulcie was stung by Maryanne's tone in front of this man who was likely no better than a snake.

R.J. frowned. "My dear Miss Crowder, be so kind as to consider Mrs. Greenwood's feelings."

Dulcie shot a look at Maryanne, who seemed to be holding up

just fine. The two of them crowded her out of the discussion. Clearly her help wasn't needed.

Dulcie swallowed hard and stepped back. She'd keep her yap shut. She wasn't about to be spoken to twice.

"I'm sure you are aware that a farm this size would be difficult to run alone." A touch of impatience rushed his words.

Maryanne clenched her hands tighter. "I'm sorry. I've no intention of selling."

Mr. Buchanan reached inside his jacket and brought out a small piece of paper. "You'll find the offer is generous."

Maryanne took the paper and tore it into pieces.

R.J. Buchanan shook his head. "I see my visit is inopportune. Again, I apologize. If you change your mind, I'm staying at Mary's Hotel."

Maryanne turned away. "Good day, Mr. Buchanan."

Mr. Buchanan stood, put on his hat, and left. Dulcie was glad to see the back of him, but she followed him outside.

"Good-bye, Miss Crowder." He drew up his reins and mounted his horse.

She snorted. When he'd gone a fair distance, and she was certain he was gone for good, she went back inside. Maryanne poked the fire, the last pieces of the contract blackened by the flames.

"Are you all right?" Dulcie asked.

"I think so."

"He won't bother you anymore," Dulcie said.

"I didn't mean to be rude, but I just couldn't face that man a minute longer."

"I know."

"Do you think he'll come back?" Maryanne asked.

"I hope not. If he does, Tom will persuade him to take his business elsewhere."

Maryanne shrugged. "Maybe selling out would be for the best."

"Don't talk such nonsense."

"Mr. Buchanan made a good point. I can't run this place by myself," Maryanne said.

"You won't have to. Stuart will be home directly."

"You can't be certain of that."

"I'm as certain as anyone can be."

Maryanne didn't look convinced.

Dulcie left for Mrs. Walker's house within the hour. She was reluctant to leave Maryanne, but her friend would be in good hands with Elias Steptow at her beck and call. And Dulcie would be back in time for evening chores.

The team kept a steady pace. Riding astride would've been quicker, but she couldn't show up at Mrs. Walker's wearing britches.

The weather was sunny for a change. The air smelled of pine and cedar.

Dulcie looked forward to seeing Mrs. Walker, even though they'd a difference of opinion about Tom's ambitions to be sheriff. She'd wanted to repay her for the kindness shown her when she'd arrived in Hangtown, and she realized the best gift to give in return was friendship. Hopefully, Mrs. Walker would consider it enough.

She arrived in good time. Mrs. Walker sat on her porch sewing. When she saw Dulcie, she waved.

Dulcie stepped down from the box and loosened the ribbons on her bonnet.

Mrs. Walker rose slowly to her feet.

"Hello," she said in her friendly way. "I didn't expect a visit today."

"I'm here for some of my things."

"Come in."

Dulcie saw Chester standing in the paddock and Baron using him for shade.

"There's a sight I thought I'd never see," Dulcie said.

"Your Chester and that old dog have become the best of friends," Mrs. Walker replied.

"I'm glad they put away their differences," Dulcie said sincerely.

Mrs. Walker opened the door and let Dulcie pass.

The interior of the big house was warmer than outside. "How is Maryanne?" Mrs. Walker asked.

"She's only fair, but that's to be expected."

Mrs. Walker nodded. They went into the kitchen. "Sit down, and I'll fix you something to eat."

Dulcie remained standing. "If it's all the same to you, I can't stay."

Mrs. Walker eyed her with concern. "What in the world is going on?"

Mrs. Walker might overworry about most things, but Dulcie never doubted her ability to handle any kind of trouble that came her way.

"There's going to be a trial for Stuart Greenwood, come Tuesday," Dulcie said.

"I heard. It's a disgrace," Mrs. Walker replied.

"Seems R.J. Buchanan heard as well."

"The city fella who bought your land?"

"One and the same," Dulcie replied. "He's just been out to see Maryanne Greenwood. He offered to buy her farm."

Mrs. Walker gasped. "What an outrage!"

"That's how most people around here will take it," Dulcie agreed.

"I hope she showed him the door," Mrs. Walker said.

"That's why I'm here. Now that I'm staying out at the Greenwood homestead, I'll need my pa's rifle."

"You're a good friend," Mrs. Walker said, "but do you think a rifle is necessary?"

"I'm not taking any chances." She retreated to the room where she'd slept. She pulled her saddlebags and Pa's muzzle loader wrapped in his bedroll from underneath the bed. She slung the bags over her shoulder.

Mrs. Walker stood in the hallway. Her hand went to her throat when she saw Dulcie toting her pa's gun.

"You can't go riding into town looking like a gunslinger."

"No doubt I'll upset a few people, Tom included. But even he admits there are dangerous men roaming these hills. Men who'll stop at nothing to become rich."

Mrs. Walker rested her hand on her bosom and seemed to be giving the situation some thought.

Dulcie admired her for her gumption and owed her a debt of

gratitude, but on this particular matter, Dulcie wasn't going to give in.

"I've got a better idea," Mrs. Walker said. "You wait here."

She climbed the stairs. What she was up to, Dulcie didn't have a clue. Everybody always seemed to be asking her to wait. The wait in her was about used up.

Mrs. Walker didn't take long. She came down those stairs as if she was twenty years younger and handed over her tiny pistol.

"Better take this. Nobody will know you have it."

Dulcie took the peashooter. It was as light as a feather. "I appreciate the offer . . ."

"Leave the muzzle loader with me, Dulcie. Thomas will probably confiscate it if he sees you with it."

Dulcie knew she was right. She set the weapon against the hall tree. She hiked up her dress and tucked the pistol under her blue garter.

"I reckon no one will be the wiser," she said.

Mrs. Walker laughed, as she was prone to do.

"Your pa's rifle will be here for you to hang above the mantel of that house you intend to build," Mrs. Walker said.

Dulcie thought the prospects of owning her own place might be slipping farther and farther away.

"I'd better say good-bye."

"You be careful," Mrs. Walker said.

Dulcie wrapped her arms around Mrs. Walker's neck and gave her a squeeze. The lady hugged Dulcie as if they'd never see each other again.

"Don't be afraid," Dulcie said. "I know how to take care of myself, and so does Tom."

She kissed the lady on the cheek and left her standing in the hallway.

Dulcie drove the Greenwood wagon into town at a quick pace. The main street of Hangtown was busy with freighters and wagons going about their business, forcing her to slow the team to a frustrating walk.

Miss Porter's school was out, and children spilled out of her white clapboard home shouting and laughing. One of them found a tin can and started kicking it around an oak tree. He was joined by a group of older boys, shouting and carrying on.

Dulcie couldn't help thinking how different their childhood was from what hers had been. She hadn't had the opportunity to go to school, even though there'd been a good one in their town. The cost had been too high, and she'd been needed to help out at home.

She thought about her own children and how they'd grow up strong and smart here in Hangtown. They'd have opportunities to make something of themselves, with a little prodding from Dulcie if need be.

There were other towns that were grander, she'd been told. Places where tall buildings reached to the sky and people roamed the streets in droves. She'd heard amazing stories about Sacramento City, the capital of California, and San Francisco, next to the sea.

None compared to Hangtown. This was Tom Walker's town, and now it was hers. Hangtown would be a good place to be from.

As she approached the sheriff's office, Tom came out the door, frowning. That was his way, to watch and worry.

She pulled the team to a stop, and he reached up and put his hands around her waist. He picked her off that wagon as if she were a china doll.

They stood toe to toe in the street. His manliness built up a powerful urge in her.

"You still sore at me?" he asked.

"No, and I realize my mistake. You're trying to stay impartial like you have to, and I'm sorry about my behavior."

"I'm glad you understand what I'm up against."

"I don't suppose it'll ever be easy."

"Why didn't Maryanne come with you?" he asked.

"I expect she'll want to come in later. I've just been over to your ma's house. I needed my gear, since I'm staying with Maryanne."

He nodded.

"There's something you should know. R.J. Buchanan paid Maryanne a visit. He made an offer on her farm."

Tom frowned. Of course, he didn't like hearing that Buchanan was back in town. "I'm sorry she had to be bothered."

He took the words out of her mouth.

She threaded her hand around his arm. His muscles tightened like the string on a bow.

She looked up at him. He didn't meet her gaze.

"Why do I have the feeling you're not telling me something?"

Tom grimaced. "You have an uncanny ability to read my mind."

"Don't credit me with abilities I don't have," she answered. "When you scrunch up your face, I know there's bad news to follow."

She was grateful he didn't hold back.

"It's about Buchanan. When you sold him your claim, I did some checking," he said. "The railroad intends to buy up the land around these parts, and they're offering top dollar. More than you got from Buchanan."

Dulcie was mystified why he'd not told her before. "Why'd you keep this information to yourself?"

"You'd already completed your deal with him. There was nothing more to say."

Dulcie chafed at the news. She would've liked to have known.

"Are you going to arrest him?" she asked.

"I can't arrest a man for making a legal offer for property," Tom countered.

"No, I suppose you can't."

"I'll speak to him," Tom said. "Although there's not much else I can do."

"I'll be watching to make sure he behaves himself."

"Don't go provoking the man. I don't trust him."

"I'll act like a lady," Dulcie said. "R.J. Buchanan won't guess otherwise."

He smiled. They'd little to smile about of late, and Dulcie liked what she saw.

"I should head back to the Greenwood place," she said, wishing she could stay a little longer. "R.J. might come back to pester Maryanne some more."

When they reached the wagon, Tom untied the reins and helped her up into the box.

"Keep Maryanne out of town until tomorrow, will you?" he asked.

She liked that he was depending on her. "I'll do what I can, but I'm not promising."

She released the brake and shook the reins, and the team started off.

Chapter Twenty-one

That evening Dulcie rocked and rocked in the swing chair on Maryanne's front porch. She'd had no trouble convincing Maryanne to stay home. Her friend was worn through.

A coyote howled in the distance. It was a lonely sound and reminded her of the times she'd been by herself at the claim. She'd been ready to howl for want of companionship when Tom Walker came calling. That would be a day she'd forever be thankful for.

Elias had bedded down in the barn, and Maryanne had taken to her bed as soon as a fretful George Arthur had finally fallen asleep. His ma was exhausted, but Dulcie guessed her sleep came in fits and starts. The deep smudges beneath her eyes were constant now.

They all dreaded what tomorrow would bring.

Dulcie was proud that Tom was doing all he could to help Stuart.

She thought about how they'd stood toe to toe on the main street of Hangtown. This was their town, sure enough.

There were things that needed correcting. Calling their town Hangtown, for instance. Such an appellation would keep desperadoes thinking twice about a visit, but the name Hangtown lacked hospitality and friendliness. How was a place going to grow with such a frightful name?

Ezra Dixon intended to take over for the old sheriff. Now, there would be a mistake. He believed in a different kind of justice, one born on the frontier. She understood his frustration, but no man had the right to take judgment concerning life and death into his own hands.

Whether Tom intended to run for office, he hadn't mentioned

of late. She hoped he would, despite the demands the job took on his time. Tom Walker was the kind of man this town needed.

The wind kicked up, and she drew her shawl tighter. Fingers of lightning lit up the dark underbellies of rain clouds. She rose from the chair and went back inside the house.

Dulcie took a seat in front of the fire and listened to the wind screeching. Not even the warm fire comforted her.

Rain began to tap on the roof, reminding her of Mr. Smalley's telegraph machine. Those telegrams surely were a wonder, traveling a great distance in no time at all.

Morning would be here quicker than she'd like. She propped her feet up on the stepstool, settled down into the softness and warmth of the upholstered chair, and closed her eyes.

What seemed like ages ago since she arrived in Hangtown had been only a little more than a week gone by, Dulcie realized as she rousted herself from sleep and prepared for the day ahead.

She had all the chores done by the time Maryanne woke and prodded George Arthur awake. The boy suckled without much interest and promptly fell back asleep.

When Dulcie heard the jingle of harness outside, she knew it was time to go. They bundled up against strong gusts of wind that blew from the north and rain that threatened to deluge them at any minute. Maryanne held on to the baby tucked inside Stuart's duster. They'd all yearned for spring to come, and it had now arrived with a vengeance.

"Morning, Elias," she said.

Elias tipped the brim of his hat, which he'd pulled down to eye level. Maryanne didn't say much as she climbed aboard the wagon. Her thoughts were deep inside her. She wore her Sunday best dress, a dark green, and a matching green bonnet. She'd sewn a piece of new lace around the wide brim to frame her face. The white lace only served to show how drained of color Maryanne's skin had become in the last few days.

Seeing Maryanne look so pale tied knots in Dulcie's stomach. She wished she could take her friend's burden from her, but at best a burden could only be shared.

Thankfully, George Arthur slept as peacefully as an angel. It'd surely be a blessing if he'd have no recollection of the events of this day.

Dulcie rode in the back in her second-best dress and with Mrs. Walker's pistol secured in her garter.

Elias shook the reins, and the team jolted forward. Maryanne gripped the back of the seat as they swayed from side to side on the washed-out road.

Just as she'd predicted, the rain came down in buckets. It dripped from the brim of Dulcie's bonnet and soaked into her shawl, causing her considerable misery. The horses labored in the deepening mud. Progress was slow.

They didn't arrive in town in style, but they did arrive. Hangtown teemed with activity.

"Looks like everybody in El Dorado County has come to town," Dulcie said. Harnesses jingled, and wagons squeaked. Folks called out to them in greeting.

Dulcie answered back, calling each and every citizen by name. She swelled with pride because she'd become one of them.

Their friends were long-faced and sober. This wasn't a time to celebrate and enjoy one another's company. They'd come to witness a murder trial, and the outcome was far from certain, especially with a hanging judge presiding.

Elias pulled the team to a stop in front of the sheriff's office.

Plenty of folks offered to help Maryanne and George Arthur. Maryanne jumped down before anyone had a chance. Mrs. Paisley took the baby from his ma's arms. George Arthur grew wide-eyed at all the commotion and looked ready to cry, but Mrs. Paisley's gentle words soothed his fright.

"I'll take him over to the Mercantile," Mrs. Paisley said.

The arrangement was agreeable to Maryanne. She hurried up the steps and disappeared inside.

Tom came out of his office without his hat. His hair was tousled, and he looked bleary-eyed. His day-old whiskers made him look dangerous.

Yet Dulcie had never seen a finer specimen of a man. She let him help her from the wagon.

Elias greeted Tom and then headed to the livery.

Dulcie opened up one of Maryanne's parasols. Raindrops began to drip off the frilly edge.

She and Tom Walker stood under the parasol as if they were the only two people in the world.

"I didn't expect you so early," he said.

"Maryanne wanted to be with Stuart," she said. "Have you heard any more news from your telegrams?"

"The sheriff won't be here, if that's what you're asking."

"So you're in charge?"

"Looks that way."

"What will you do if Stuart's found guilty?" It was a question she needed to ask.

"It'll not come to that," he said. She could see he was sidestepping the answer. She wouldn't let him.

"It's a possibility we have to face," she said.

He took a deep breath and let it out slowly. "If Stuart is found guilty, then I'll have no choice but to resign."

"I'd hoped you'd say that."

"Not that I don't believe in law and order."

"You don't need to explain. I know who you are and what you stand for," she said.

They walked together, arm in arm, and he opened the door for her. It was something a gent did for a lady.

Maryanne was sitting in front of the jail cell with another man, talking to Stuart.

Stuart wore a clean, dark blue flannel shirt. He'd been freshly shaved and had washed. His oiled hair was parted on the right side.

Dulcie's gaze shifted to the other man.

"This is Mr. Bottle, the lawyer from Marysville we sent for," Maryanne said.

The lawyer shot to his feet. He was a slightly built man. His dark brown hair had been parted down the middle like a freshly plowed field.

"John Bottle." He bowed. "Please to meet you."

"Same here," Dulcie replied.

Mr. Bottle offered her his chair. Dulcie obliged and sat down. As she did, she caught a whiff of a strong scent she couldn't put a name to. The lawyer didn't smell like any man she'd ever come across.

"Now, I don't want you to worry," Mr. Bottle said. "Stuart clearly acted in self-defense. These proceedings are just a formality."

Maryanne looked at him with adoration. "We're depending on you, Mr. Bottle."

Dulcie sat back in her chair, relieved that the man believed Stuart's story. Tom had explained how the law considered a man innocent until proven guilty. She tried to have faith that the law meant what it said.

"Rest assured, I'll have your husband out of here and eating a home-cooked meal by noon," Mr. Bottle said.

Mr. Bottle's confidence seemed to rub off on Maryanne. She managed a thin smile. "Thank you. I look forward to having him home."

Mr. Bottle took a gold watch out of his vest pocket and looked at the time.

Dulcie stood. She knew what Tom needed from her. "Come on, Maryanne. I could use a cup of coffee."

Maryanne grabbed hold of Stuart's hand and didn't look like she'd ever let go.

"You go on with Dulcie," Stuart said.

Dulcie put her hand on Maryanne's shoulder. Her friend was trembling.

"Come on, now," Dulcie said gently. "Let's leave the men to their palaver."

Maryanne rose and turned away. Dulcie looked over at Tom. He smiled one of his generous smiles.

Her pride hitched up a notch.

To her surprise, the lawyer fella followed them out the door.

"There's the matter of the fee," he said apologetically as he buttoned his coat.

"We'll pay you when Stuart is out of jail," Dulcie replied.

"I'm afraid this is the only opportunity I have to collect. I must return to Marysville directly after the trial. I've other clients to attend to."

Maryanne sniffed. "You believe there's no hope?"

Despite his confident words spoken minutes before, the lawyer looked guilty as charged.

"I reckon we agreed to pay you fifty dollars," Dulcie said. "We expect Stuart to be set free."

"I'll do my best."

His sudden lack of conviction sickened her. Nor had he been truthful with Stuart just now when he'd told them the trial was only a formality. This Marysville lawyer was nothing but a two-faced scoundrel. Still, there wasn't time to find another lawyer to take the case.

"Turn around," Dulcie said, making no attempt to disguise her contempt for the man.

"What for?" the lawyer asked.

"Turn your back so I can fetch your money."

He had the decency to color up, and he turned around without another word.

Dulcie pulled up her shirtwaist and used Maryanne as a shield while she retrieved fifty dollars cash from the money belt around her waist.

"Here's your money," she said.

The man swung around. He took the money and counted the bills.

"Thank you, ladies," he said. He stuffed the money inside his coat and tipped his hat.

"Could you ladies tell me where I might find the Blue Stocking?" he asked, slick as you please.

Dulcie pointed down the street.

He stepped off the boardwalk and headed in that direction.

"Guess his throat is dry," Maryanne said.

Dulcie snorted.

Maryanne chewed her bottom lip. "I hope he stays sober. He won't do Stuart any good if he's drunk."

"How much can Mr. Bottle drink before the trial starts?" Dulcie tried to sound encouraging, but she had her own doubts about Mr. Bottle.

Chapter Twenty-two

Mary's Hotel was the last building on the main street. It stood two stories, one of the tallest structures in town. Painted up in canary yellow, the hotel was a sight to see. An Irish lady owned the place, Mrs. Walker had told Dulcie, and ran a respectable business.

Dulcie guided Maryanne through doors painted with gold curlicues. The dining room was half full with folks eating their breakfast.

Dulcie had never been in such a fine-looking place. The room was even grander than Mrs. Walker's front parlor. The walls were papered in pale yellow with drawings of green leafy plants. Sky blue curtains with gold fringe graced the tall windows and were held back by braided ropes. Each and every table had a white tablecloth.

A woman with russet curls piled on top of her head pushed through a swinging door and told them to sit anywhere they'd like. She introduced herself as Mary O'Brian. She wore a milky white ivory-and-pearl brooch at her throat pinned to a lavender dress with white lace at the neckline and sleeves. She was a lady, all right.

Mary excused herself and returned the way she'd come.

Maryanne sat down on a dainty little chair that looked as if it would break in two given any weight. Dulcie sat down carefully.

Mary came out of the swinging door carrying two plates heaped high with steaming corn grits and biscuits.

"Maybe you should have some vittles," Dulcie said.

"I don't think I can eat," Maryanne said.

"It'll do you no good to starve yourself," Dulcie said.

Dulcie caught Mary's attention with a wave of her hand and asked her to bring them the same.

Maryanne's lower lip trembled. She took out her hanky to stem a fresh flow of tears.

Dulcie tried to find comforting words but choked back her own grief and anger.

Mary brought out two platefuls of vittles. The hot food smelled as good as it looked. Dulcie reached for a biscuit.

Then she saw a sight that made her stop. R.J. Buchanan came into the lobby of the hotel. He didn't take time to greet a soul or even look around to see who was there but headed straight upstairs as quick as you please.

Dulcie wondered what he was still doing in town. She pushed back her chair and stood.

"Where are you going?" Maryanne asked. She still hadn't touched her plate.

"Go ahead and start eating. I just saw Mr. Buchanan go up those stairs."

Maryanne looked behind her, but the wily land agent had already disappeared.

"You must leave him be," Maryanne said. "Let Tom deal with him."

Dulcie gave a reassuring smile. "Tom has his hands full. I won't be a minute."

She headed out of the dining room. She knew what propelled her. Curiosity and the suspicion that R.J. Buchanan's arrival meant he was still after the Greenwood property.

She climbed the carpeted steps. They curved into a landing. There were three doors down the hall to the left and two doors on the right.

Dulcie had no idea what room R.J. had gone into. She decided to find out.

She heard men's voices coming from the first room on the left. That was the room she went to first.

She raised her hand to knock. Two men were talking, and she heard Maryanne's name mentioned. She rested her ear against the smooth wood.

"You've got to move on this quickly," came a booming voice Dulcie didn't recognize.

"I'll head out to the Greenwood place as soon as Mrs. Greenwood goes home," R.J. replied. "It'll take some effort to convince her."

"Women can be unreasonable at times like these. I'm depending on you."

"She's got a friend in Dulcie Crowder," R.J. answered. "You know, the woman whose land we already bought."

"Will Miss Crowder be of any use to us?"

"Could be. She sold me her land easily enough, although she can be prickly."

"I'll be on the noon stage," the other man said. "See that Mrs. Greenwood signs the bill of sale as soon as you can."

"You can count on me," R.J. said.

The conversation seemed to be over. Dulcie backed away from the door, her heart thumping. R.J. Buchanan had told her he represented a buyer in Sacramento. And that buyer was here in town.

To her horror, the door opened. A man with white whiskers and dressed in a fancy black suit, white starched shirt with a high collar, and string tie came out of Mr. Buchanan's room. She took him to be about the same age as her pa but with the look of prosperity about him.

He doffed his hat. "Ma'am."

She lowered her head, unwilling to meet his gaze, but watched him descend the stairs. She leaned over the railing and watched him exit.

Her suspicion had been correct. Two snakes-in-the-grass were in cahoots, buying up land to sell for a quick profit to the railroad. They were still after Maryanne and Stuart's farm.

Dulcie hurried down the stairs. When she took her seat, Maryanne looked at her with a spark of interest in her eyes.

"Is everything all right?" Maryanne asked.

"I don't know," Dulcie answered truthfully.

Maryanne arched an eyebrow.

"Mr. Buchanan was conferring with a man who told him to make another offer for your home."

"I won't sell," Maryanne said.

"No, you won't."

Maryanne huffed. "What gave him the idea I would?"

"I'm not sure, but with Stuart in jail, these men see an opportunity."

"We should find Tom." Maryanne bunched up her napkin and tossed it next to her plate.

"We will, but it'll keep. Tom will thrash around like a caught trout when he finds out R.J. Buchanan is still in town. He needs to give all his attention to the trial."

"I suppose it wouldn't hurt to wait."

"Right now you eat up," Dulcie said. "We can't let these vittles go to waste, and Mr. Buchanan can't leave without us knowing about it."

Maryanne sat up straight and picked up her fork. "I can't believe anyone could be so bold."

"Me neither." Dulcie managed a smile.

The court was held in an empty warehouse building near the jail.

"Let's go inside," Dulcie said, wanting to get these proceedings over with.

Maryanne balked. "I'll wait for Stuart."

"Tom will bring him when it's time."

"I've never been to a trial before," Maryanne said with such touching innocence, Dulcie's heart ached.

"That makes two of us," Dulcie replied, fighting back tears. It'd do nobody any good to go all blubbery. "There's neighbors and friends in there. They're here to help."

She clasped Maryanne's elbow, and they walked side by side through the doorway.

The air in the room was stale. Threads of light filled with dust motes floating in glittering patches filtered in from the high windows.

Dulcie's pulse raced. They were the only women in the room.

Where the other ladies of Hangtown had gone off to, Dulcie had no idea.

Men stood around talking, but when their eyes lit on Maryanne, they grew quiet. Nobody offered any howdy-do's or murmured kind words of sympathy. Nobody had to.

Jasper collected firearms and set them against the wall in a far corner. He'd looked up when he heard Dulcie and Maryanne enter but made no move to question them about whether two ladies clinging to each other carried a weapon.

The room had been outfitted with rows of chairs. A big oak desk had been brought in for the judge. A solitary chair was set next to the desk. Twelve straight-backed chairs had been placed in two rows on the right side of the desk.

Maryanne looked around. Her face bunched up in wonder as if she didn't know where she was.

"Let's take a seat in the front row," Dulcie said. She wanted to get a close look at the man folks called a hanging judge.

She steered Maryanne down the center aisle. Maryanne was slow to put one foot in front of the other.

Dulcie urged her forward, nodding at those who looked at them with pity or shame and others who were just plain curious.

Dulcie didn't fault them for their nosiness. It would be a wonder to anybody how a lady held up under these circumstances.

They reached the first row of chairs, and Maryanne sank into the nearest one. Dulcie took the seat next to her. Across the aisle sat Mr. Bottle and another man dressed in a black suit. Dulcie hadn't seen him before and guessed he was another lawyer.

To Dulcie's relief, Mr. Bottle appeared reasonably steady.

The room filled up with citizens waiting to see the law run its course. The room began to smell of heated bodies and tobacco-soaked woolens. Dulcie loosened the ribbons on her bonnet.

She was reminded that her pa had met his fate in this very same place. Had he seen a friendly face? Had he been afraid?

There was a grumbling of voices, and Dulcie turned to look behind her. She saw Tom leading Stuart into the room wearing handcuffs and leg irons. The leg irons rattled with each step. Stuart didn't look to the right or left of him.

Dulcie's temper flared at seeing Stuart shackled up like a criminal, but she kept her mouth shut. It'd do Maryanne no good for Dulcie to speak her mind at that moment.

Tom's face was blank, but his lips were drawn into a thin line. He looked worn out. No doubt none of them had slept since last Saturday night, when all that had seemed important was greeting friends and filling their bellies.

When the two men reached the front row, Tom paused. Maryanne's gaze connected with her husband in a tender embrace.

Dulcie looked away. The moment was too precious to be shared.

Tom sat his prisoner down in the chair next to the oak desk, his back to Maryanne and the others in the audience. He hadn't acknowledged Dulcie sitting there. He hadn't even cast her one of his scrumptious smiles.

She wished this trial would be over and done with in short order.

He pulled up a second chair from the end of the row and set it facing the window. He took his seat within easy reach of Stuart and with the ability to keep watch over the crowd.

As they waited for the judge, Dulcie couldn't help but stare at Tom. He looked ahead, his jaw set and his expression unreadable. He looked cold and hard with no sentiment to him.

The night of the social, he'd asked her if she could stomach being a lawman's wife. Amid the frivolity of the evening, it'd been easy to believe she had the gumption that would be required of her.

But this was a side of Tom she'd never get used to, a side that no woman could.

The crowd hushed up. All eyes shifted to the back of the room as the deceased's brother walked in. Bert Chase had brought half a dozen men with him. That bunch challenged everyone in the room with narrowed eyes and mouths twitching.

Jasper stepped forward and asked them for their weapons. They removed their six-shooters from their holsters and handed them over without a grumble. The six-shooters were added to the pile.

Maryanne shivered when she saw Bert Chase take his seat.

A side door swung open, and Dulcie spotted Riley Gibbs standing there. He held a shotgun and wore a shiny badge.

Tom hadn't left anything to chance. Both doors were covered, the people in the room disarmed. Nobody would interfere with this trial as long as Tom Walker had a say in the matter.

She realized what comfort she took from Tom's presence in the room. She reckoned they all did, whether they disagreed with him for putting Stuart in jail or hoped to see Stuart hang.

A man entered from the side door. He carried the Good Book under his arm and a wooden mallet in his other hand.

"Is that the judge?" Maryanne whispered.

Dulcie gulped.

"He doesn't look as bad as everyone says," Maryanne said.

They'd expected a monster. The judge looked like an ordinary man. And Dulcie had no doubt this was the man who'd been talking with R.J. Buchanan in his room at the hotel.

Everyone in the room stood, even Stuart. Dulcie understood why it was proper to do so. They stood not for this man but out of respect for the law.

The man removed his hat. He looked over at Stuart, then at the crowd. He scowled at the assembly of men and two women, and Riley shut the door behind him.

He took his seat and set his hat on a corner of the desk and the Bible and mallet in front of him. He bid them all to take their seats. There was the scraping of chairs.

Dulcie wasn't sure what to do. Should she tell Tom what she'd overheard? Surely he'd want to know what the judge was up to.

"Good morning. My name is Judge Raymond T. Hennessy." The judge's voice boomed as if it was Judgment Day, deep and full of consequence.

"I'm the circuit court judge for the Eleventh District, State of California," he continued. "The deputy sheriff in charge will act as bailiff. The jury will come in now."

The side door opened again. Twelve men shuffled into the room. Dulcie didn't recognize anybody. They came from all walks of life, by the look of them. They headed for those straight-backed chairs to the right side of the judge and stood behind them.

Tom stood and picked up the Bible. He asked the jury men to raise their right hands and swear to do their duty. They all answered that they would and sat down.

Dulcie marveled at how an ordinary citizen could participate in a trial and how each and every one of their votes would be equal. Pa had told her stories about the Old Country, where justice was at the whim of the landlord, and judges worked for the wealthy man.

"Come forward when your name is called to witness," Judge Hennessy instructed the crowd. "Otherwise remain seated and silent. I'll not tolerate any disruption in my court. This will be a fair trial, and justice will be served."

Authority rang out with every word. Judge Hennessy was a take-charge kind of fella.

Dulcie squeezed Maryanne's arm.

"The judge is the man I heard talking with Mr. Buchanan."

Maryanne turned rigid. "Are you sure?"

"Sure as I'm sitting here."

"We've got to tell Tom."

Dulcie remembered what Tom had said. "There's no law against a man buying up property."

Maryanne wouldn't be comforted. "But Stuart won't get a fair trial."

"Now, don't go thinking there's no hope," Dulcie answered. "We have the truth on our side."

Maryanne looked at her wistfully.

"And Tom Walker."

Chapter Twenty-three

Finally, for Dulcie couldn't count how many *wherefore*s and *whereas*es had been spoken, the judge asked Mr. Bottle to bring his first witness.

Mr. Paisley was called to the chair next to Judge Hennessy's desk. Mr. Paisley put his hand on the Good Book and swore to tell the truth. He looked over at Maryanne, smiled briefly, and then sat himself down.

He and his wife, Lyla, owned the A. Paisley Dry Goods and Notions and had organized the social, he told the court. Mr. Paisley had been talking with Stuart when Judson Chase arrived. Those two had started arguing almost immediately, he explained.

"What was said?" Mr. Bottle asked.

Mr. Paisley scratched his whiskered cheek. "Stuart asked Judson if he knew anything about a fence that'd fallen down out at his place." He turned to the judge. "Stuart was sure somebody'd pulled the fence down and let the Chases' steers wander onto his property."

"The two men argued about a fence?" Mr. Bottle scanned the jury.

"Yes, sir, and Judson denied he'd had anything to do with Stuart's fence coming down."

Dulcie knew Judson had flat-out lied. She'd seen the broken fence with her own eyes. The Chase brothers had pulled it down to let their cows wander wherever they pleased.

"Is that all?"

Mr. Paisley shook his head. "There seemed to be some other

business. Stuart claimed that the water for his animals had turned bad the day before, and his milking cow had gone sickly."

The lawyer paused, most likely for this information to sink in.

"What did the deceased, Judson Chase, have to say in reply?" Mr. Bottle asked.

"Why, he was offended by the accusation and not shy about saying so."

"What happened next, Mr. Paisley?"

"Stuart told the fella he didn't believe a word he said."

"How did the deceased react?"

"He pulled a knife. Told Stuart he'd better hold his tongue or he'd cut it out."

The lawyer looked alarmed. "Those were his exact words?"

"Yes, sir."

Mr. Bottle looked over at Stuart, who was bent over and staring at the floor.

"Was Stuart Greenwood armed?" the lawyer asked.

"No, sir," Mr. Paisley said soberly.

Dulcie's gaze flew to the judge. Was there any doubt that Stuart had acted in self-defense?

Judge Raymond T. Hennessy sat there stone-faced. He had to remain impartial, just like Tom. It was what the law required of him.

"Did you see what happened next?" the lawyer asked.

"Yes, sir, I did. Stuart told him to put the knife away."

"Did Judson Chase do so?"

"I reckon he didn't; otherwise we wouldn't be here," Mr. Paisley replied.

The men in the room chuckled, and Mr. Paisley looked pleased with himself.

Judge Hennessy pounded on the desk with the wooden mallet, which brought silence quickly enough.

"What happened next, Mr. Paisley?"

"I saw Stuart's hand bleeding."

"From a knife wound?"

"Yes, sir."

"Did Stuart pick up the knife?"

"He did, and that's when Judson Chase lunged at him."

Mr. Bottle looked at the jury. "Did you see what happened next?"

"Yes, sir. The knife went through him—Judson, that is."

The jurors exchanged glances.

"I don't have any other questions," the lawyer said to the judge, and he took a seat.

The other lawyer stood and buttoned his coat. He'd a long mustache that had been waxed into two perfect points. He represented the people, he explained, which meant every person sitting in the room.

He had a great responsibility, to Dulcie's way of thinking. She couldn't help but dislike the man anyway. He meant to argue that Stuart was guilty of murdering Judson Chase.

"Mr. Paisley, did you see when Stuart Greenwood was cut?" the State's lawyer began.

"No, sir. I was looking away at the time."

"How do you know who was holding the knife?" He spat out the question.

"I . . ." Mr. Paisley faltered.

Dulcie didn't see how it mattered. Stuart hadn't cut himself.

"Mr. Paisley, are you and Stuart Greenwood friends?" the lawyer asked.

"Yes, sir, I like to think so."

"How long have you been friends?"

"Since that boy came to the valley, I suppose. Year before last, as I recollect."

"Do you like Stuart Greenwood?"

Mr. Bottle jumped to his feet. "I object to the question, Your Honor. What relevance has it?"

"Let me hear what the witness has to say," Judge Hennessy answered.

Mr. Paisley nodded. "I surely do. He's a good provider for his wife and youngster, and a good citizen."

"People in this community help each other out in hard times?" the lawyer asked.

Again Mr. Bottle jumped to his feet, but Judge Hennessy waved him to sit back down.

Mr. Paisley beamed with pride. "We do."

"Thank you." The State's lawyer addressed the judge. "That's all the questions I have for this witness."

"That will be all, Mr. Paisley," Judge Hennessy said. "You may step down."

Mr. Paisley got out of the chair, clutching his short-brimmed hat, and smiled feebly at Maryanne.

The rest of the witnesses Mr. Bottle called up told the same story. Nobody had actually seen Judson cut Stuart, it'd happened so fast.

Again, the State's lawyer asked if the witness knew Stuart. They all replied that Stuart Greenwood was a good friend and well liked in the community.

Dulcie knew the questions had nothing to do with the accusations, but Judge Hennessy allowed them to be asked anyway. The State's lawyer seemed determined to make a case that the witnesses favored Stuart because of his strong ties with the community.

Mr. Bottle finished with his string of witnesses and took his seat. Dulcie wondered why the lawyer hadn't called Stuart to the witness chair in his own defense. Shouldn't Stuart be able to tell his side of the story?

The State's lawyer rose to his feet. He told the judge he'd only one witness. He called Judson Chase's brother, Bert, to sit in the chair.

Bert Chase walked down the aisle, hat in hand. His coat was too short in the arms and tight across the shoulders. He laid his hand on the Bible and swore an oath to tell the truth. He took his seat in the witness chair.

He glanced over at Dulcie. She hoped he was remembering their conversation of the other morning when she'd paid him a call. She hoped he'd taken to heart the sincerity of all she'd said and found forgiveness to be the better choice.

Bert Chase rested his powerful arms on the chair's armrests.

He bounced his left leg. The people's lawyer smiled to put Bert at ease, but Bert was nervous, and it showed.

"State your name and relationship to the deceased," the lawyer said.

Bert addressed the jury. "I'm Bert Chase, and Judson was my brother."

"Were you at the social the night of April fifteenth?"

"I was."

"Mr. Chase, in your own words, tell the jury what happened that night between your brother and Mr. Greenwood."

Bert cleared his throat. "Those two were arguing. Threats were made on both sides. I saw Stuart Greenwood with a knife in his hand. Before I could stop him, he stabbed my brother in the heart." Bert turned to the jury. "Judson dropped dead to the floor. No doctor could save him."

Dulcie grasped the edge of her seat. The Chase brothers didn't know their way around the truth. Bert's version of what had happened was so at odds with what the rest of them were saying, those twelve jury men had to know he was lying.

The lawyer motioned for Jasper Jenkins to come forward. Jasper walked down the aisle and handed over a knife. The knife had a six-inch curved blade and a deer-antler handle.

The lawyer showed the knife to Bert. "Is this your brother's knife?"

Bert looked at the knife briefly. "Yes."

"This is also the knife that was used to kill your brother?"

"Yes."

The lawyer thanked him and sat down.

Mr. Bottle stood up and pulled down on his coat. He looked worried, more worried than a lawyer defending an innocent man should look.

"Your brother carried a knife?" he asked.

"Most men do in these parts."

"Was Stuart Greenwood armed?" Mr. Bottle asked.

"How could we know for sure he wasn't?" Bert looked around the room. Some of the jurors nodded in agreement.

"Did you see him with another weapon?"

"No, sir."

"Did Stuart Greenwood threaten you?"

"Yes, sir, he did."

"What, exactly, was the nature of those threats?"

"I don't remember what exact words he used."

"Did he tell you or your brother he'd kill you?"

Bert looked over at the people's lawyer.

"Did he say those words, Mr. Chase?"

"No, not exactly."

Dulcie shot another look at the judge. Again, he gave no indication how he felt about what was being said.

Mr. Bottle thanked him and took his seat amid the soft murmur of voices. Dulcie reached over and patted Maryanne's hand. It was as cold as spring water. Maryanne smiled but without any warmth. They both were close to falling off their seats.

The judge banged his mallet again. The sharp sound made Dulcie jump. He dismissed Bert Chase. Bert lowered his head and stumbled from the chair.

Dulcie hadn't thought it possible that Bert Chase would be cowed by anything, but he surely looked meek and mild-mannered when he left the witness chair.

She saw from the expressions on the jury's faces that they'd come to a similar conclusion. They felt sorry for Bert and his trouble.

The opposing attorney stood. He had a fierce look about him. His nostrils flared as he took a breath to start his speech. He pointed a long finger at Stuart.

"There's no doubt Stuart Greenwood has good friends in this room, and they've come to his aid in his hour of need." The lawyer turned to the crowd as if somehow they were at fault, that showing kindness and lending a hand to a neighbor was a defect.

Would the men of the jury believe the witnesses had all lied about what had happened that night to save Stuart Greenwood from the hangman's noose?

The lawyer grabbed the lapels of his suit and turned back to the jury. He looked at every one of them in turn.

"The Bible says 'Thou shall not kill,' " he said in a matter-of-fact

way. Several of the jurors nodded. "A man died at the hands of
Stuart Greenwood."

The jury listened intently, and their gazes followed the lawyer
who paced in front of them. Had they begun to doubt the truth of
the matter? Did they believe Bert Chase?

"The consequences are clear. An eye for an eye," the people's
lawyer continued, his voice rising as if he'd just discovered the
truth himself. "Stuart Greenwood should hang for what he did."

Dulcie could hear no more. Her learning from the Bible needed
work, but she was certain that wasn't what the Lord meant at all.

She shot to her feet. All eyes turned to her. She'd made a fist
without realizing it. "Now, you see here. You've called on the Bible
to make your case, but the Good Book also says it's wrong to bear
false witness against a neighbor. Bert Chase has done just that."

The judge hit the desk with his mallet. "Sit down, or I'll have
you removed from this room."

A hand clenched her shoulder from behind and tried to pull
her down.

"Calm yourself, Dulcie," said a male voice.

Dulcie wasn't finished, and she shrugged free. "Everybody in
this town knows Stuart came to the social unarmed. He picked
up that knife so Jud Chase couldn't use it against him. He never
intended to kill Judson Chase, but he wasn't fool enough to give
the man a chance to cut him again."

The people's lawyer looked at the judge. All the men in the
room started talking at once.

"And furthermore," Dulcie shouted to be heard, "Stuart never
had a chance to tell his side of the story."

"Deputy, take that lady outside." The judge banged his gavel,
which did nothing to quiet the ruckus.

Tom was in front of her and reached for her arm. Dulcie side-
stepped him, but he grabbed her by the elbow and strong-armed
her down the aisle.

The judge kept banging his gavel. They exited amid an uproar.

Jasper had been leaning against the hitching post. He came to
attention when he saw Tom and Dulcie.

"You stay out here," Tom told her. There was anger in his eyes and a fury so unlike him. He held her arm in a viselike grip. "If you come back inside, I'll have you put in the jail cell."

She glared at him with all the contempt she could muster. "You wouldn't dare."

She knew that Tom would do as he said. Tom Walker was a man of his word.

He let her go. Her arm hurt where he'd held her, and she rubbed her smarting flesh, exaggerating a mite, but she wanted Tom to regret manhandling her.

"You shouldn't have come," Tom said.

"I have every right to be here!" she yelled back.

"A courtroom is no place for a lady."

"I wasn't going to let Maryanne face this alone."

"You should've taken Maryanne over to Mrs. Paisley's parlor, where the rest of the ladies are waiting."

"You know as well as I do that she wouldn't go."

He turned to leave, but she blocked his way.

"Are you going to let the people's lawyer say those things about Stuart?" she asked.

"He's presenting the other side of the argument."

"He's got it wrong."

"Hopefully, the judge and jury will figure that out for themselves."

"What if they don't?"

Tom's dark-eyed gaze bore through her. It frightened her to see him at the brink, to see him about to lose control.

"You're not helping Stuart by interfering in his trial," he said.

His sharp words cut her to the bone. "Interfering?"

"That's what I said."

"I suppose I was interfering when I saw R.J. Buchanan at Mary's Hotel and followed him upstairs?"

"You did what?" Tom was actually red in the face.

"I just wanted to talk to him, but I never got a chance." She gazed at him defiantly. "R.J. had company. I found out he works for none other than the Honorable Judge Raymond T. Hennessy. Appears the judge is the businessman buying up land around the El Dorado."

"You're making a serious accusation."

"One I don't make lightly."

Tom grimaced. "You stay away from R.J. Buchanan."

"Don't you fret. I won't go near him." She stepped aside, giving him room to pass.

He slammed the door behind him.

She glared at Jasper. Jasper backed away. She'd a mind to include him in her anger with a few choice remarks.

Tom was mistaken. She'd had every right to speak up. Only she'd picked the wrong time and place. She'd never been a woman who could hold back.

"What's got you all riled?" Jasper asked.

"The lawyer representing the people is saying that Mr. Paisley and all the others are lying about what happened at the social because Stuart's their friend. You were there that night. Why didn't you tell them what you saw? You'd make a good witness. The judge and jury would believe a deputy."

Jasper scuffed one boot on the ground. "I didn't see those two quarreling or Judson with a knife. Me and a pretty little gal had stepped out for a few minutes."

"Nothing we can do about it now," she said, shaking her head. "The trial's about over. All we can do is wait for the verdict."

She began to pace. The sun had peeked out from behind a cloud overhead, the better part of the morning gone. No telling how long the jury would take. She walked the length of the boardwalk, turned, and came back again. There must be something she could do, but she was at a loss as to what.

She had a bad feeling Hangtown was about to live up to its name.

Jasper held on to his shotgun, resting the barrel on his shoulder like a sentry would. She could wrestle him for it or use her feminine wiles to coax him to put it down so she could snatch the shotgun from him. She also had Mrs. Walker's pistol to persuade him to give her his weapon.

She could hold the shotgun on a roomful of unarmed men and bust Stuart out of there. She reconsidered. Her skills with a firearm were considerable, but her chances of success were slim to none. Tom wasn't about to let her take Stuart away, and where would Stuart go anyway?

Tom expected her to believe in the law, and that's what she needed to do. Those jurors would see the truth of the matter, and justice would be served.

When she heard the unmistakable booming voice of the judge, she stopped dead in her tracks. She looked at Jasper, and he perked up.

"What's happening now?" Jasper asked.

"Don't know, but I aim to find out."

They hurried to the door and held their breath so they could hear what Judge Hennessy had to say.

Chapter Twenty-four

Wหile they waited for the jury's decision, Tom stewed.

What Dulcie had told him would put any lawman off his feed.

Accusing a judge of not conducting a fair trial for his own personal gain was a serious charge. One that he would be sure to pursue as soon as this trial was over.

Even so, Tom thought the trial fair. The evidence had been in dispute but weighted heavily in favor of Stuart.

He wished Stuart had shown some grit and gumption. Mr. Bottle hadn't called on Stuart to explain to the jury what'd happened because Stuart looked defeated, and the jury had seen that in him.

The jury shuffled in. Tom took his watch from his vest pocket. They'd been outside for only ten minutes.

Tom took that to be a good sign. The men had agreed on a verdict without an argument, but Stuart continued with his hangdog look as if he'd read the jury's mind and accepted a guilty verdict as his due.

Tom looked over at Maryanne. She was as pale as the whitewashed walls of the room.

Judge Hennessy instructed Tom to collect the pieces of paper from the jury with their verdict. He did so and handed them over to the judge. The judge unfolded each scrap of paper and set them in a pile. The room was silent.

When he finished reading each vote, he looked up, pokerfaced.

"The defendant will stand," he said sternly. He left no room to doubt he was a man who made pronouncements, and the people of California lived by them.

Tom helped Stuart to his feet, thankful this travesty would soon be over so Stuart could go home to his wife and baby.

"Stuart Greenwood . . . ," Judge Hennessy said.

Every man in the entire room leaned forward, even though the judge's voice was loud and commanding.

Tom was put in mind of a ship's captain, giving orders and requiring obedience. It was how the system worked. A court of law was how civilized people dealt with disputes and lawbreakers. There'd be no frontier justice today.

"In the case of the killing of Judson Chase . . ."

Tom chanced another look at Maryanne. She was wide-eyed and hopeful. She'd always been a gentle soul. She'd befriended Dulcie at a time when others had held back.

Maryanne didn't deserve this.

". . . this court finds you not guilty."

Tom snapped his head front and center. The judge banged his gavel, finalizing the verdict.

There wasn't any glint of satisfaction in his eye. No smirk of contentment on his lips. He'd announced his verdict as normally as if he was reading a stockman's report out of the *Mountain Democrat.*

Maryanne cried out and began to weep. Stuart wavered. Tom clapped him on the back.

"This court wishes to thank the jury," Judge Hennessy continued. The crowd wasn't listening.

Again the gavel came down like a crack of lightning, but no one cared. Twelve men had seen the truth of the matter. It was over.

Tom removed the handcuffs and leg irons. Maryanne broke free of those who tried to hold her. She flung her arms around Stuart's neck. Most in the room, including the jury, cheered.

Judge Hennessy shoved his way to the exit. He escaped through the side door with the two lawyers right behind him.

Tom had to find Dulcie and tell her. She'd been angry with

him about putting her out on the street; hopefully she'd forgive him.

Dulcie hadn't been able to hear the verdict. When cheers rose up inside the courtroom, she guessed at the outcome.

The crowd grew noisier, and she and Jasper jumped back just as the door burst open and exuberant men spilled out of the room. They talked loudly as they nodded their heads and shook hands with members of the jury.

Dulcie saw Maryanne and Stuart inside, surrounded by their community of friends. There were smiles all around. Nobody was frowning.

Dulcie was overjoyed that Maryanne had her husband back, but she didn't join them. The only place folks didn't congregate was under the shade of the hanging tree. So there she dawdled, feeling like the frayed end of an old shawl.

The judge was a scoundrel, which she'd been in the middle of pointing out, when Tom had showed her the door.

He'd been plenty irate with her, but she'd make no apologies. Like her pa, she couldn't abide excuses. She'd said what needed to be said, whether Tom agreed with her or not.

Dulcie wasn't sure what could be done about the judge. She knew one thing for certain: the men who wrote the laws back when California became a state wouldn't have thought kindly of his kind of shenanigans.

She had plenty more to say to that judge, given the chance.

Tom had warned her off R.J. Buchanan, but he hadn't said anything about her talking to the judge.

Wouldn't that put a burr under Tom's saddle?

"Have you seen Dulcie?" Tom asked.

"Can't say I have." The livery man spat a wad of tobacco into the grass and wiped his chin off with the back of his hand. "She must've gone over to Mrs. Paisley's place to be with the Greenwoods and their young'un."

"I reckon."

"Congratulations on the verdict," the livery man said.

Tom frowned. The verdict wasn't his doing, no matter what folks believed.

"If you ask me, somebody should be guarding the judge," the livery man said.

"What have you heard?"

The livery man pushed his hat back on his head and scratched his scalp. "Only talk so far. There's folks unhappy with the outcome of Stuart's trial. They were looking forward to a hanging."

Tom hated to hear such talk.

"I'm headed over to the Blue Stocking for my noonday meal," the livery man said. "Care to join me?"

"Not just now," Tom replied. Tom needed to find Judge Hennessy and warn him.

"Whatever you say, Sheriff," the livery man said, and he started off at a canter.

"*Deputy!*" Tom shouted after him, but he was already out of earshot.

Tom continued down Main Street. Judge Hennessy came out of the stage agent's office. He stuffed a ticket inside his coat and turned in the opposite direction. He seemed to be in a hurry. Tom intercepted him.

"Deputy," the judge said cordially.

"Judge, I've come to tell you there's vengeful talk being bandied about Hangtown. You need to be careful."

Judge Hennessy didn't break his stride. "I'm used to such talk."

Tom had seen such confidence get a man killed. "This here is a dangerous town," he explained. "I've seen men murdered for no more than a few coins in their pockets and a worn-out pair of boots."

"I'm carrying a pistol," the judge said, "and I'm a very good shot."

"With all due respect, a pistol won't impress an angry mob much."

The judge stepped off the boardwalk and started across the street.

"I'd like one of the deputies to stay with you," Tom said, following him.

"A bodyguard?" The judge looked amused.

"Yes, sir."

"I really don't think that's necessary," the judge replied firmly. "Now, if you'll excuse me."

Tom wasn't about to go contrary to a judge's wishes, but he'd make sure Judge Hennessy was on today's stage.

Tom kept a fair distance behind him. Nobody followed or paid any undue attention to the judge. He watched until the judge stepped inside Mary's front door.

Tom turned around and headed for the Dry Goods.

Mrs. Paisley was standing in the doorway. She was a small woman. Her gaze raked over him as if he was a truant schoolboy.

"Dulcie Crowder here?"

"I haven't seen her."

"Do you know where she could be?"

"I'm afraid I couldn't say. Won't you come in and join us for some refreshments? We're having a little celebration."

Tom tipped his hat. "Thank you, ma'am, but I have to find Dulcie."

Mrs. Paisley shut the door.

He turned to survey the street. Where had that woman gone?

Chapter Twenty-five

Dulcie found Judge Hennessy tucking into a plate of scrambled eggs at Mary's Hotel dining room. She was thankful she wouldn't have to confront the judge in his room.

R.J. Buchanan wasn't with him.

She steeled her courage and headed in the judge's direction.

Deputy Riley Gibbs sat by the window eating a plate of fried potatoes while reading a book. He greeted her with a nod.

There were several other diners, folks Dulcie recognized from the town social. Having them and Riley around assured her there'd be civility when she gave the judge a talking to he wouldn't soon forget.

Despite her bravado in the courtroom, right this minute she was as scared as a rabbit.

Dulcie clasped her hands behind her back as she reached his table. She supposed the judge was used to folks around him struggling with a case of nerves, but she hated that it made her look weak and uncertain.

"Mind if I join you?" she asked.

"Be my guest," he said, looking up from his grub. He wiped his mouth with his handkerchief.

Dulcie pulled out a chair and took a seat next to him.

"Would you like some coffee?" he asked.

"No, thank you," Dulcie replied.

Judge Hennessy put on a show of pretty manners as if he was a gentleman. Dulcie wasn't fooled.

He rested coiled hands on the table. "How can I help you?"

"My name is Dulcie Crowder. My pa was Willie Crowder."

"Yes?"

"You bought my land."

He gave no sign of recognition, but he knew who she was, all right.

"You're mistaken, Miss Crowder."

"There's no mistake. You sent R.J. Buchanan to Hangtown to buy me out. I heard you two talking upstairs in this very place about buying the Greenwood farm."

She had his attention now.

"What do you want?"

"I'm here to ask a favor," she said.

The judge leaned back in his chair. He was a man whose will would be done, his expression seemed to say, but he was big enough to do a kindness for a lady.

"I'd like you to quit being a judge for Hangtown and all the rest of the towns trying to make the law something we can respect," she said.

"On what grounds?" he asked, attempting a smile.

"Isn't it obvious? You shouldn't be buying up land from folks you've sentenced to die."

Judge Hennessy fished around in his vest pocket and took out his pocket watch. He opened it and looked at the time. "I'm a businessman. I haven't broken any laws."

"Maybe so, but you shouldn't be a judge, and soon the entire State of California will agree."

Judge Hennessy shoved his watch into his pocket and set a fisted hand on the table with a thump. His gaze shone with menace, like a rattler getting ready to strike. "Are you threatening me, Miss Crowder?"

"No, sir." Dulcie could stare down the meanest of critters, and she didn't flinch.

After a breathless moment, his anger fled.

"The stagecoach will be here any minute now," he said. "If you'll excuse me." He hefted his bulk from the chair and grabbed his hat. He stormed out of the room, pushing Mary, who'd just come into the room, out of his way.

Mary squawked as she tried to keep her footing.

"See here!" Riley Gibbs jumped to his feet and ran to her aid.

Judge Hennessy stopped in front of the door and cast a hateful look at everybody in the room before he pushed through the front door.

Dulcie rose from her chair and hurried after him. Judge Hennessy hadn't heard the last of Dulcie Crowder.

What she saw when she got outside stopped her cold. Bert Chase stood in the middle of the street. He aimed a six-shooter at the judge, who'd put his hands up in the air.

Bert glared at Judge Hennessy, his dark eyes wild and full of rage.

Dulcie thought she'd feel triumph or something akin to it, seeing the judge in such a state, but all she felt was fear.

"What do you think you're doing?" Dulcie asked Bert.

Bert's gaze stayed fixed on the judge. "I want to see justice done."

"Don't talk foolishness, Bert."

Bert ignored her. "You're coming with me, Judge. If this town won't abide by its duty, then it's up to you to put the rope around Stuart Greenwood's neck."

Dulcie couldn't let this happen. "It'd be a terrible injustice for you to take the law into your own hands, Bert."

The judge reached inside his coat. A volley of shots split the air. Mary's big front window shattered, raining shards of glass.

Dulcie dove back inside the hotel and slammed the door behind her. Deputy Gibbs was sprawled on the floor. Blood oozed out of his chest, soaking his shirt crimson. Mary knelt at his side, the front of her skirt spattered with blood.

Dulcie ran over and crouched down beside him. Mary touched two fingers to the side of his neck.

"He's gone to his reward," she said, and she closed Riley's eyes.

"Stand clear of the window!" Dulcie shouted to the others. "There's bound to be more bullets flying, and they don't know the good from the bad."

"What's happening to our town?" Mary asked, staring, teary-eyed, at the dead deputy.

"One of you ladies, take her away from here," Dulcie said.

Someone grabbed Mary by the hand and dragged her away from the body. "The rest of you too."

They moved away and stood corralled at the other side of the room.

Dulcie hiked up her skirt for all the world to see and removed the pearl-handled Derringer secured by her blue garter.

She opened the door a crack. Judge Hennessy's body lay draped over the hitching post, his head dripping blood.

She opened the door wider. Bert had dropped his gun in the dirt.

"You saw what happened," Bert said to her, panting heavily. "The judge was going to shoot me. I was only defending myself."

She shrugged. "Doesn't matter. Riley Gibbs has been shot dead inside. You'll be held accountable for that."

Tom and Jasper came running up the street. Tom's scowl could blister paint.

When he reached them, he grabbed her by the shoulders. "Are you hurt?"

"No, Tom."

His red-hot gaze went to the pistol in her hand.

"Don't look at me that way." She shook out of his grasp. She could feel her own heat rising. "It was Bert Chase who decided to give the judge his due."

"You're under arrest," Tom said to Bert.

"I didn't mean to kill him," Bert said.

"That's for a judge and jury to decide," Tom answered.

Bert went the color of ashes.

"Lock him up, Jasper," Tom said as he slapped on a pair of handcuffs.

Jasper took hold of Bert's arm and led him away.

Tom looked at Dulcie. "What were you doing here?"

"Giving the judge my rightful opinion," she said.

"The judge wasn't your concern."

She stung with such grievous hurt, a protest died on her tongue.

Tom walked past her and climbed the steps, spurs ringing. He disappeared into Mary's Hotel, and everybody inside called out his name.

She could hear him talking in his soothing way, calming their fears and taking charge of the situation.

Dulcie wanted to follow and stand by his side. Good sense stopped her. Nobody had to tell her twice. She was an outsider. There was no pretending otherwise.

She looked back at the judge's body. It'd begun to draw flies.

"I've come to find out the name Hangtown suits this place," Dulcie announced to nobody in particular.

Chapter Twenty-six

Dulcie borrowed a nag from the livery man and rode hard to the Greenwood place, grieving for young Riley Gibbs, who'd had a lot of life ahead of him.

She'd thought to make herself useful, but that had been a mistake. Although Bert most likely would've tried to take the law into his own hands anyway, Dulcie felt responsible for what had happened. She should've put a stop to Bert and his vengeful ways. She'd failed, and the results had been deadly.

She'd no doubt that Tom had come to the same conclusion.

Dulcie hurried inside Maryanne's house. She gathered up her worn-out saddlebags. She didn't have much in this world, a poor showing by most accounts, but what she did have was precious to her.

There was the yellow Sunday-go-to-meeting dress Mrs. Walker had sewn up for her and the Good Book that'd belonged to her pa. There was the big Bowie knife she'd carried since she was a girl and had set aside now that she was a lady. Finally, there was the red bandanna Tom had given her when they'd first met. She clutched it to her heart.

Her love for any other man would never equal her love for Tom Walker.

She counted out what was left of her money. She'd spent most of what she'd gained from selling her land on the Greenwoods, but she had no regrets.

She'd always be a working girl, earning her own keep. She put what was left back in the pouch secured in the waistband of her skirt.

She took one last look around the room where she'd known friendship and kindness. She'd wanted a homestead just like this one, but it wasn't to be.

The trip back to town took forever. When she reached the hay yard, Dulcie stopped the horse and jumped down. She untied her saddlebags and pulled them off.

The livery man came out and doffed his hat.

"Thank you kindly for the loan of this horse," she said.

"Ma'am," the livery man said.

She handed over the reins. There wasn't time to say good-bye to Chester, but she knew he'd grow fat under Mr. Eng's care. No time for her pa either, who'd been promised regular visits.

"Good-bye, miss," the livery man called after her.

Dulcie retreated as quickly as her legs could carry her. The boardwalk in front of the stagecoach office held a jumble of people waiting for the stage going to Sacramento.

"What are you doing here, Miss Dulcie?" It was Mr. Paisley.

"I could ask you the same."

"I meet every stagecoach comes into Hangtown," he replied. He looked down at the saddlebags in her hand.

"I'm going out on the stage," she said.

"Do tell."

"Yes, I've decided to travel."

Mr. Paisley nodded. "You'd better get a move on. The stage will be here shortly."

Dulcie made a beeline for the front door of the stagecoach station and didn't take the time to greet the rest of the Hangtown citizenry. Folks would be asking questions out of nosiness. She'd leave Mr. Paisley to tell them.

The station agent wrote out a ticket, and she paid him with one of her paper bills. The agent looked up at the large clock on the wall. "The stage will be here any minute now, if you'd like to take a seat."

She sat in a captain's chair next to the potbelly stove and put her saddlebags on the floor.

The door opened, and in came a draft of cold air. Tom Walker filled the doorway, hat in hand.

Dulcie turned away, giving him her back. She heard the scraping of wood. He'd brought up another chair and took a seat next to her.

He settled down in his chair. She spared him a glance. He was wearing a clean red bandanna around his neck.

Dulcie looked over at the agent, who pretended to be busy with his stack of papers.

"Don't you have some criminals to attend to?" she asked.

"Left Jasper in charge."

"What'll happen to Bert?"

"He'll stand trial just like anybody else."

"I'm so sorry how the judge came to meet his end," she said.

"I know."

She turned to face him. "Riley's death is my fault. If I wasn't such a busybody, such an interfering banty hen . . ."

"Don't take the blame on yourself. Judge Hennessy wasn't fit to judge. The truth of that came out, thanks to you."

It was a small consolation that he didn't lay the blame on her. She'd have a more difficult time forgiving herself if he had.

"I appreciate your coming over and telling me," she said.

"Where you off to?" His face bunched up in a dreadful scowl, but that was to be expected.

"Sacramento City. Maybe even San Francisco, if I've a mind to," she said. There was no use in keeping information from him. He'd find out soon enough.

"That's a distance," he said.

"I mean to see a bit of the world."

"Why would you want to do such a thing? I thought you liked this town."

She squared her shoulders. "A hanging town isn't a place for a lady."

"I'd make a poor farmer."

Dulcie grimaced. "Do you think I want you to change?"

He looked surprised. "I thought you and my ma were working together to get me to quit my job as a lawman."

"I can't speak for your ma, and you'll have to settle your differences with her yourself, but as for me, I can think of no better man to be sheriff than you. You're just the kind of man this town needs."

"This town needs both of us."

She heard bellowing in the street and the jingle-jangle of harnesses.

"Stage's here," the agent said reluctantly. He shrugged on his black coat and went out the door.

"Have you said all you came to say?" she asked Tom.

Tom reached over and took her hand. His hand was cold and chapped but branded her like a hot iron.

"I'm not one for making speeches," he said. "But I reckon I need to make this one. I'd never forgive myself if you left town thinking you weren't needed here."

Dulcie withdrew her hand. "Tom Walker, you know as well as I do that you're talking nonsense."

She stood. Tom sprang to his feet beside her.

He wasted no time as he gathered her into his arms and planted a kiss firmly on her lips.

There was no doubting the man's ability or his commitment or—and this was important—the shivers that kiss sent up and down her spine.

"Does my kiss convince you?" he asked as they both came up for air.

"What do you reckon?"

"What do you say we get married?"

She leaned back to get a good look at his face. He was grinning. She matched his grin with a grin of her own.

"Is that a yes?"

"You know it is."

Right then the door was flung open, and a whole crowd of people looked in at them from the boardwalk. They'd caught her and Tom in a delicate situation. Tom made no move to let her go.

There was Mr. Paisley and Tom's ma in her buggy with Mr. Eng driving, and Stuart, Maryanne, and little George Arthur in his ma's arms, and so many others, she couldn't count them all. They all looked at her with apprehension.

"I asked her to marry me," Tom said.

"Please say yes!" Stuart yelled. "I'll start on a porch swing for your wedding present as soon as we get home."

"She said yes," Tom told them.

Every last one of them began to cheer, whoop, and holler.